dead drop

JACQUELINE BOYLE

ISBN: 0615730396
ISBN-13: 978-0615730394

Library of Congress Control Number: 2012921978
Skyway Avenue Publishing
Saint Charles, IL

To my four real partners in crime on this great adventure

chapter 1

It was 7:00 on a Wednesday morning and, as usual, my life was breathlessly running at least ten minutes behind as I slid with stocking feet across the hardwood floors into the kitchen. I snatched the brown sack lunch my dad had made for me while juggling a stack of textbooks in my other hand, throwing my backpack over my shoulder, and mentally running through my French vocabulary and my schedule of after-school meetings. Breakfast would necessarily resort to nothing.

"Dad, I'm off to school, and I will—"

"Quiet," my father snapped from his standing position in front of the television in the open living room, causing a perplexed look on my face at the reaction from my normally easygoing father. With his back turned to me, it was impossible to tell how serious the reaction was meant to be.

"At seven forty-three last night, a seven-forty-seven commercial flight bound for Denver International Airport crash-landed in the upper peaks of the Rocky Mountains a hundred miles from the city of Denver. At this time, it has not been determined if this crash was associated with terrorist motives. A lack of transmission activity from the plane remains in question. Unfortunately, there were no survivors of…" droned the Channel 7 morning newswoman.

I interrupted the voice on the television. "Dad, I'm late, so I'll text you if I do anything. Bye."

As I turned to bolt out the back door, a guilty feeling came over me for leaving my father straining against the voice of nothing more than a typical news report, with coverage of an unfortunate accident in the skies. Unfortunately for me, unless I knew someone in that plane, there was not a chance the deans were going to accept another tardy to first hour. Time management is really not one of my best attributes, and as senior year passed, my ability to be on time was receiving a shining F. At this point, 7:06 a.m., I'd only make it through the crowded, winding streets of my Naperville suburbia if I had my own helicopter, plus a landing pad on the roof above my first-hour class, and I could pull a James Bond through the window. I looked down to see that the only things on my feet were a polka dot blue sock and a solid orange one, instead of a pair of combat boots. Seeing that my fantasy of being MI6 was not going to happen, it was "Hello, Dean Gonther."

School in no way deterred me from my typical routine. I spent the day with all my friends because, even in a school of eighteen hundred students, the administration could not grasp an alternative class schedule aside from just changing the classroom number and professor with each subject. I accepted that likely we were not the only school where a selective group of students took classes just because they were labeled "Advanced Placement" or "AP." Therefore, we all had the same classes and the same schedules. At my school, I was a part of that group, and they happened to be my friends. It is not that

2

we put ourselves on an academic pedestal; it just made sense to have a group of people who actually understood an over-commitment to school-related tasks. Our version of fun on a weekday involved studying at our favorite cafe downtown until the owner kicked us out at 10:00 p.m. A nice middle-aged woman with an ever-changing slew of boyfriends always made sure to supply us with day-old bakery items and the best cinnamon scones. It worked for us, and our parents sure appreciated it.

By sixth hour I had already downed two tests, with more planned throughout the rest of week. Like all of the best students and now seniors in high school, we were the masters of procrastination, so it was going to be a long week. During weeks like these, motivation came from the promise of pints of vanilla ice cream, frozen California Pizza Kitchen pizzas, Doritos, and movies on Friday night. For now, I would be chugging the burnt coffee from the school cafeteria and sending farewells from afar to my abandoned bed.

By the last class hour of school, the reduction and titrating of chemical solutions looked closer to a foreign language of subscripts, numbers, and oddly combined letters. While normally I am one of the few mildly insane people who enjoy and understand chemistry, despite my refusal to read any of the textbooks, I took to copying the data from my friend, Alec, in the seat next to me. It was a bit of an unspoken rule at this point among our tight-knit group that sharing was an obligation to each other because we would all eventually learn it, and the debt would always be repaid. As I mechanically washed the last couple of beakers, in the deep-welled sink with the constantly changing water pressure that sprayed droplets of water throughout a ten-foot vicinity, the final bell rang. I turned off the faucet and placed the last wet beaker on the black countertop before shoving my lab notebook into my backpack and slinging it over my shoulder. Although it was the end of the mandatory school day, my time in the building would not be ending for another couple of hours after a Relay for Life committee meeting until 4:00 p.m., followed by French and calculus tutoring for two hours. My commitment to such activities could be defined as a love and hate and then, deep down in a small crevice of my heart, love relationship.

"I'm home," I yelled from the back laundry room, kicking off my purple chucks and throwing my backpack to the ground next to the mountain of shoes, which included my UGG boots and flip-flops. The back laundry room clearly maintained no regard for the season. On second thought, neither did the weather gods in the Midwestern part of the United States. Meandering into the kitchen, I went straight for the fridge to grab whatever food was easily accessible: leftover pizza and carrots. Food in hand, I flopped onto the worn, chocolate-brown leather recliner in the living room. Slumped on the couch was my dad with his BlackBerry, also known affectionately as his Crack-berry, and his laptop humming on the coffee table, the creases on his face appearing deeper, giving him the look of a man of many more years.

"Hi, Devon," my dad said, acknowledging my presence with a weary voice. It was obvious he had not slept, which would explain all the commotion and lights that filtered upstairs through the cracks in my bedroom door last night from the main floor. The character of our historic home may be worth a pretty penny in the eyes of a realtor, but there is no value in the amount at which it moans and groans with the sneeze of a mouse.

Chowing down on the cold, mushroom and black olive pizza, I browsed the coffee table, and my eye caught sight of a couple of newspaper articles, including, "Couple Dies of Jellyfish Poison on California Coast." I instinctively reached for the article with my empty hand and skimmed across the text, with vague interest as to why my father would have found it significant enough to print off. What connection would a jellyfish poisoning at a beach all the way across the country have to my father? I determined there was no use in bothering him with such trivial information. He looked to be pouring through his phonebook in vain, the roller ball on the BlackBerry in overdrive. I set down the article, grabbed my backpack, and heard the floors creak as I made my way back into the kitchen, and then up the stairs to my room to plow through another night's mountainous pile of homework.

At about 1:00 a.m., I decided it was about time for a snack, which is most often a giant scoop of peanut butter straight from the jar, or two, depending on how many pages are still left on my United States government paper. Crawling over the top of Zeus—my hundred-pound guard dog, who sleeps faithfully on his bed next to mine—I landed on the floor. He acknowledged my movement by raising his head before dozing back to sleep. Our other German Shepherd would, without doubt, be curled up next to the back door. Thank goodness we were not fans of little accessory dogs with yipping mouths sounding the alarm whenever they heard the slightest sound. Tiptoeing down the groaning and cold wood stairs under my bare feet, I entered the already lit kitchen to find my father with the peanut butter jar, the discarded remains of a sandwich on the table, and a shuffled stack of the papers lying across the counter.

"Same idea, I see," I said with a grin, jumping up to sit on the counter.

"It always tastes the best this time of night," he said while handing me a spoon.

"Why don't you just go to bed? You look like a zombie. You're not a zombie, right? Because if you are, then we are going to have some serious issues. I don't have time for this, and my guns are not loaded."

"You always wanted the world to end in a zombie apocalypse. Haven't I taught you to always be ready?" he joked. He then grew serious. "Things have just come up. There is no need for you to be concerned. Now stop working, and get some sleep. You may believe it is possible to live on two hours of sleep, but it seriously will catch up to you."

"Sleep is for the weak. Well, I got my peanut butter, so good night. Love ya."

"Love you, too."

The next day while falling asleep in my government class due to a dull lecture, a monotone voice, and a lack of light, my eyes opened for a brief second to see my phone screen glowing with a message from Dad. My high school graciously purchased desks properly designed for a cell phone to be placed in the cubby under the table counter: we can text, and yet the phone is completely out of the vulture sights of certain teachers hell-bent on enforcing school rules. Sometimes I have to wonder what they were thinking, or more like not think-ing. Regardless, my dad's message asked me to please not go to my friend Anya's house for the weekly chemistry review and to come home ASAP. At this point, I was officially concerned that whatever had been causing him stress was suddenly going to be dumped onto my plate like a scoop of undistinguishable cafeteria food. It wasn't like I had hours of spare time to devote to more obligations. "What's up?" I texted in response. Two hours passed. No response.

The next three hours dragged on, but every line of thought in my paranoid mind somehow circled back to the situation surrounding the reason I was being summoned home on such short notice. My tendency is to overanalyze, which often works rather well for school-work, but was of no use in this situation. Regrettably, my thoughts were focused primarily on the possibility of a horrific accident where someone was dead or going to die. *It could be that there is a surprise waiting at home*, I told my unsettled mind. That optimistic theory vanished as quickly as it was created, due to my father's known lack of spontaneity.

Walking down the vacant hall between our half-period switch between classes, I mentioned to Anya, "I'm not going to be able to make it to your house today. Sorry about the late notice, but I am sure you all will survive without me."

"Is there anything going on, my dear?" she replied, with concern.

"No. No, I'm fine," I denied quickly.

"You are not as talkative as you usually are," she observed, under-standing me all too well.

"No, it's not a big deal. My dad just needs me home, and it sounds like an emergency," I said, with false confidence.

"OK, but you know I am always around if you need anything."

I grinned. "Of course, *mi amiga*."

When I pulled into the driveway after school, everything appeared to be status quo. No unexpected cars were parked along the street. No police tape. No new reporters. Our two German Shepherds, Zeus and Poseidon, were in the front yard. As soon as I pulled in, they came bounding toward me. Zeus dropped a slobbery branch from one of the old oaks growing in the small yard, at my feet, and Poseidon was content to receive a pat on the head before he headed back to a shaded spot as the official guard, no security alarms neces-sary. Animals are notoriously good at reading moods, and these two were as content as a small child with chocolate ice cream dripping down his face.

It all started to spiral into a realm of confusion when my father opened the front door and told me to hurry inside because, looking at his Crack-berry, "We have about eight minutes before we are running on negative time."

Before I was able to utter a single question, he threw a suitcase in my direction, and he instructed me to grab everything that I might need because "We may not be coming back." The empty suitcase weighed heavily in my grasp. Was I hearing correctly? My aunt would swing by later for the two mongrels outside. Yes, my ears were still processing correctly. The situation had now reached the point where I needed to know what was going on, and I wanted to know now, but my father had disappeared into his den with the look of a wanted criminal on the run. Let us hope to God that he was not a criminal. (Although, it seemed highly unlikely, considering the worst he does is drive like Mario Andretti in the Indy 500.)

I figured in my moment of panic and unanswered questions that it might just be best to fly up the stairs and pack my life into a single carry-on suitcase, in five minutes. Ripping through my already chaotic room like a tornado, I wished for once I had attempted to defy the theory about chaos and actually had cleaned up some of my clothes, books, and junk so I could find what I was looking for. I instinctively reached for my collection of well-worn jeans and high school-labeled T-shirts and folded them neatly to maximize space in my quickly filling suitcase. Why am I always thinking overly practical? Zeus was utterly confused by my hectic scramble and whined lightly at me from my door, not wanting to be left behind. He was my shadow, and trips were not his idea of fun when I left him behind. As I threw my weight on top of the suitcase to ensure closure of the zipper, I looked over at my antique wooden dresser with all of my pictures, my memories, and my life for the past seventeen years. If

Dad was right and we were not returning, I found it hard to swallow the idea it would all be abandoned here. Throwing the suitcase on my floor with a massive thud, I snatched up my laptop and the one picture that mattered most: my dad, my mom, and me, when I was two, hugging each other in our boat while the sun set over the horizon of the lake. Enough admiring. My dad was yelling at me from the base of the stairs.

I looked at Zeus's begging eyes. "Come on, Zeus. I promise I will be back soon. Watch over my stuff. Okay?"

About twenty minutes into the mad dash down the tollway, with my dad's black Jaguar pushing ninety, he finally clicked off the head-set jammed into his ear. No longer could I contain the anxiety and the questions that had been pounding through my mind and clouding my thoughts since less than an hour ago. "*What* is going on? You won't talk to me, and now I am being driven to who-knows-where with supposedly enough stuff for me to survive for who-knows-how-long. And without a 'Hey, you might want to be prepared for some things to change,' or even the slightest explanation."

"I'm sorry. I never thought everything would result in this. I thought the past was behind us fourteen years ago, but…one minute." He faded out, while the sonar ringer on his phone sounded.

He had completely forgotten his phone was automatically wired in his car with the radio speakers. We had never kept anything secret between us. It is hard to do when there are only two of us in our family, and unlike most teenagers, I happened to get along well with my father. Today though, the call picked up, and all I heard before he snatched up his phone to disable the speaker was a man's voice in a quiet, but shaky tone masked by a massive amount of static. I thought I caught something along the lines that someone had arrived. Great. Now, we had other involved parties and someone or something after us. With that, my mind went reeling off into a world of unknown possibilities for my near future, where no amount of ice cream and movies would remedy the situation. I kept staring dead straight at the road in front of us, eyes unblinking until the road became a blur, and letting my breath out in a forced sigh.

He continued his rapid conversation and veered into the right lane toward the Chicago O'Hare Airport. At this time of day, a minimal amount of airport traffic allowed us to weave in and out of cars at racecar pace and blast through the tollbooth much faster than the allotted fifteen miles per hour. With the jets taking off and landing only right above the power lines on I-90, I was just glad to be headed in a familiar direction. It also meant that our identities were not completely red-flagged if we planned on flying.

"Here is your boarding pass and an explanation. I know you are an intelligent and bright young lady and will understand. For your own safety, read this in the best security possible and before the plane lands in Denver." My father handed me a home-printed boarding pass for a direct flight from Chicago to Denver, and a crumbled envelope. I stared at them in my hands, wanting to tear them open right that instant. Then, we were at O'Hare, and he was reaching over to hug me.

"You're not coming with me?" I asked.

"I love you," was all he managed to say with a single tear rolling out of his eye and down an exhausted face.

"You're not coming?"

"I wish I could, Devon. It would only put you in greater danger. All I want to do, all every parent wants to do, is protect their child."

"Protecting me means not abandoning me here." I was on the verge of a complete meltdown.

"I promise it's only for a little while- a week or two. The letter explains everything- who you are meeting and why I have to do this. It shouldn't have been this way."

"Then, why is it this way? Give me one good reason to get out this car and board that plane."

"Because I love you and I need you. If you still don't find a sufficient reason in the letter, please do it for me."

"Where is the return half to the ticket?"

"I promise I will see you very soon. You need to trust me. I love you, Devon."

I let myself out of the car and gave him one last, enduring embrace before he handed me my suitcase from the trunk.

"Who am I meeting there? Are you going to be safe?"

"Don't worry about me. I'll be fine as long as you are. See you soon. Love ya." He kissed me on the top of the head.

"I love you, too."

Ten seconds later, I was standing in shock as the shiny, black Jaguar peeled away from the curb, and I was left to fend for myself with nothing more than what I had in my hands. I felt tears forming, and then falling easily from my blurry eyes. I quickly pushed them away with my sleeve and told myself to make my father proud. It would only be for a little while.

chapter 2

After threading my way through the masses, I found myself at the Starbucks between terminals H and G ordering a Grande Chai latte. I still managed to arrive at the gate exactly as the loud speakers called for passenger boarding in preparation for the departure of my 5:35 p.m. flight to Denver. I was flying into uncharted territory, with an unknown reason, yet I had surprisingly mellowed out in comparison to my panic when I was dropped off earlier. It was probably the old familiarity of O'Hare Airport and my headphones blasting mellow country notes through my head. *Just another flight;* I just kept telling myself. The only voice in my mind was the nagging curiosity over the plain envelope weighing down my backpack since I had jammed it into the front pocket. The urge to tear it open was intensified by my demanding tendency for instant gratification. I figured though it was best saved for my undivided attention on the plane.

At least one thing was in my favor: an emergency row exit seat alongside the miniature oval window overlooking the sky. Considering the ticket was most likely purchased this morning, such benefits were made entirely possible by my father's excessive travel requirements for his job and corresponding mileage. Settled into my seat, I gazed out onto the third busiest runway in the world. An assortment of jets from regional to double-decker international ones performed a synchronized pattern among various runways and terminals. There is something begging description about taking off in a plane. You forget about the crowded, noisy, and stuffy re-circulated air of a commercial flight with the piercing wail of a small child three rows behind you. When the wheels lose contact with the friction of the pavement below, it is like taking off from everything in life and entering a realm not belonging to people. Like the birds, we borrow it from the fleeting wind and tumbling clouds. Flight is only a theory and has never been proven. By flying, it is as if we scream to the universe that its laws scratched out in logical proofs are simply restraints put on us by the world, and the only way to really fly is to jump off the cliff, shouting challenges at Newton.

Since I was going to be gliding at a few hundred miles per hour toward the mountains for approximately two and one half hours, I figured that the sooner I knew what I was in for, the better. I cautiously pulled the envelope from the front of my bag, freeing it from the stranglehold of the electrical snakes that powered my variety of electronic devices. Never having experienced such a feeling before, I could only assume that what I felt was the suffocating and gut-dropping sensation you undergo before a part of your life is shattered into pieces that scatter into the darkest hiding places.

On the front of the envelope was my name in small, blue lettering in the chicken scratch that characterizes my father's handwriting. I tore off chunks of the envelope to the point of destruction before I was able to pull out two sheets of standard, white computer paper with a typed letter. When the paper was free of its envelope, something else fell out: an antique skeleton key about two inches long, dulled from age and whatever story it held secretly inside its cleverly crafted teeth. After twisting it around my hand a couple of times, feeling the smoothed edges of its worn notches, I took off the ever-present silver chain from my neck. The chain delicately held safe my mother's silver Victorian locket with a small etched bird on the exterior that opened up to reveal a black-and-white image of my mother and grandmother, both whom I've never had the pleasure of meeting. I had been too young to remember my mother, and on my sixteenth birthday, a year and a half ago, my father had given a piece of her to me. From the moment I lifted it from the simple, maroon velvet bag, I wore it as she had every day. Next to the locket now hung the key, like ice on my skin. They looked at home next to each other with their imperfections from age. Prepared, as I would ever be, I started to pour over the words found in the letter.

Devon,

It has taken too many hours, although it continues to be not enough. Nothing can describe how much you mean to me; you are my entire life. If I could wind back the clock, I would never have chosen this life for you. I can only hope you will not consider your mother and my decision to think we could have a family without it affecting you, as selfish. I apologize for the secrets I have kept from you, but they were only to protect my little girl. Despite how you will be living on your own at college in the fall, you will always be my little girl. The little girl who held my hand crossing the street, but always told me she was big enough to do it all by herself. And the same little girl who still listens to her music too loud, singing and dancing for the audience of her stuffed animals and the dog. Despite what happens, remember I created this mess, and it breaks my heart to see that you will have to be the one to fix it.

Many years before you were born, your mother and I took a job with a private corporation. We had met each other previously at NYU. Although recently graduated with majors in finance and economics, they marveled at our extensive experience with the economic undertakings of the United States and, to our young eyes, it was a job of big promises and brighter financial payment. We were not the only type of people hired by the various branches of a corporation known internationally as Brecker. The individuals swept up in their hiring spree varied from security personnel and law enforcement, to computer specialists and politicians. No one questioned the lack of focus and purpose the corporation maintained. When questions were not answered, it was easier to simply focus on one's own work and turn a blind eye. A few years down the road, news surfaced that Brecker was operating under the private funds of the Langer family. You are well aware that Alfred Langer was president a few years back; his son Arthur Langer was president only eight short years later, and now his grandson, Landon, has taken office this past year. Not to mention the dozens of other positions within government the extended family continues to maintain. If none of this appears suspicious, then a mandatory reevaluation is in order. Under their distinctly separate private corporations, including the expansive branches of the Brecker Corporation, we were unknowingly manipulating the system in their favor and creating a reputation designed to promote their image and allow the nation to run according to their standards. Everything was proceeding without a hitch. That was all until a couple of us saw past the enormous paychecks and fulfillment of our unrestricted demands not always needed to accomplish our jobs and to what we had created: a monster with a map of influence clutching at every part of American politics and life.

There was a group of us who had become close friends in our few years together. One day, after months of debating and keeping thoughts quiet, except off the job, we decided to jump into shark-infested water. By jumping in, we vowed to do anything in our powers to slay the monster we were responsible for creating. For the next thirteen months, we collected data and found loopholes in our own programming and daily tasks to sneak information beyond the walls and security gates of the corporation. We maintained our normal Thursday night gatherings at the local bar, but instead of just enjoying a few beers over a recent football game, it was about strategy and how much information we would need to safely hide for our day in front of the Supreme Court. The risks were enormous. The tangled and nearly untraceable manipulation by the Langers created a phony system. If that system were to fall apart, the structure we all knew would find itself suspended in midair before an inevitable crash. If those documents were brought to light, the entire United States might be brought to her knees. However, as this weighed down on us, we all knew. We knew that sitting there meant turning a blind eye to corruption of a democratic system and perversion of power. The risk to our lives was nothing compared to guaranteeing the future of a free United States.

Two months premature of our intended departure from the corporation, things took a turn for the worst, although none of us could say it completely blindsided us. They went after one of us. All this time, I persistently explained to you how your mother died in an unfortunate car accident. I did it for you because our life was not yours to pay for. It was ruled an accident by investigators and served as a warning to the remaining five of us. We could have dropped the mission and just played ignorant. The decision, decided around a smoky bar table and a couple of untouched beers, was a unanimous vote on behalf of your mother and her life that had been unjustly taken. That night, we packed our lives and the lives of our families in a few bags and left everything we loved for a couple of bad new names and untraceable destinations. Every word collected in the previous month was copied, encoded, divided among us, and whisked off to foreign destinations with hidden keys until the day we vowed to return for them.

Fourteen years have passed the world by, and with the election of the newest Langer nearing, someone in the Langer inner circle finally navigated through the web we used to disguise our lives and is knocking at our doors with loaded guns. Yesterday, two "accidents" took the lives of three of the remaining five of us. It is a now-or-never moment for our knowledge to crash to the surface. It is apparent as well that we remaining two from the original group cannot be the ones to retrieve and expose the truth, due to the fact they know who we are and what we are planning. Here is where you, along with four other children born to our group of self-proclaimed operatives, come in.

There are four vastly separate international locations where the documents have been stored for safekeeping. If all four sets can be obtained, there is no doubt the Langer family and their partners will come plummeting off their self-proclaimed pedestals. Simply put, the five of you will travel the world and collect them. Each one of you will have a key to unlock a box. Devon, put the key found with this letter on the chain with your mother's locket. Consider it a part of both of our memories. The key will unlock a hidden compartment under the opening/closing bell at the São Paulo Stock Exchange, or Bovespa, in Brazil. Look hard and you will find it. You will find all the supplies and initial transportation details needed upon arrival, in Denver. Please remember if they do not find you now, they will find you soon, unless the utmost care is taken. Stay hidden and avoid anything that can transmit a signal or be traced by documentation. With your love for spy shows and old James Bond films, you should excel as a covert operative in the field.

Upon arrival at the Denver Airport, there will be two of your partners waiting for you by the names of Riley and Rowan. Their father was the pilot of the flight that crash-landed yesterday near where they live in Denver. Rowan is hard to miss with his red hair, and he is the same age as you. His little sister is a petite fourteen-year-old with dirty blonde hair. In addition, you will be responsible for receiving Gavlin Fleet from his international flight returning from Japan. He should require less effort to find considering he is the nineteen-year-old snowboarder you asked me to watch on television during the Olympics. His parents are the ones you read about in the article with the jellyfish poison on the California coast. After Denver, you will find your way to Florida to pick up the final member of your group, Falon. Her father was involved with the entire process and is the only other surviving member of the original group. For her safety, he left her with family friends once we dispersed throughout the country.

From here, there is nothing more I can directly tell you. When you touch the tarmac in Denver, there will be ten days at maximum to make it to the Hague, or Peace Palace, in the Netherlands: your final destination. The court is only in session until this point. If you can make it into the building, you will be on the sovereign ground of the International Court of Justice and in the presence of the United Nations.

You are on your own now, and I will be waiting for you when you cross the street toward home.

With infinite love,
Dad

There was not a moment while reading that I stopped, thought, or took a breath. I was unsure if I wanted to pretend this was all some horrible dream, and Zeus would soon be barking in my face after barging up the stairs to wake me to the smell of homemade blueberry pancakes, or if I wanted to scream. In one short letter, my dad had dealt me a hand greater than he had been capable of handling. Fair or not, there was no way I was going to fail my father after the years he devoted to me. He always preached that if you were going to do something, then you might as well do your best. Cheesy words to live by, but those clichés stay around for a reason. Deep down, my instinct would never permit me to jump ship even when everything was headed toward Davy Jones' locker. Being one's own toughest critic is no doubt a double-edged sword. I needed challenges, but this might be overloading my sinking ship with lead weights. On the brighter side of my grim future, if I survived being chased by men with power much greater than my own and most likely ammunition, it would be worth enough stories to last a lifetime. I sighed deeply and looked out on the dark ocean from my position behind the stationary wheel, the eerie calmness surrounding me with a chill.

Upon landing at the Denver Airport, I rolled my black suitcase behind me with my backpack slung over my shoulder, in preparation to meet my newest companions. I must have looked like the spitting image of beauty in my typical wardrobe of ratty Converse sneakers, a high school branded T-shirt, a brown North Face fleece jacket, and jeans that hung over my slender five-foot-three body. I have never been a fan of makeup, which always complemented my shoulder-length brown hair being thrown into a messy bun low on my neck.

Just off to the side of the gate, I saw the pair I had been sent to meet. If it had not been for the boy's flaming red hair and accompanying pale skin with freckles, it would have been significantly harder to spot them among the hustle and bustle of the airport. Other than the hair, he wore worn-out and well-faded loose jeans with a gray and navy-blue printed Colorado Springs hoodie. His stretched out six-foot stature stood tense as a dog waiting to defend his own against an intruder, green eyes soaking in every detail of his surroundings. As I looked closer, I could tell it was taking all his energy to maintain his defensive presence. Everything had obviously taken a toll on him, and considering the circumstances surrounding what the past twenty-four hours had been for me, there would have been no talking me off the tower if I had needed to also cope with the death of my father. Standing to his left was whom I presumed to be Riley. Her dirty blonde hair curled loosely around her pale face, while she waited anxiously. Standing about the same height as me, with obviously a lot more growing left, we sharply contrasted. She wore slim-fitting jeans tucked into brown cowboy boots and a cherry red, sheer, dressy shirt that one would find at a downtown boutique, complemented by a brown leather jacket. Minimal traces of makeup brought attention to her bright chestnut eyes, which gave her face an innocent glow. Catching sight of me, she tapped her brother on the arm and pointed in my direction with a bright smile on her face. Her cheerful expression slightly perplexed me, considering our lives were practically in limbo. Ten more steps forward, and I had parked myself in front of them.

"Are you Rowan and Riley?" I asked with almost certainty.

Rowan was the first one to immediately respond. "Yes. You must be Devon. Nice to meet you. I'm Rowan, and this is Riley," he said in a casual manner, gesturing over to his sister who waved her hello.

"Well, we better get going then, my accomplices. We need to go find our other friend," I stated, chasing after Rowan who was already one step ahead of me and headed off at a brisk pace.

"Bruce, who will be our escort, already found him at baggage. We need to meet them at the plane," he explained while looking over his shoulder and weaving through the airport as if it were his second home. Logically, his father did work as a pilot at this airport, and he likely shared his father's love of planes. Personally, I was more impressed that he managed not to careen into anyone while looking behind him and walking forward. I am unsure I could have managed such a feat even walking through a vacant airport.

"We have a plane?" I said, surprised, causing a lapse in awareness. Unfortunately for the overstuffed luggage of a middle-aged woman, this sent my rolling bag careening into her luggage before I yanked it to freedom and scurried after the other two.

"Actually, it's a Gulfstream G-five-fifty, which is a jet," he said with a brief boyish grin before we came to a door marked "Designated Personnel Only. No Exit." He rapidly whipped a key card out of his pocket and slipped it through the scanner on the door. We stood on a walkway leading down onto the black asphalt of the runway. The rumble and vibration of the planes was overpowering, along with the smell of fuel and what I suspected to be burning rubber as the planes touched down prior to screeching to a halt. A few hundred feet ahead, in the land of metal workhorse giants, our luxury transportation with wings waited patiently. Although I knew not an ounce about the capabilities of our Gulfstream, its sleek body style, sharp nose, and large rear engines still gave air to a sense of unmatched speed and performance. One hundred feet and millions of dollars. This must be how the other half, the rich and famous, live, I thought absently. Standing at the base of the staircase descending from the jet's door, Rowan reached behind me and grabbed my rolling suitcase.

"Thanks," I mumbled as I scurried up the steps after Riley. I could have handled my own suitcase. When I reached the top of the metal staircase, a man in his late fifties with a professional suit and sunglasses perched on a full head of silver hair, greeted me.

"'Ello. You must be Devon. It is a pleasure to meet you," he said with a thick British accent and shook my hand.

"Nice to meet you, as well," I replied, politely.

"Make yourself at home." He motioned to his left at the rest of the stately jet interior. He then turned to join Rowan in the cockpit in preparation for our takeoff.

chapter 3

I stood staring in awe. On each side of the jet were five plush, taupe leather seats with each pair sharing a secured wooden table between them. Behind the seats, on the right, was a leather sofa, which would look super comfortable as a bed if we were still in flight tonight. The back was home to a small kitchen, and I could have sworn my stomach growled. The chai latte had not replaced my lack of dinner or absent mid-afternoon snack. Please let there be food, I mumbled as a quick prayer. Aside from the major elements, the small details of the jet included deep, rich, mahogany-colored wood accents and elegant, yet simple cream-colored curtains and carpeting. I was just waiting to find a trace of 18 karat gold or diamond accents.

After looking about, there was no doubt why these Gulfstream jets were the choice for the rich and famous. Thinking of celebrities, my eye spotted Olympic gold medal snowboarder, Gavlin, in the farthest back seat on my right. Right now, the combination of the death of his parents, and jet lag, must have gotten the best of him. He appeared to already be sleeping, reclined completely back in the cushioned recliners that replaced the standard blue cramped, poorly cushioned commercial airliner seats, his shaggy black hair falling over his face. From the media coverage I had seen of him surrounding the Olympics only months earlier, it was not surprising to see him in black skintight jeans and a yellow flannel button-down covered partially by a black jacket, with his white iPod headphones threading out of his ears. It was quite amusing to find that while all luggages had been stored away, he could not part with his beloved board bag advertising countless sponsor logos propped against another seat. A couple of seats in front of him, Riley's fingers were rapidly moving across her laptop keyboard, with her eyes glued to the flashing symbols on the screen. Her feet pulled underneath her, a black comforter became an anaconda wrapped clear around her shoulders and suffocating her in the world of her computer. A world existing without all the pain and confusion of seeing a plane take your most valuable things into the ground of a vacant field. It occurred to me that I had yet to hear Riley utter one word. Regardless, we had known each other for less than thirty minutes, and I hadn't had the chance to have a conversation with her. For now, I don't think anyone here was mentally prepared to make small talk with the others on this plane. We were the personification of the years of secrets holding us together and tearing the world apart.

I decided to take a seat across the aisle from Gavlin, grabbed my royal purple iPod out of my backpack, plugged in one ear bud, and gave it a light shake to engage shuffle mode. *Owl City*. I allowed the cheerful beats to play, only half listening to the clear high voice and magical imagery of alligator skies auto-tuning my mood a couple of pitches higher. About ten seconds later, Rowan came striding back from the cockpit and fell into the seat across the table from Riley, who did not even glance up from her glowing computer screen.

Bruce came over the speakers throughout the cabin. "Ladies and gentlemen, it is currently 9:17 p.m. in Denver, Colorado, and we will be departing shortly for Ocala, Florida. Help yourself to the food and drinks in the rear of the cabin, sit back, and enjoy the ride." I guessed Bruce was not only our chaperone for the time being, but also our pilot.

Before settling down for my favorite part of the ride, I quickly glanced across the aisle to watch Riley and Rowan in a halfhearted conversation. The only difference was that if my eye had not seen them, I would have missed their silent exchange. Their hands glided through the space around them with facial expressions worthy of complete sentences. It was mesmerizing. Never in my life had I seen people use sign language and could not recall any experience with a deaf person. If she were deaf, it would explain one reason why Riley had not uttered a word since I'd met her. My lack of knowledge about this whole different way of life made me instantly unsure how to talk with her. I had no clue how to act, how we would understand each other, or what questions were acceptable to ask. As a child, we are taught not to stare or to ask people about such personal things, but my curiosity had wheels turning. While I was awkwardly staring at their conversation, Rowan caught me in dead stare. For a moment I caught his vibrant green eyes glaring in my direction before he stood up and disappeared back into the cockpit to serve as our copilot. I whipped my head to face the other direction and watch the world grow smaller through the window. Cars and illuminated night streets turned to Tonka toys beneath us, until it was nothing but darkness on our way to Florida sunshine.

A couple of hours later, having sacrilegiously thrown away my iPhone at the Chicago airport for fear it would be traceable, and never having worn a watch a day in my life, I guessed it was around midnight without the time changes we experienced from mountain to eastern time. I was starving and decided to scavenge around in the back kitchen for food. In addition to my rumbling stomach, my left foot was painfully asleep to my knee, and the muscles throughout my back needed to be stretched from sitting with my feet stuffed underneath me. Meandering a few steps toward the back, half-dragging a foot that had fallen asleep and had no intentions of waking up any time soon, I was not the only one with food in mind. Gavlin was already crouched at floor level, foraging like a raccoon through an unlatched garbage can around the cabinets and successfully pulling out a variety of pretzels, chips, and cookies.

"I see they have a nice healthy selection there," I joked. Gavlin practically levitated straight up and around to where I was propped against the counter with the small sink, a bag of trail mix still clutched tightly in his hands.

"Hey. Sorry. I didn't see or hear you come over here. Looks good to me," he said, overcoming his fright quickly, and grinning after realizing who it was. "We haven't met. I'm Gavlin."

"Devon," I replied. My pulse raced slightly, and my mind ceased normal function at the sight of an international celebrity standing only a couple of feet away from me. I was not the type to be obsessed with celebrities and never thought of myself as someone who would completely freeze at the presence of anyone, no matter how famous. Thankfully, my mind slowly started to process full thoughts, and I quickly jumped back to the conversation. "I normally will not eat this crap, but since it is about midnight, I am on a plane, I am starving, and this has been a hell of a day, I say what the heck."

"Want to join me? It'd be nice to have some company," he said.

"Sure. Considering we will probably be sharing a lot of quality time together for at least the next few days, we might as well get to know each other," I said, my pulse fluttering out of my chest at how normal he was treating me. I know that celebrities are regular people, but never having been in contact with such a group of people, it came as a weird shock. We were only a year and a half apart in age, and I am sure plenty of girls my age would have practically died to meet him. Surprisingly, he did not automatically push me away fearing that I was some obsessive girl with the screen name "Mrs. Gavlin Fleet."

After moving his board bag, I sat across from Gavlin with a collection of cheap, processed junk food and a couple of water bottles consuming the small table between us.

"For someone who lives in the public eye, you are really laid back," I blurted out, immediately regretting how it sounded.

"Um, thanks?" he said with a carefree laugh that momentarily erased the sunken features of his face.

"I am assuming you know what we are really gathered for," I stated, trying to avoid the topic of his parents' recent death.

"I have details, but being in Japan and coming back makes all the details a little shuffled. Yeah, kinda."

"Where is your wonderful stop on the list of secret document hiding locations?" I jumped straight into the newest adventure. A trick I learned long ago. If I could just keep myself preoccupied, I could evade the mental breakdown.

"Zermatt, Switzerland. Some of the best boarding in the world. I might get lucky and be able to ride a bit."

"That would be unbelievable to actually ski any form of powdery snow. In the Midwest it's hard to find anything that is not a frozen sheet of ice," I managed to mumble, while chewing a handful of SunChips and smiling, surprised at how easy it was to talk as just two teenage kids. Clearly, I was not the only one on my mental plane ride above reality until the engine coughed through its last drop of gasoline.

"If it's the right time of year, it's sick."

"Then, I hope we get to."

"We will," he assured me with joking seriousness.

"Sweet. I have no doubt that the fan girls eat up your dashing smile." "I could not help mentioning his continual, yet genuine way of speaking, despite the ghosts hanging over him.

"Thanks. Yeah, I know."

The next couple of hours involved me falling for his contagious laughter and constant smiling, in a schoolgirl crush fashion, while we talked about anything the conversation connected to: anything but the here and now. Slowly, Gavlin slouched back farther in his seat, and I crossed my feet under me, allowing the leather seat to transform into the recliner found in my living room at home. For someone I had a celebrity crush on since he burst into the spotlight surrounding his Olympic win, he was one of the easiest and more open people to talk with. He was clearly not concerned that I would take any of his secrets to the first tabloid reporter I could find when our "vacation" ended. He was envious of the calm of my life, and I was envious of his worldly travels and lack of fear for anything, where the chance of living was only slightly higher than that of an epic death.

When Rowan walked up to the table, which looked like the remains of a war between hungry, unmannered giants, it took Gavlin and me a couple of moments to gain our composure from a story Gavlin had just narrated about the culture shock of traveling for a snowboard competition in Japan at the age of fifteen. Needless to say, he was naïve and thrown under the bus by older snowboarders regarding traditional Japanese etiquette. Rowan appeared slightly fed up with our nonsense, but he waited while we calmed down before spilling out the plan for the next few hours.

At least someone had a plan, because my life decisions were often based on a play-it-by-ear program, which worked with varying and unpredictable success. Right now, it just kept me away from freeing all the questions struggling to break free from the shackles of the envelope in my backpack.

"In twenty-five minutes, we will land in Ocala. There will be no leaving this plane. We have to pick up one more person, and then this flight heads straight to Costa Rica." With his couple of direct statements, Rowan simply walked back toward the cockpit of the plane without acknowledgment of any agreement to his decisions.

"I guess that is what we are doing," I said, looking back at Gavlin's face, who also seemed slightly taken aback.

"Guess it doesn't matter what we say," Gavlin said.

"Now, I am not sure my story is going to top yours about Japan, but my father and I spent a couple of weeks in the Netherlands," I offered, claiming another tale of culture shock to a sheltered American teenager.

We had been sitting in the plane, as directed, at the airport, for a little over an hour. In that time, I became shockingly aware what a horrible idea it was to engage in a game of Texas Hold 'em with Riley. For fifteen, the kid was a poker wiz with a face convincing enough to make you second-guess your own gut instincts. Gavlin seized a couple of bags of Skittles and M&M'S from the back cabinets for collateral. An hour in, Riley sat perched in her chair with about every highest-valued red Skittle and M&M in the pot, while waiting patiently for me to either raise her my last couple of green M&M'S by going all in, or folding for the round.

"Fold," I sighed with exasperation at my losing streak and slapped the cards down on the table.

"*Good game*," Riley wrote in her flowing handwriting on the notebook she held up to us. We had all learned quickly that Gavlin and I were hopeless at reading lips or understanding her signs, so the paper and pen method worked out brilliantly. Throughout the game, the look on Gavlin's face moved quickly from irritation to frustration as the silent, but deadly killer in an angelic disguise took all our cash. As he'd mentioned earlier in our conversation, his unsurpassed competitive drive could not be turned off, even if it was only a game of candy poker to pass time and keep the distractions at a maximum.

"I am out," I said and popped the candies into my mouth with a jokingly defeated grin. "You look like you still have some change there, Gavlin." I pointed out the meek presence of three green Skittles and a single blue M&M.

The sound of footsteps on metal stairs caused me to look around the side of the chair into the aisleway. Riley caught the fact that we were both looking for the source of some noise and held up her hands for the universal sign of "what?"

"I believe your brother and whatever-her-name-is, are here," I replied.

Rowan entered the plane, followed by the final member of our mission group. She was sporting deep azure designer jeans with a belt entirely covered in shimmering stones and designs. Her crisp polo shirt was embroidered in the fashion of team polo uniforms, with a scripted number "3" in the top right corner and a lavender purple strip running diagonally across a pastel blue shirt. Chestnut-brown ankle boots lent another inch to her already five-foot-eight frame.

Pulling her Dolce & Gabbana glasses off her straightened jet-black hair, her ice blue eyes were a stunning and slightly spooky contrast to her Hispanic skin tone, as they scanned the jet in approval. Rowan, once again, went straight to the cockpit.

Waltzing up to the table, she introduced herself. "Hello. I'm Falon. Nice to meet y'all."

"I'm Devon, and this is Gavlin," I said while giving him a bump with my shoulder because we had both jammed into the same seat across from Riley. "And Riley," I said, pointing across the way.

"It is nice to have faces for the names. I have heard from the gentleman who walked me here that we will be flying down to La Universidad de Costa Rica de San Jose first," Falon explained in a way that indicated a native Spanish accent.

"Nice accent," Gavlin commented.

"My aunt and uncle, whom I live with, are from Costa Rica. I see you are all busy with your card games. If no one minds, I am going to make an international call to Costa Rica to guarantee everything will be prepared upon arrival."

"*Call?*" Riley gestured with her hand, miming a phone to her ear, and showing concern.

"Actually, we do mind," Rowan stated while walking down the aisle, obviously having been listening in on our conversation. Riley was still looking for an answer and clarification as to what she believed Falon had said. Earlier, Riley had informed Gavlin and me, reading our curiosity and not wanting to be rude, that she could not hear a sound, though she could read lips if we spoke normally and faced her. In addition, she would have a much easier time once she started to understand the way we each talked. When Rowan came to a halt next to Falon, Riley rapidly signed something to him. All he did was take his fist and move it in a downward motion with the nod of his head, which indicated "yes" and satisfied his sister.

"I see no harm in ensuring he will be available when we arrive," Falon said defiantly, her hand holding an iPhone encased in pink and accented in shiny stones.

"There is not a chance I am going to allow these people to track us any more than they already have," Rowan spat vehemently.

Falon's eyebrows immediately shot up as she defiantly shifted her weight back on her left hip. "Fine, but when he is not there and we have no access, do not come complaining to me or expect me to solve the problem." Following her declaration, she spun around and delicately lowered herself into a chair across the aisle and rapidly texted away on her phone with the little pinging sound of her manicured nails hitting the screen.

Rowan had caught sight of this as well, took a half a step in her direction, snatched the phone from her grasp from above, and even at the sound of her screaming, took a few steps toward the front of the plane before launching it out the open door. He waltzed back to find Gavlin and me snickering in an attempt to hold in the laughter, and Falon glaring at him with a gaping mouth. For a second I wondered if someone was going to have to tear her claws out of him in the next twenty seconds. As he casually glared back at her, she let out a frustrated yell, snatching her purse from the ground and turning toward the window with both arms and legs crossed.

"Sorry we took your seat. Your little sister just managed to slaughter us in Texas Hold 'em," Gavlin said to Rowan as he stood up, forcing me to awkwardly stand up as well.

"I should have warned you she has a bit of a knack for cards. In case you didn't know, the plan is to land in Costa Rica at the San Jose Airport, drive to the university, and grab the documents Falon was instructed to receive." He spoke and signed for his sister at the same time.

"Sounds good, man."

"Here. I brought some real food," Rowan said, holding up a couple of bags of Chipotle. None of us questioned how he had acquired that type of food at this hour and, honestly, it really did not matter.

"I see we are setting the mood for the trip south of the border," I joked and shoved a tortilla chip in my mouth while unpacking one of the bags on the table. Although it was only about 6:00 in the morning, I was not opposed to a couple of burritos, chips, and tacos with some of the best guacamole I knew of in my homogenous, white suburbia. I made a mental note that we needed to make some time and enjoy some traditional Costa Rican cuisine when we arrived in San Jose, temporarily forgetting that this was not a vacation.

Riley signed something to all of us, which was lost on everyone except Rowan, who helpfully interpreted. "Riley says it was a good choice to take the food because she is not giving her candy to you." Then Rowan snatched up a handful of candy, only to be playfully punched by his sister before he snuck back into the cockpit for takeoff.

chapter 4

As we descended toward San Jose, it appeared we were planning a landing straight into the dense rainforest in *Jurassic Park* movie style, complete with screeching, bloodthirsty dinosaurs. The lush, tropical forests blanketed the ground for miles until suddenly we flew into the airspace of San Jose, one of the larger cities in Costa Rica. From above, the city panted with the life of small cars, crowded buildings, and people scurrying about the maze of intersecting roads and buildings cropped from the ground that was once teeming with the life of various other species.

As quickly as the city emerged from the forest, we were abruptly headed for a thin line of pavement on the city limits. With our intended runway destination close to the highway, I could see individual people in the cars as our landing gear skimmed only a hundred feet above them. The first bounce of the tires as they grabbed hold of the cavernous crevasses in the pavement, long overdue to be paved, lead to an abrupt and turbulent landing. Luckily, before our arrival, Bruce had reminded everyone over the loud speaker to fasten our seatbelts. If not, I would have been slammed into the table in front of me instead of just my stomach suffering the choking clutch of the seatbelt. We taxied over to a quiet spot away from the commercial jets near a couple of other smaller prop planes on the outskirts of the airport tarmac. Even with the larger planes, ours might as well have sported a flashing neon arrow sign when compared to the little planes, whose engines were questionably suitable enough to make it to the next major city. My own mind was suddenly paranoid about how vulnerable we actually were.

"Everyone, take only the few things you may need. It is going to be a short ride to the university," Rowan directed.

"I'm ready to stretch my legs. Where better than a place I haven't seen!" Gavlin said while handing me my backpack.

"Stay safe. I will be waiting when you return, fueled and prepared for departure," Bruce assured us from the door of the cockpit as we descended the stairs.

Unsure if anyone had a clue to our desired direction, I took the lead toward the airport building. I headed for the path being used by several airline passengers, as they entered a set of glass doors after walking off their flight with carry-on luggage in tow. The airport personnel directing traffic appeared unconcerned with our presence when we walked clear from the opposite direction of the arriving passengers and through the doors. Entering the airport, I observed it was smaller than one gate at the Denver Airport, with people permitted to wait for arriving passengers directly at the gate. Clearly, airport security was either not an issue in Costa Rica or a slightly neglected issue in airport management. Regardless, we wove our way through a couple of hallways until we were standing directly on the curb in front of the airport.

"To make this easier, I have one rule. I do the talking," Falon insisted when we were all gathered together.

"Riley says she thought that was her job," Rowan said, and we all laughed slightly. For the sake of communication between everyone, Rowan had developed a habit of interpreting for his sister.

No one could contest Falon's self-proclaimed position as spokesperson for the group considering she grew up in a Costa Rican family and spoke fluent Spanish. The most I could have managed was "hola" or "gracias." Gavlin flagged down a taxi, and once the car pulled to a stop, Falon bent over to the window to instruct the driver in her brisk Spanish tongue. After a quick conversation, she indicated that we all needed to pile into the taxi. Our taxi was a decrepit compact car with probably an excess of two hundred thousand miles. I only had to wonder if, at this point, every warning light on the dashboard was disabled in order to evade the time and funds required for the mechanical repairs. Regardless, I pried open the scratched, dented, and bent door and climbed into our chariot. Clearly, not all legs of this trip were going to be as posh as our million-dollar jet, which was fine by me if it kept us off the radars.

"The three stick people are going in back," Gavlin voiced in reference to us three girls.

While he was clearly over-complimenting us on our size, in reality, a couple of us were relatively short and compact. Four people squished into the back seat of a car make for intense closeness, and even more fun, for the forty-five-minute to drive into *la ciudad*. I congratulated myself for picking up another word in Spanish. Once off the straighter highway, the taxi jolted as if we were on a rusted, teeth-rattling carnival roller coaster, as the driver alternately stomped on the gas, slammed on the brakes, and then floored it around a couple of hairpin turns on our way into town. I most remember watching Riley turn ashen as I buried my face in my hands to ward off the queasy feeling in my stomach. When we finally came to a lasting halt, I looked up to see the front of an ornate, ancient stone building. The sign on the front lawn indicated it was part of La Universidad de Costa Rica. The first story was built from almost black stone, while the second floor was a faded white. The windows stretched out from floor to ceiling and were accented by columns. After realizing we had arrived, Gavlin threw open the door to a rush of fresh air and practically fell out.

"I can breathe again!" he celebrated with a dramatic breath. Next to me, Riley laughed a little, legitimately relieved to breathe in the cool, clear air, mimicking Gavlin's deep breaths.

"And I thought New York cabs were bad," I added.

"That is something I could not agree more with," Falon said after she finished paying our driver.

"Where did we get that money?" I asked.

"Our parents didn't leave us without some help. There is a stash of money in the plane's safe, of various currencies," Gavlin answered before Falon.

"That is reassuring," I replied.

Pulling out a piece of paper from her black purse, Falon said, "Now, in a letter I got yesterday from my father, who was supposedly dead long before then, he told me to enter the building for judicial studies, on the southern side. Then, on the second floor, find the office of Professor Andrés Gallegos."

The fact that her father rose from the dead a day ago added a plethora of questions to the unanswerable list in my head.

Being a university, it was not entirely abnormal to see a mismatched group like ours entering through the stiff wood doors of the building. For all they knew, we were four big-eyed gringo exchange students with our guide. Once inside, it was apparent the recent designers managed to maintain the same authentic aura found on the exterior, with modifications to assure durability against the foot traffic associated with a college campus. Across from the entrance, a staircase led us to the top of the building, which was the second story. The muddled echo of footsteps followed us the short distance up. The second story was a simple, straight hall with doors lining the corridor for the length of the building on both the right- and left-hand sides.

"I think we should split up, take separate sides of the hall, and look on the doors for his office. How about Riley and Rowan go left, and the rest of us will head right. Okay?" I asked the group expecting no rebuttals.

"Great! Let's go," Gavlin said and walked off to begin looking at name placards on the right wall of our side of the building.

For a weekday afternoon, when one would expect there to be classes, the building was fairly quiet. In the entire time we wandered, I saw two students exit a professor's office and meander down the wooden hallways. Falon, Gavlin, and I scanned all doors, with no sign of "Andrés Gallegos" on our half of the hallway. Finishing at a dead end, we headed back toward the center staircase, with disappointment. Before we walked the length of the hall to the center, Rowan and Riley were headed back in our direction, and by the look on their faces, it appeared they had found something.

"Last door on the right," Rowan said, pointing.

"Lead the way." I hoped our professor was in his office.

Tucked in the corner at the end of the hallway was a plain wooden door with a simple name placard screwed to the right of it. Gathered around the door, we all just stared. The sound of quick breathing floated down the silent hall. If Gallegos could not be found in his office, or worse, lacked any knowledge of why we had flown thousands of miles to meet him, it would be the end. The end before it all began. Staring at the door, we all knew it was the first test.

"This is mine, so I shall knock," Falon finally offered. We all jumped back and allowed her to rap gently a couple of times on the door.

After a couple of seconds, we heard feet walking toward the door, and then the handle turned. In the doorframe stood a man of Hispanic descent who appeared to be in his early seventies, although he moved with the strength of a seasoned athlete, gray hair cut short, and a strongly defined face.

"Hola, mi nieta. Tu padre me llamó y dijo que vendrías."

I had not the slightest clue what he'd just said. Regardless, Falon looked to be a deer in the headlights of an oncoming semi-truck. With her mouth open to say something, shock grabbed every syllable away.

"No, no. Qué diablos…¿Papi?" Falon stumbled out after a couple of seconds.

chapter 5

In response to her mumbling, the man in the doorway opened up his arms to embrace Falon. I spun my head to face Gavlin with a "What the heck is going on?" look. Not only was there a language barrier, but Falon and the man she had supposedly never met were embracing as family.

"Sorry, I forgot that our other friends do not speak *castellano*. Come in, and I can offer an explanation," he said, switching to only faintly accented English. "Take a seat, please."

We looked around the office, which was probably no bigger than one hundred square feet with ceiling-high bookshelves on every spare wall space. Three diplomas hung proudly behind the professor's desk, but were slightly overshadowed by the precipitous amount of literature on the shelves. It was not that it was unorganized, but the sheer number of leather-bound books shoved onto the shelves overwhelmed the room and caused the shelves to look as if they were bent-over old men, moaning in discomfort. Gavlin, Rowan, and I settled on the worn, maroon leather couch jammed in the corner.

Riley opted for a seat on the arm of the couch. Falon sat on a wooden chair the professor pulled out from behind his desk. He joined our circle of non-conversation on his swiveling chair that now resided in front of the desk. Falon clearly had not recovered from seeing this man, to whom none of us had been formally introduced, and like the rest of us, she simply continued to look at him in shock. She was seeing a ghost, and the rest of us were just wondering who was behind the illusion.

"I apologize for the clutter," he said, motioning to the stacks of papers where the top of his desk must have existed. "My deepest apologies for not formally introducing myself. Professor Andrés Gallegos, and the grandfather of Señorita Falon," he said and stood up to shake our hands.

"Falon, how could you not know we were visiting your grandpa?" Gavlin asked, confronting the elephant in the room.

"I would have told you if I had known."

"So, you did not know your grandfather's name?"

Falon dropped her gaze to the floor to avoid an answer she could not form.

"If you do not contest, it would be best if I approached the situation from the beginning," the professor calmly said. Without a word of yes or no, he must have taken our puzzled and questioning faces as the indication to proceed. "Many years ago, your papá, Falon, came to live at this university. He lived here for two years as an exchange student from The University of California in Berkley before returning to the United States. He spent his second year in Costa Rica, at my home. The same age as my children, he became another member of the family. He was enrolled in my department to study law, and I was privileged to teach him. He was a magnificent student. We grew accustomed to discussing the cases after my lectures. Despite my questions and statements against his ideas, he defended them with passion. His ability to reason an argument was better than any student I'd had; still, I like to say he learned how to listen from me. These two concepts must be equal if you are to succeed in any area of study in your life. Carry this advice with you for life.

"When he returned to the United States, we stayed connected. He would come to visit Costa Rica at least every year and was always pleased to lecture to my students. It was a privilege to watch him interact with them. It was in those moments I realized how he had grown from the young scholar sitting in my lecture years prior. He told me about you, Falon. You were the only one that kept your father alive after your mother died before you were one year old. A year and one half following the tragedy of your mother, a panicked call came from your father. The knot in my stomach upon answering at 3:00 in the morning threatened to choke me upon hearing his voice. Never one for small formalities, he asked me bluntly where I would hide the two most valuable things in his life: you, Falon; and the box. As far as the box, it resides with me and brings you here today.

"Never did I receive nor ask for further details, but it was my responsibility to see that no harm would come to the daughter of *mijo* or this invaluable box. By the hands of God, my daughter and her husband had recently relocated to the United States, and I approached them with the idea of raising you as their own. With limited details and still adjusting to their new life, my daughter immediately agreed. Less than a day later, your papá flew with you to their home in Florida, the one he had personally found for them only a month earlier. Please believe my words when I tell you your father left his world in the crib at a small home off the Florida coast. Their newest title as your aunt and uncle, and mine as your grandfather, was never a lie to anyone. Your father was the son God blessed me with late in life, and you were my granddaughter. Fortunately, the physical resemblance between you and my daughter was pure coincidence. None of the times they tucked you into bed at night with words of love, or when I hugged you good-bye after you spent *La Navidad* in Costa Rica was a lie. The lies we wove around your father and mother were meant to maintain a safely detached life for you. A life where you could become everything they imagined for their beautiful daughter."

I looked across the room at Falon, taking my eyes off the bearer of this grand dream-like sequence. A couple of tears were rolling down her delicate face. If this was only the beginning, what were the other four faces in this room going to find about our lives when we arrived at the other locations? How many more lies precariously wove our lives together? I needed to know. Was the letter from my father just scratching the surface of our past, and more importantly, my future? I needed my father on the phone now. Falon needed her father on the phone. We all needed the answers. Right now we were lost in the woods. Hopefully, we would slowly see beyond the dense forest, though I had some serious doubts. I was going to need a floodlight for that. For now, I watched Riley slowly stand from her perch on the arm of the couch and approach Falon for a reassuring hug. Falon was slightly taken aback before she slightly smiled and returned the embrace. A couple of hours ago, I wanted to knock her pampered behind off her pedestal. Actually, I still did. For these few moments, though, she needed someone and, not being the most empathetic person myself, I was pleased to see Riley take control of the situation.

Professor Gallegos reached behind his desk and handed Falon a box the size of a folder and only a few inches deep, decorated with the vibrant colors of traditional Central American art. The image of a field, a couple of grazing horses, and a lush tree with vibrant, yellow tropical fruit embellished the top. She opened up her purse—the size of a small suitcase—and dug around until she found a plain silver key. The key fit seamlessly into the keyhole on the box. Falon unlocked and opened it briefly with the lid blocking our view of its contents before, without touching a single item, she shut and locked the mysterious package.

"Your father told me yesterday that this box would bring peace to his life."

"Thank you," Falon said, sniffling, while she held the box tight to her chest. "Can I speak with him now that he exists?" she asked sheepishly. I'm not sure I could have contained a venomous stream of thought upon hearing my own father still existed.

"I wish you could," he said solemnly. "I have no number to offer, although in our brief words he assured me it was time for him to see his little girl." I detected a glint of frustration in Falon's eyes. "*Tú abuela* would love to have you all over for dinner, though I fear time is of the essence, and you must not stay too long in one location. Falon, and the rest of you, if you need anything, please call me."

Falon embraced her grandfather. A few brief good-byes passed between the rest of us; then we shuffled out of the office and walked in silence down the hall. We were all wondering how to address Falon and, personally, I was on the verge of fashioning an excuse as a way to see the contents of the mysterious box clutched in Falon's arms. Riley walked next to me, looking down at her boots that echoed sharply through the empty corridor. Suddenly, she shot her head up and caught my attention with a touch of her hand on my shoulder.

Between her exaggerated gesturing and multiple guesses in our game of charades, I finally deciphered that she was looking to find out where our jet would be taking us to next on our "around the world in eight days" trip.

Until now, it never occurred to any of us to plan a route bearing some logical flow from destination to destination and within our ticking time bomb-like deadline. My only knowledge of the topic stopped with the need for the jet to fly me deeper into South America, to Brazil, and Gavlin to Switzerland. We needed to have better travel management, which automatically eliminated my "play it by ear" mentality, and Falon's idea of planning on "Falon time."

Riley appeared to ponder a thought before turning around to her brother and starting a conversation.

"What are you two talking about?" Gavlin asked Rowan.

"We need to figure out the next stop. Everyone knows their city, right?" Rowan asked the entire group.

"Um, Zermatt, Switzerland," Gavlin answered.

"Bovespa in São Paulo, Brazil."

"We are Boyle Abbey in Northern Ireland." Rowan spoke for both him and his sister.

"Well, commons sense says we head south to mine next, then Zermatt, then Ireland, all prior to being in the Netherlands in a matter of a couple of days," I said. "This could be interesting," I inserted, with a hint of sarcasm.

Blinking against the intense sunlight of day as we walked out of the building and into the outskirts of the campus of La Universidad de Costa Rica, everyone nodded heads and agreed to the intended itinerary. If the entire trip ran this smoothly, we could be on Netherlands soil in a couple of days, with time to spare, which I fantasized spending flying our air limo to a beautiful village in rural Europe, far away from everyone. Riley waved us down a taxi, and we all jumped in for what was sure to be a super enjoyable ride back to the airport. My stomach was already doing flips in anticipation.

Settled, or more like smashed into the back seat of the cab, Gavlin asked, "Falon, you fine?"

"I'm good. Thanks for asking," she politely articulated next to me, though they were the first words any of us had heard out of her since leaving the office. Riley reached over to give her a quick hug, which was a bit challenging while crammed into the back of a taxi. Falon replied with a polite "thank you," which was lost completely on Riley, obvious by her head tilt. In a couple of seconds, Falon noticed her quizzical look and repeated her statement. This time she looked directly at Riley so that Riley could read her lips. Riley responded by sweeping a flat palm starting from her chin and down in front of her. Falon looked slightly puzzled, but mimicked her action, to which Riley gave her a huge grin: "Thank you."

"You're lookin' a little pale," Gavlin said to me.

"I need to get out of this taxi." I tried concentrating on his face instead of the scenery blurring past the front windows behind him.

"There will be no chucking if I am in this car. Look, we're pulling in."

"Thank goodness." I probably only sounded somewhat relieved, just wishing to be standing on any solid ground. Upon my comment, the taxi screeched to a halt along the curb, the momentum violently throwing us forward and then back against the un-cushioned seats.

The amount of foot and luggage traffic in the airport had exponentially increased since our departure a couple of hours earlier. Standing on the curb and waiting for the world to stop spinning, I was unsure how security would handle our ticketless entry.

"*Tickets?*" Riley signed, recognizing my concern.

"Bruce said to show them this." Rowan showed us a pilot's badge and an additional sheet with an official letterhead, from his back pocket. "And we should be able to walk straight to the runway without an issue."

With Rowan leading the way, we waltzed directly to the front of the security line, past dozens of faces glaring in disgust or with puzzled expressions. Not a single airport security member questioned our motives when Rowan flashed the badge. We were escorted in a celebrity-like fashion, without tickets, bypassing the metal detectors, to the other side. It was slightly unnerving to see how easily their form of flight security could be avoided. A security guard in his late twenties and no taller than five-foot-five swept us through a private doorway a couple of hundred meters down the hall. Once inside one set of doors, we were confronted by another door demanding authorization. The scanner on the door, which was in Spanish and which I could only marginally assume the meaning of, readily accepted his badge, with a green flashing light. Ahead of us, he pushed open a metal door leading to a set of narrow metal steps down to the tarmac. We mumbled "gracias" to our escort as he walked back inside.

Exiting through a different door than we had previously entered, we all stood on the steps, scanning around to get a sense of our bearings. The burning rubber, raw airplane fuel, and other chemical smells assaulted my stomach, empty and still struggling to recover from the taxi drive. Falon was casually fixing her hair, while Gavlin had propped himself against the metal railing hiding behind oversized, gold-lens sunglasses, in no rush to make a decision. Riley was making a valid attempt to locate our plane, her hand shielding her eye from the intensity of the mid-afternoon sun casting shining mirages on the ground. Putting on my red Ray-Bans, my eyes were thankful for no longer feeling the fire searing my corneas. I only hoped the engines on our plane were humming loudly and prepared for takeoff very soon.

Oddly enough, Gavlin was the first to identify our jet, and our eyes followed his hand as he pointed off in the distance to the left. "Guys, we have company."

"Isn't that just wonderful," I remarked sarcastically, straining forward to make sure my eyes were not seeing a heat mirage.

On the steps of our plane was a well-muscled, tanned man dressed in black, sporting dark sunglasses and wielding an automatic gun across his chest. Shoulders sharply pushed back, feet spread apart ready to spring forward, his eyes no doubt were scanning the open pavement lying barren in front of him. In the States, that weapon would have drawn swift, unwanted attention, and it would probably be illegal to blatantly displaying this type of force. But we were in Central America, and clearly their perspective on guns was a little bit different. Actually, their policies on many safety concerns were generally a little bit different. I could not help but wonder what their airport crime rates were. Was there any form of law enforcement in our general vicinity? And, more importantly, if these men were already allowed on our plane, should we trust them? Did they belong? Or should we be running? To add to the fun, a few hundred yards away, an additional unmarked jet about three-quarters the size of ours, stood patiently, the identical twin to the man on our jet stood erect on its staircase.

"Damn it," I heard Rowan mumble under his breath before he turned around to instruct. "We need a plan, and it needs to involve getting on that plane."

From behind me came Falon's falsetto voice. "I have an idea. While the general idea may have its flaws, seeing our current situation, it may be our only chance."

chapter 6

Gavlin, Rowan, and I had, after a hop, skip, and a couple of sprints among the various aircraft, managed to sneak around to the backside of our plane and hide as shadows among the foliage lining the outskirts of the airport's paved landing area. Trying to keep my heart from pounding out of my chest was no easy task. Even more challenging was trying to breathe quietly, not to mention simultaneously crouching over in statue formation as to not disturb the foliage. Clenched tightly, my muscles were beginning to shake in rebellion. Every loud breath or sound of rattling leaves from the slightest movement on our behalf caught the breath in my throat as my chest clenched tightly, fearful we would find guns pointed in our direction within the next twenty seconds. I could not help but panic over the idea that there were possibly poisonous mutant-sized bugs in the trees surrounding me. If I saw a bug, it would be a dead giveaway that I do not do creepy crawlies. After watching hundreds of spy movies, I knew we did not have editing, lights, cameras, stunt doubles, or second takes to get this one right. Maybe I could consider applying for the CIA as a covert operative after my newfound field experience, beginning right here in the middle of the Costa Rican jungle. Our signal was unexpected, unpredictable, and undetermined. When the distraction came, involving some form of screaming girls, it would be a matter of seconds to decide when the three of us could make a move. One second in either direction could trigger an avalanche of unfortunate gunshots and unavoidable capture. No pressure. No pressure at all.

Brisk movement from where we had previously emerged at the low airport building caught my eye. Falon came bursting onto the runway from our original location on the stairs with her hands flailing and legs attempting a choppy run toward the two jets. Her ability to look like a duck trying to run, body ill-equipped and without any practice for such action, was a beautiful portrayal of how it looked to "run like a girl." Ironically, I believe she was actually "running." To enhance the performance, a piercing scream rang through the air, filled with a sense of pure panic. Eyes wide open, mouth gaping, and face taut, she embodied panic, with the ability of a fine-tuned actress. Of course, some of it might have been real. She fearlessly flew toward the man standing at the door of our jet, loaded machine gun in hand. With her approach, he spun the weapon into position, with both hands prepared to fire if necessary, and shouted his warnings in English. Instincts kicking in, with a loaded weapon in her direction, Falon halted. Her foot propped on the first step, she screamed, "¡Señor! ¡Señor! Mi amiga…," which was all I heard before her Spanish turned into a rambling mess of more screeching than words. The man obviously had no clue what she way saying and put up his hands defensively to stop her from proceeding up the stairs. Yet, she kept coming with no hesitation, talking at a roadrunner pace and gasping for short bursts of air between the occasional words.

Since he was not responding, she grabbed onto his arm that was not holding the gun with one hand while pointing in the distance with the other. If he had any sense, he would have twisted his arm around, grabbed hers, and dragged her into custody. Initially, his stunned look indicated his uncertainty in how to handle the "native" who had run to him for assistance. Initially, he shook his arm, which Falon had no strength to hold onto, and remained parked two stairs above Falon on the staircase. He scanned in vain for anyone else to assist in the situation, though he felt her dire stress and was reluctantly dragged off with her. With step one in motion, we anticipated he would radio another guard to take his watch over our jet. This gave the three of us, crouched between the leaves, only moments to dash under the plane, jump in, and get her rolling down the tarmac.

When Falon and her prisoner were about fifty feet from the plane, we darted from the underbrush. My pulse was pounding in my throat, and although I was in excellent shape, I was breathing as if I had run a few miles by the time we traveled a couple of hundred feet to the underbelly of the jet. Standing in the protection of the wheels, the distinct smell of burned rubber clogged my airway, and I roughly pushed back the strands of my hair that had escaped ponytail captivity on my head. We scanned the surroundings in separate directions, and with no guns pointed at our skulls, Rowan lead a final dash to the front of the jet. I followed Rowan, and Gavlin flew up the stairs, skipping steps as we went, and praying no one was inside. Safely inside, Rowan ran straight for the cockpit, where he immediately stopped short. I watched with hands on my hips, attempting to slow down my breathing, and I could hear him swearing under his breath.

"Bruce is not here," I heard him call from up front.

Just as Rowan walked back toward me, Gavlin took two steps toward me and, without warning, dive-tackled me to the ground and into the cockpit. I crashed into Rowan with the force of Gavlin behind my own unsuspecting body mass. In my rapid descent toward the ground, I was prepared for impact between the unforgiving ground and Rowan, with Gavlin slamming into me from the other direction. Thankfully, Gavlin's cat-like reflexes kicked in enough that he half caught the both of us before we collectively landed on the floor in a Devon sandwich. Not awkward at all.

"What was—" I started to scream before Gavlin clamped his hand over my mouth and put his finger to his mouth to quiet Rowan and me. When he finally removed his hand, I shot him a dirty look, rubbing my stinging shoulder that had made contact with the metal frame on the pilot's seat a couple of seconds earlier. We silently untangled ourselves in the limited aisle space we all occupied. Rowan appeared moderately displeased, but quickly brushed that look away in exchange for a furrowed brow as he peered out the side of the front glass. Probably a bit on the hasty side, I popped my head up to eyeball our newest situation. Low and behold, our friend's replacement was approaching the foot of the stairs, with his trusted artillery friend.

Huddled together in the cockpit, I whispered, "Now, what are we going to do?"

"We're going to leave," Rowan answered in a matter-of-fact tone.

"I knew you were sitting up front, but have you actually flown anything like this before? I would also like to emphasize there are supposed to be *two* pilots," I added, frightened for my life.

"Not exactly. As soon as I cue the both of you, I need you to get that guard off the stairs."

"Got it, captain," Gavlin said, with a salute. Rowan's consistent, complete confidence in all his intended plans had me ready to strangle him. If the sky Gods were not on our side, then we were all going to pay for his decision.

Slightly hesitating, Rowan jumped into the pilot's seat and starting rapidly checking the systems on the control panel. To me, it looked like a thousand buttons and levers randomly lit like a faulty Christmas tree. I personally prefer cars where there is a steering wheel, a key for the ignition, and a GPS navigation system. Instead, he was programming numbers and flipping switches to create an eerie red glow. Nervously, I thought, *I would rather see a green light over a red one any day*.

"Now," he whispered and swept his hand in a "go" motion around the top of the seat, still concentrating on the controls.

Gavlin and I stealthily walked out toward the main door. Before the guard could turn around, and on my quick head nod, we gave our gunman a shove to the back. Unprepared, he went hurtling down the stairs, bruising every part of his body and crashing to the ground in a heap. Deliberately hurting another person felt terribly wrong, and the unpleasant and regretful gut feeling that we might have killed him sank in.

The rumble of the jet's engines beneath my feet, and Gavlin's voice, snatched my eyes away from the scene. "Devon, get in the plane. We gotta go! That guy down there is gonna kill us. Fuck! Where are those two?"

I had little time for my feelings to linger as we watched the guard slowly start to rise from the dead, body shaken and disorientated. Then, there was the realization he was a human, but he was also a human with a gun, and I was sure he would not be shy to use it.

"I don't know, but they need to hurry it up," I said while I panned my eyes over the runway. There was no sign of the girls, and we needed to get this hunk of metal air-bound.

Suddenly, I threw out my arm to catch my balance on the wall as the jet roared to life, and we were tossed backward. The plane stated to taxi down the runway, progressively increasing speed at a pace that would be impossible to maintain on foot in less than a minute or two at maximum. I could feel the engines revving to their maximum power, and the ground was quickly disappearing behind us. When sparks started erupting from the dragging staircase, Gavlin was given no option but to search around for the power switch. We needed it down for the other two; still, neither of us was sure how much damage we would be doing to the door attached to them. If it were forcibly bent open, it would create a personalized flying coffin. With the bottom half of the stairs retracted, the top half became a steep, slick, and flat platform. Where were they? Thirty more seconds and we would be moving too fast for anyone to run alongside us. Gripping the wall in a death-hold and bracing against the wind, I leaned out the door. We were rapidly running out of viable runway in front of us.

"Rowan, they are not here!" I screamed up front.

"Twenty more seconds and we have to pull the power," he responded, distressed.

Suddenly, I saw two girls emerge from the backside of a commercial plane, sprinting down the runway. One of them was running like a girl with her purse clutched in both arms across her chest, and flailing her feet non-efficiently. The other was behind her, following in a graceful but manic sprint toward the plane. With Riley's slightly heeled cowboy boots, and Falon's small heels, I was utterly impressed they were still running with two good ankles.

"Rowan, do we have a rope or something around here?" I yelled.

"How the hell would I know!"

Gavlin was already one step ahead of me, rummaging around the back cabinets. There were chips, a first aid kit, blankets, and other things flying behind him like the dirt from a dog digging for a gopher. I joined him in the back just in time to unsuccessfully dodge a bottle of glass cleaner before it smacked me in the head. It took me a moment to rub the pain from my temple and regain composure. A few seconds passed before the floor was strewn with every object imaginable.

To my relief, Gavlin, beaming, jumped to his feet with a red and black rope ladder. "Will this work?"

"Perfect!"

When we returned to the door, my eyes had to do a double take. I fought to stay balanced in the open doorway as the wind funneled through. Ten seconds ago, Falon and Riley were sprinting toward the plane. Now, surprisingly, Falon and Riley had reached the tail of the plane. However, also in the picture was a four-wheeled, off-road Jeep, on steroids. It carried three men on their own steroids with guns loaded and balanced on the top of the open frame of the Jeep. Far enough back that I could not make out the distinct look on their faces, I could tell by how fast they were gaining speed that they were out for us. A single bullet had yet to be fired. Maybe we would be lucky and they were following instructions to bring all of us back alive. All good plans involve hostages as leverage, so the spy movies say.

"Gavlin, do you see that?" I yelled over the wind.

"We needed one of those! It is nice of you to join us!" Gavlin screamed to the girls as he threw the ladder outside the door, laughing a little.

Falon grasped on o the ladder and kept running alongside, gulping in air, gasping with every shallow breath. Her once well-done hair was wrapped around her face and trailing behind her from the wind forced around the nose of the plane. The cement pounded under her feet, yet she refused to jump onto the ladder. For a moment, it was as if her mind just told her she could not go any farther. Gavlin immediately lay down on the floor with his arms reaching out to meet her. I knelt down to grab onto his ankles for extra leverage when he would grab onto Falon and Riley.

"Climb!" I could barley make out Gavlin's voice.

Falon looked behind and saw Riley still running, then finally caught a better glimpse of the vehicle closing down on us. She jumped. With only one hand free, she moved up the ladder too slowly until Gavlin grabbed the purse with the precious information and chucked it into the plane, directly in my direction. But I have the reflexes of a sloth on narcotics, so on Gavlin's second attempt today, he successfully nailed me in the head. Luckily, it was a toss that only skimmed the side of my head. With me still rubbing my newest injury with one hand, Gavlin proceeded to pull Falon into the aisle next to me. Stunned from her sprint down the tarmac, she did manage to drag herself away from the door. Under her dark skin, her face was flushed. If she had been any older, I would have been concerned about a heart attack and the possibility of her rolling over dead in the next ten seconds. Almost immediately following, Gavlin dragged Riley, who was huffing and puffing, into the plane. Just as I helped her in the last few feet, I caught a look at our entourage holding guns instead of cameras. They had gained considerable ground. Their rusted Jeep was clearly keeping up with our million dollars of flying metal. Then, the party really got started with a bang—the bang and pop of automatic guns as they opened fire. Clearly now within shooting range, they were out for blood. I could vaguely detect the harsh lines across their faces and the deadly concentration they were using to aim their weapons for a disabling contact with our escape vehicle. The driver was pushing the Jeep, and it screamed in protest, it's engine not forced to such great speed in probably the last twenty years of its life.

"Rowan, we need to get off the ground. Now!" I screamed from the door.

"Shut the door! I still need clearance."

I jogged up to the cockpit to find him absorbed in his job. "Gavlin is shutting the door. In case you failed to hear the gunshots earlier or check the rearview mirror on this vehicle, a Jeep laden with machine guns is chasing us. If we don't get off the ground now, we are not going to have a flyable plane!"

"No clearance still. We could crash into someone, which would be worse."

"That is a risk I am willing to take."

"I'm not, and I'm the pilot."

"Have you seen the mess behind us?" Gavlin interjected, pointing out toward the back of the plane to emphasize my previous point.

"I know, but I need clearance."

"Clearance? Let's go!" Gavlin said, stunned at our reasoning for sticking around. Just as he finished his sentence, another round of bullets came raining down on us. It was unmistakably the hired guns attempting to stop us. If one of the bullets managed to pierce the plane, we would be done.

"Damn it! Everyone, hold on!" Rowan said as the engines whined to a higher gear and we hurtled down the runway to what I was convinced was going to be my death. If anyone believed in any type of gods, this would have been the perfect time to pray. Gavlin ran toward the back, and I braced myself against the wall.

Over the radio, I heard, "Gulfstream five-fifty, no tiene permissión," which I assumed meant, "You cannot leave." No one in this plane clearly cared about words spewing from the radio, in distress, neither did we understand. Suddenly, the hum of the wheels ceased to exist, and we were air-bound.

Rowan wasted no time with a steep nosedive toward the sky. The little jet climbed and climbed until there was nothing more than the specks of some planes, and the Jeep, where I was sure they were cursing obscenities. The comical scene from *Madagascar 2*, when the group of rogue penguins fly the plane and the engines gave out, kept replaying in my head, with the lines: "This is your captain speaking. I have good news and bad news. The good news is that we will be landing immediately. The bad news is, we're crash landing." And then the plane goes into a dive as it hurtles toward the earth. "When it comes to air travel, we know that you have no choice whatsoever, but thanks again for choosing Air Penguin." This is how I imagined our own fate in the next twenty seconds, minus the comedy. "We know you had no choice, but thanks for choosing this mission." I stood board-flat against the wall behind the pilot seats, my hands pressed to the walls on my sides. For a person who enjoyed the feeling of weightlessness from taking off in a plane, I sure was ready to pass on doing it again any time in the near future. When I thought we were practically in outer space, Rowan eventually decided to level out the plane and remove his death grip from the handle controls. Our breathing was shallow and quick. Rowan pushed his hands through his hair, uncovering a face similar to mine. Are we actually alive? For the first time, I breathed a sigh of relief. With no adrenaline left to sustain me, I allowed my shaking leg muscles fold under me as I slid down the wall and slumped onto the floor.

"How's my sister?" Rowan said, the first words uttered since leaving the ground.

"She's fine. A little winded, and she will probably sleep after coming off a running and adrenaline high, but everyone is in one piece. I do not think Falon ever sprinted that much in her life. Your sister came in a few seconds after Falon. Contrary to Falon, I was not as worried she was going to die."

Gavlin came striding from the back, looked down at me with his yellow cat eyes and broke out in a puzzled smile and his typical laugh. "Hey, guys. That was like unbelievable. Next step, we find ourselves a bigger one, and you do it with your eyes closed. How's it down there, Devon?"

"It's actually very nice."

Gavlin offered me his hand and helped me to my feet before sitting down in the other captain's chair on the right of Rowan. I decided it would be best to check on the two marathon sprinters in the back and leave the guys up front. My kneecaps trembled as I braced myself on the walls toward the inviting recliners.

chapter 7

A couple of hours later, we were flying over some part of the Southern Hemisphere toward South America, contently surrounded by clouds, when Gavlin and I decided we should piece back the contents of the cabinets, instead of tripping over ropes, boxes, and tools every time we walked down the aisle.

Holding up a blue bottle of chemical cleaner, I sarcastically commented, "And this is what you threw at my head."

"That is what hit you? Too bad, because I was aiming for this," Gavlin replied as he reached into the piles surrounding us on the floor and pulled out the metal first aid box.

"Well, I would say Falon's massive suitcase-purse hybrid made up for it. Thanks for the love."

"Any time," he said with his smile that could kill any teenage girl.

"Are those other two still sleeping?"

He looked toward Falon and Riley, curled up in their seats. "Yeah."

"I'm surprised you haven't crashed."

"With all my travel, I never sleep at the same time. I can sleep wherever and whenever. It's a great skill to have."

"You just came back from Japan, right?"

"Yeah. We went off the beaten path for this one. No lifts. We had to walk up in four feet of snow just to drop down. It was worth it. I would sometimes just look around and think about how you could never see this on a normal day. Pretty heavy."

"I'm jealous."

"It's all kinda crazy. I spend so much time with everyone watching me, and the pressure to deliver for the crowd drives my competitive nature. Still, in Japan it was like I got a glimpse of normal."

"Well, what is the definition of 'normal' anyway?"

"Only crazy people ask that kinda question."

"Might as well call the funny farm and have the straight jacket waiting, because after this trip I will be certifiably insane."

Gavlin gave me the "come on" look and said, "So far, this has been the best adrenaline rush in a long time. It's a totally different feeling from landing a run. People with guns chasing you in their Jeep while you are in a jet flying down a runway is wicked."

"I'm going to have to pass," I said seriously.

He pointed to the seats where Riley and Falon were crashed out. "At least you didn't have to run in those heels."

"Good point. There is a reason I own Chucks. You never know when you may have to sprint after a moving plane." In my experience, I cannot even manage a brisk walk in one-inch heels. "I swear, heels were made so that girls cannot run away fast."

"Along with other positive effects on the way a girl looks," Gavlin added, reminding me how much of a teenage guy he was.

"No comment."

"It's a compliment."

"Okay. Do you tell your girlfriend that?"

"Are you asking me if I have a girlfriend?" he said with a mischievous smile.

"Actually, no," I halfway lied, my curiosity piqued.

"No."

"No to me, or no to the question you thought I asked?"

"No to the girlfriend. Haven't had one in a while."

"I am sure there are plenty of bombshell blondes just waiting for you to call them."

Gavlin smirked. "Yeah, but I'm lucky to be home for maybe a couple of months in the year."

"But you cannot tell me the idea does not slightly interest you. Most guys would give a lot to be in your position."

"Never said I had anything against it."

I smiled a little before changing the topic slightly. "Do you have any siblings?"

"Two sisters and a brother. Kallie is twenty-six, Brynn is twenty-six, and Sian is twenty-one."

"Sian? Your parents were creative with their names, because Gavlin is not very ordinary either," I commented.

"Better than Matt or David. Your name is pretty unusual, too. I might have heard someone with the name once, and it was a guy."

"Touché. It's quite nice not to be confused with anyone. So, are you close with any of them?"

"Kallie is a little more than six years older, so we weren't really close until I was in high school. She lives in Florida now with her fiancée doing marine biology stuff with rescue dolphins. She's the oldest. She is the one always calling back to check on everyone else, and I think my parents wish she'd never left. Brynn is the typical older brother, and he is the one I call when I need to figure stuff out. Yet, it doesn't matter what, but everything is a competition with us. I only see him when he flies to see me compete, or for family stuff. He is playing the markets in New York, and doing pretty well. Sian and I have the normal 'little brother' relationship. She hated me for years. I annoyed her, and she always told our parents. The pattern never stopped. Now we're past the teenager stage. She still has a little while longer to finish at Stanford. She's the smart and logical one in the family. She's always asking me what I plan to do when I stop boarding."

"And what do you plan to do when *this* all ends?" I was genuinely curious.

"I don't know. I'm just so stoked snowboarding has been this good. My parents gave up a lot to get me here. I do it for myself, but now the only thing I can think about is getting back on the mountain. It's that last connection I have to them." His voice dropped a few notches.

"Well, we'll hopefully be there in a couple of days. On a side note, I think we should have had a camera to film that last action sequence. This is only the beginning. Well, I'm gonna see what our pilot is doing about getting us to São Paulo, considering I have no idea where we are," I said, handing Gavlin a small plastic box, one of the last things left strewn across the floor.

"Think fast!"

I flew around, reflexes tensed to catch something. Just as my body rotated enough to be facing Gavlin, something light wacked me in the side and fell to the ground: a bag of chips.

"Your reflexes are horrible," he mocked.

"You jerk." I grabbed a pillow on the seat and chucked it at his head.

In front, Rowan had his headphones on and was still staring at the controls. I sat down in the chair next to him and looked to my left where I met his forest green eyes.

He pulled one of his ear buds out. "You need something?"

"Just seeing what you're doing."

"Keeping us in the air. We should be landing at about o-one hundred hours, in Jundiai, Brazil. It is the closest I'm willing to get to the city." He looked straight ahead again at the glass windshield of nothing more than white clouds.

"It's fine with me. I love guns about as much as the next person." I had hoped that Rowan would have at least talked with me. Considering we had only heard him talk when it was necessary for instructions or to deal his demanding opinion, I was ready for a real conversation. There must be a human inside the robot shell doing more to keep things in than out. Instead, he replaced the ear bud and kept listening to whatever noise was on the other end. Figuring I was not going to have a conversation with a wall, I got back up, trudged my way to the back of the plane, and found a home on the couch to recover from my earlier adrenaline high.

Someone shook my shoulder and awoke me from my slumber. I slowly opened my lids and saw that it was bright-eyed Riley. She indicated for me to wake up, so I slowly sat up, with the blanket still wrapped around my shoulders. I could have slept for another ten hours, but as five teenagers on the run, sleep was not a top priority. Satisfied that I was awake, she tapped Gavlin on the shoulder, where he was bent over, hidden by the seat directly in front of me.

"The sleeping beast has risen," he said as he stood up and turned around.

Still curled up in the blanket on the couch, I said, "Now tell me why I am up, before I really act like a hormonal teenage bear awoken from hibernation."

"Rowan and I decided it would be best to pack a little lighter. I don't know what you started with, but you can have whatever you can carry on to a plane. No checked bags, because we're going on the radar to jump a plane to Switzerland," he said while grabbing clothes out of his bag and throwing them into piles.

"I'm good then. My dad only let me bring my carry-on bag and backpack. If that's all, then I am going back to sleep." I fell back over and closed my eyes. I just wanted another ten minutes.

"Maybe you could give Falon a hand on how to pack," he said. I looked across the aisle between my slit eyes, and there was our little princess. She had two huge suitcases and a smaller one as well. There were shoes, sweaters, shirts, jewelry, makeup, a hair straightener, and more clothes than I kept in my closet, forming a three-foot-high pile around her.

"You need any help?" I said, slowing rising from the couch and stretching as I walked over to her.

When she turned her head toward the sound of my voice, I feared her blue eyes looking at me might freeze me on the spot. "No. I find this unnecessary and absurd. There is not a chance that I will have *this* all packed into *that,*" she said pointing to her carry-on Gucci bag, "by the time we land in thirty minutes."

I shrugged and pointed with my foot to the piles of shoes, makeup, and accessories. "I would get rid of that, but have fun on your own."

Gavlin looked busy switching all his suitcases into his beat-up, box-like leather suitcase. Falon was on the verge of a meltdown, and I doubted Rowan would be receptive to any form of conversation, so I sat down across from Riley. I pushed the top of her computer screen slightly forward to get her attention. She looked up, saw me, typed something down, and turned the computer toward me.

"I am getting plane tickets from Sao Paulo to Zurich, Switzerland. Not possible with this plane and no other pilot. I am good with computers, people say. =) I re-configured the system a little bit. Just a little. The tickets have our name, but the system will not know. We can go through security, and the bad guys can't follow. Good?"

I typed back for fun, *"You are an evil genius."* =P

Rowan managed to gain clearance for us to land our jet on the runway of a small airport on the outskirts of São Paulo sometime around 1:00 in the morning. We actually buckled our seat belts without being prompted and braced against the seats for the landing of our life. I still felt like seat belts would not save us if we missed the runway and went bounding into the dense jungle forest. I suspect we came in with a bit too much speed, indicated by the screaming breaks and barely completing a halt at the last stretches of runway. For a second during the landing, I saw us becoming the bug on the windshield of another jet waiting its turn for takeoff, only slightly off to the side and at the end of our possible path. The runway had obviously seen little repaving or maintenance since its creation years ago, and the plane's tires seemed to snag on every pothole and crevasse in the splitting tarmac. My body rattled against the seat, and I could not look anywhere but straight ahead at the beige seat in front of me. More screeching brakes and a slight veer to the right, and we were able to avoid any mishaps with the other jets. Regardless, Rowan proved capable in idling down the plane to a lone parking spot. Unsure of what Rowan actually told to the control tower to allow our unexpected arrival, it was a relief to be on solid ground, a common theme of our trip to this point.

Falon was beyond ticked off about her suitcase situation, but she had managed to jam a large percent of her things into one bag and drag it down the stairs. I helped Gavlin clear out the safe in the back, of cash and passports, while Rowan mysteriously tinkered in the lower compartments.

"What is Rowan doing?" I asked the group as we stood waiting for him outside the plane, subconsciously rolling my suitcase back and forth in one place. Riley shrugged her shoulders.

Rowan walked up behind us and pulled out the handle of his suitcase. "We need to catch a cab. Quick."

Before a single question could be uttered, Rowan was speed walking toward the main building. The four of us left standing near the plane exchanged confused looks. We hurried after him. About ten feet away from the door to one of the airport's back entrances, there was a ground-shaking boom, and an instant heat wave washed over us. Instinctively, I jumped and, like everyone else, flew around to see our plane dressed as a Roman candle. It was mesmerizing to watch the twenty-foot flames dance across the plane in contrast with the dark night sky as they crisped the Gulfstream to a burnt nothing. As the smoke and fire crawled into the sky, the stars took to hiding. After the initial shock, it felt criminal to be burning millions of dollars worth of engineered sky travel. We at least could have left it for someone else to savor, or maybe whomever we took it from originally would have liked it back, intact, not as a jar of ashes. Despite my disgust, this was the type of explosion good action movies are made of. If only producers could capture the vibrations from the ground traveling up through my body, the thick smoke, and the heat, hot on my skin, from hundreds of feet away. In the few seconds we stood mesmerized by our blackening jet, the fire showed no signs of slowing down; it must have loved how designer clothes burned.

"What did you do? Do you know how risky that was!" Falon screamed in Rowan's face.

"Questions later, unless you all want to spend the night in a Brazilian prison," Rowan calmly replied as the fire's glow reflected on his face, lending to the image of a raving lunatic. Most guys only dream of blowing up something to this extent. It was scary to think of what he was capable of.

The show was over. We all took one last glance back and piled through the door to the airport, acting as if there was not a raging fire on a runway with thousands of gallons of available gasoline. At this point, the entire sparsely filled airport realized what was happening. The airport passengers scattered like roaches, provoked by blaring security alarms, although some people remained near the windows to capture a video on their phones. I guaranteed myself that a video of our plane would be uploaded and sent to thousands of people via YouTube and Facebook, within a matter of minutes. I made a mental note to tag us in the video when it made it to Facebook. Employees were doing their best, but the panic on their own faces indicated that they were dealing with their own shaken mental state. There was no stopping us as we wove in between screaming children, people on cell phones, and piles of luggage to the front door. By the time Riley and I emerged from the mob scene, the others were already piling their suitcases and themselves into a nearby car. My suitcase was the last one to be chucked into the trunk by Rowan, who had not waited for the driver to come to our assistance. I dove into the back seat, practically landing on Riley. The driver did not speak but a few words in English, and although Falon spoke Spanish, it was close enough to Portuguese to give directions. Right now, anywhere aside from this airport would have sufficed.

The instant the driver put the car in gear, Falon jumped forward from the back seat to be within closer yelling distance to Rowan in the front. "What in the world were you thinking?"

"I was thinking we probably shouldn't leave a trail!" Rowan snapped back at her.

"You could have killed us!"

"I didn't. It's not like we were ever going to see that stuff again."

"You caused a scene!"

"A scene? Would you rather the airport find an extra plane, check the records, and send those people after us?" he sneered back.

"Agghh!" Falon exclaimed and fell back into her seat. She had obviously lost the battle.

Riley poked her brother from behind him and said something with a look of curiosity.

"Strategically placed C-4," he replied nonchalantly while turned toward the back seat.

"Cool. I didn't know explosives were on the packing list. I would've helped," Gavlin said from the seat next to Falon.

I laughed. "I guess you never know when you are going to have to blow up a couple million dollars." I think I saw a smile on Rowan's face from that comment.

An hour and a half later, we were standing on the side of a street in front of the São Paulo Inn, a tan, brick, red-accented four-story building that had seen many years of use. It directly faced a grey-stoned Catholic Church that stood among commercial buildings between two angled streets. The circular stained glass of the church caught my eye, even in the dim light of the streetlamps. None of us had been to São Paulo before, but gazing around at the lights illuminating the city and buildings, it reminded me of a city much like Chicago. What Chicago had in skyscrapers, São Paulo had in traditionally built, older buildings reaching closer to six stories rather than sixty. Thousands of motorbikes lined the streets even at this time of night. All of us stood there taking in the surroundings and hoping that someone would decide what we should do until the exchange opened later in the day. Gavlin pulled out part of our cash from his bag while the other part remained in mine. He found a credit card, which we figured would be safe to use one time. Taking the closest thing we had to a translator, he dragged Falon inside with him. A few minutes later, they happily rejoined us outside.

"I don't know half of what she said or what language she used," Gavlin remarked, pointing to Falon, "but we finally convinced the lady to give us a room. The catch is, it's gonna to be fun getting in."

"And...?" I questioned.

"We were not gonna push our luck, so they think it's just the two of us staying the night," Gavlin expanded with a mischievous grin.

"I take no responsibility," Falon said.

Despite all of Falon's complaining that she was going to injure her fragile back, we convinced her to take more than just her stuffed suitcase. If she mentioned another word about breaking a nail, I was going to punch her. A few minutes after Gavlin and Falon disappeared into the building dragging our luggage, we made a break for it. Considering it is not normal for a bunch of American teenagers to be walking through the doors of a hotel at 4:00 in the morning, we only made it halfway across the lobby before the front desk stopped us. In broken English, it translated along the lines that she was convinced we were a bunch of kids looking for trouble. The reaction on her face when we acted confused and showed her a key card was complete embarrassment. Her actions were no way to properly treat the hotel guests that we obviously were, or so she thought. After evading that small roadblock, we darted toward the elevators. Once the final inch of the door closed, Riley and I gave each other a celebratory high five. Rowan just looked at us in judgment and then straight back ahead. Riley's face scrunched in confusion at her brother's reaction and then must have decided it was not worth asking about. On the fourth floor, we exited into a hallway dimly lit by the few light fixtures on the wall. Without much looking, we found our room and used the room key to let ourselves in. The room was nothing more than a box with a small bathroom, shabbily decorated in beige, with a single queen bed. I was just happy to have a place for the next few hours.

"You made it!" Gavlin exclaimed as he ran to give me a hug that picked my feet up off the ground.

I laughed at how foolishly delusional we had become. "The lady at the front desk looked like she had seen a ghost when we actually had a room key."

"Sweet," he replied.

"What time is check-out?" Rowan asked.

"Twelve," Falon said. "Tomorrow, I will be in the bathroom from nine o'clock to ten o'clock, minimum."

Gavlin bowed. "We shall all work around you, your highness."

Falon looked back in distaste. "Where are we all sleeping?"

"You and Riley can have the bed. I'll take the chair, and the guys can sleep on the floor," I suggested.

A short time and the use of five brains later, we managed to set the hotel's ancient digital alarm clock. I turned out the lights, and the room was enveloped in darkness with only the muted glow of the streetlamps trickling through the curtains. The stiff hotel chair smelled of funky chicken falsely covered by commercial cloth cleaner. The muffled sound of my continual shifting was soon joined by petite sniffles drifting through the stale hotel air from the bed. My pupils adjusted to see a figure on the floor slowly rise and make his way to the side of the bed farthest from me. Crouched near the floor, his presence only caused the sniffling to develop into shuttering, gasping breaths between constrained sobs. Peripherally, I could make out Falon throwing the covers down and crawling across the bed until she sat with her hand warmly passing over Riley's back. I closed my eyes, salty water forming on them. *Not now. Don't you dare.*

chapter 8

"Bzzzzz. Bzzzzzz. Bzzzzzz." I heard sheets rustling and a hand fumbling around to disarm the alarm set for 10:00 a.m. My neck refused to move after sleeping curled up on a chair for the past six hours with my head sideways. Regardless, my feet marginally worked as I half fell out of the chair to see if the bathroom was free. All I wanted was a really hot shower. Riley was wrapped in the protection of knotted sheets, and I had to step over Gavlin, sprawled out on the floor, to get to the bathroom. Propped against the wall and trying not to doze off again, I waited outside the bathroom for a couple of minutes to see if Falon would be somewhat on time. She had given us a minimum time ultimatum, so I knew there could be no guarantees. Low and behold, the door opened. My eyes fluttered open.

"Good morning," she said. For leaving behind most of her bathroom on the plane, her hair was still straightened, and she was wearing a considerable amount of makeup.

"Good morning. You done?" my hoarse voice replied.

"Yes, do I not look done?" she replied slightly panicked.

"No, you look great. Just making sure."

I walked into the bathroom, looking forward to a relaxing shower. The lights in the bathroom were bright enough to force my eyes into little slits as I robotically went over to the shower to turn on the water. I pushed down the knob so the water would come from only the faucet, not the showerhead, to avoid being sprayed. The clink of pipes indicated a response to the demand for water. Suddenly, instead of the water just flowing out in a downward cascade, it sprayed high-pressured streams in every direction. Water was hitting every inch of the bathroom and soaking me as I fought through the explosion to turn it off. Blindly reaching for the off switch, I managed to press the shower release. The water poured out from directly above my head to drench me more with ice-cold water, stealing the air from my lungs. What a wonderful start to the day.

By a little after noon, we managed to rally the troops out of the hotel and were walking down the sidewalk, bags in tow, and admiring the city. We had done a 180-degree change of seasons upon entering the Southern Hemisphere. With the country housing a majority of the Amazon rainforest, the fall weather warmed the city with a considerable amount of humidity. The buildings were in the same proximity to that of a major city, like Chicago or New York. For a city I assumed would have the ethnic diversity of a bowl of red M&M'S, it was closer in resemblance to a Skittles rainbow. While the majority of people were of a darker, olive skin tone, there were considerable Caucasian, African, and Arabic influences. From what my underdeveloped linguistic ear could decipher, they were all speaking the national language of Portuguese. It sounded a bit like a mix of Spanish, with the rhythm of French or Italian. Upon walking, we discovered a new form of entertainment: dodging human traffic down the briskly moving sidewalks, and skirting around the overwhelming number of motorbikes zipping through any narrow opening, while toting suitcases. When the bikes were not producing the high-pitched whining noises of overworked engines, they were jammed together on the side of the narrow streets. Obviously missing the memo on tourist season dates, our Americanized clothing and accented English drew slightly more attention than we would have liked. Still, the ignorant teenage American tourist look might at least keep us from being pegged as five agents on a covert mission to break into one of the most secure buildings in the city.

We figured the only way to get into Bovespa, the São Paulo Stock Exchange, would be later when the market closed for the day at the end of business hours. With any stock exchange, one cannot just walk in, uninvited, and without identification. Therefore, we still needed a plan. It would be a matter of either evading security, which was highly unlikely without knowing what the building even looked like, or finding a way past the guards. After successfully passing security, we needed a brighter plan than just waltzing up and asking to "see the closing bell, to unlock some secret compartment to look for some secretive documents hidden there more than a decade ago." Yet, instead of being well-trained agents, finding a coffee shop and sitting down to talk strategy, we decided to simply play it by ear. Up to this point, that concept had worked, but if this mentality was going to be any indication of how we planned to conduct our entire mission, then it was bound to be an adventure. In truth, we might just find ourselves in a jail cell or somewhere much worse.

Everyone was in agreement, except Falon and Rowan, and we were without a clear direction for the next few hours. I decided to take advantage of the foreign cultural experience. Falon and Riley led the adventure off with a predicable venture into the expensive stores lining the sidewalks between corporate offices. Not very "cultural," yet still entertaining and a way to lay low. Multiple stores later, we had developed a fun game of composing the most obnoxious and ridiculous clothing combinations. The dressing rooms became transport vessels into another dimension of high fashion.

Two stores later, without buying any clothing, we found ourselves meandering the streets once more. Riley attempted to convince us to enter the next boutique, but the rest of us were listening to our screaming stomachs. Wandering along, we came across a nice café with seating along the street to bask in the sunshine. The menu was entirely in Portuguese, but our waiter spoke English and offered to bring a collection of his highly suggested dishes. With the lunch rush subsiding and dinner not for a few more hours, the food still arrived slowly. Clearly, Brazilian culture deemed we would be in no rush.

Waiting around the table, I was surprisingly content to be sitting, talking, and sipping on a cold Coke with a much more sugary taste than its American counterpart. Still in a giddy mood from earlier, the conversation was a rapid combination of voices jumping in before one was done talking. Drifting away from the current situation, our minds began to retrieve the stories of our lives with at least one person having a tale to connect one idea to the next. Falon composed images with much greater urgency and more dramatic elements than the situation probably justified, aided by her verbiage that often included the word "like" as a connector. Gavlin's adventures surpassed what most of us hoped to accomplish in our entire lives. His adrenaline junkie personality never failed to keep him immersed in situations most people would never consider attempting. Free-jump off a bridge or jump out of a helicopter to snowboard down a mountain? No problem. I think someone would have had to tie me up, and then forcibly push me out of the helicopter or off the bridge to accomplish those tasks. And I would probably kill myself in the process. Riley's facial expressions, even with her oversized "Jackie O" sunglasses, revealed her emotions painted by her hand movements. Just watching the way she varied her body language, I forgot entirely the voice I was hearing was Rowan's. Rowan was the true storyteller in the way he intricately strung together a highly varied vocabulary to put you standing next to him in a memory. For his guarded nature, his ease when talking at those moments carried above the noise of the lively city. Long after the food arrived and was devoured too fast to even savor most of the Brazilian spices, the plates disappeared while the conversation still remained abundant.

At the end of my narration, I decided we needed to come up a plan that coincided to why we could be found on a São Paulo street on a late March afternoon. "Before we start into another anecdote that will lead to another, which will, in turn, last three more hours, we need to at least move closer to the exchange in hopes of slinking in."

Riley pointed at me and then toward her brother across the table and shook her head in disapproval.

"I take it you are tired of us ruining all the fun with actual work. If you ask me, I would say that has been your brother's job," I remarked sarcastically pointing at her brother. Rowan bestowed upon me a death stare, and Riley just giggled at his reaction to my comment. In exchange, I smirked in his direction, which did nothing to his stone face.

"I guess we should," Gavlin agreed, pushing back his chair, jumping to his feet and anticipating us to follow suit. "Your bag, my dear." He handed Falon's luggage bag to her, bowing down with the wave of his hand above his head. She looked slightly offended, but she politely took the bag from him. I think it was her way of finally beginning to understand Gavlin's playful personality.

It was around 5:00 when our roaming finally brought us to Bovespa. The six-story, crisp, white-stoned building stood regal on the corner of two sharply angled streets framing it. The doors were tucked between high arching windows accented by the heavy outcroppings of the pillars extending up the wall of the building. A Brazilian flag hung proudly between two of the pillars, the bottom corners catching the gusts of wind and rippling quietly. With no other options, we waited to see if any brilliant opportunities would present themselves. It was practically a hopeless shot in the dark, but no other options were viable. The constant hum and sharp whine of human and scooter traffic whizzed by, and the thick air smothered my senses as I sat quietly on a bench, fidgeting with the zipper on my backpack. Gavlin paced around everyone, which was habit for him if we sat in one place for any length of time. Following ten minutes of sitting in front of the building, Falon made a comment under her breath.

"What did you say?" I asked.

"Those three seem really happy about something, and they are now going to get drunk. Typical," she said with disdain about the three guys in their late twenties or early thirties heading out of the entrance to the stock exchange. The exchange was closed for the day, and there was nothing too special about the three of them in comparison to the workers filtering out the front door, a colorful array of trading jackets. I watched one of the three men unclip a card-sized identification from the front of his hunter-green trading jacket and place it in his side pocket.

"Wait, where are they going, Falon?"

"How should I know? I speak Spanish, not Portugúes."

"Wall Street Bar," Rowan responded, like he had casually been eavesdropping on their conversation. He did not know a single word in Portuguese.

I stood up abruptly, dropping my backpack to the ground and jogged toward the street to call a cab. "Guys, I have an idea!"

About forty-five minutes after the sudden onset of my completely insane plan, Gavlin and I were sitting on a bench in the thin shadows as they grew slowly across the city. Gavlin and I were the only ones who had piled into the cab that took us about a block away from the entrance to the Wall Street Bar. Sitting there, we reviewed the plan for the thirtieth time, if nothing but for my own sanity. By process of elimination, Gavlin and I were chosen to run the gauntlet into the bar. Riley looked too young; a ginger would have stood out too much against the typical crowd in these parts, and while Falon could have gotten us by with the language, we needed to bring a guy along. Finally, I was the author to the crazy idea. It was my stop after all, and Rowan was not going to be the one who took any credit for our success in Brazil. Falon threw a chestnut leather jacket in my direction, along with the slim-fitting frilly white shirt prior to Gavlin and me leaving them at Bovespa. The shirt felt restricting as I pulled repeatedly at the unforgiving seams. Falon had a valid point about looking the part. I was just thankful we were not the same shoe size. In the event of a possible quick exit, no amount of convincing would have me running in heels. I pulled my hair down, fluffed it around, hoping it did not look like a complete kinked and wavy mess, took a deep breath, and looked at Gavlin.

"Wow, look at you," he said, giving me a once-over, approvingly.

"Do not push me. Falon is not convincing me to wear this any longer than necessary," I remarked sarcastically as I started to walk off. Following the hint, Gavlin jogged a couple of steps to catch up. Something inside me skipped for a second.

We easily made it through the door of the bar, and were greeted by a green neon sign stating "Wall Street Bar," with the outline of the Wall Street Bull statue from New York below. It was only a short walk down a poorly lit, steep flight of stairs before a thick wall of smoke assaulted us. The United States may have been thinning out the smoking habit; however, it remained customary in Brazil. The bar stools were lined with people, while others mingled around tables with drinks in hand. Ticker strips created an electronic border on the top of the walls, displaying the value of various stocks when the market closed hours earlier. It was a parade of red- and green-letter abbreviations and numbers I was mostly unable to decipher from a quick glance. On the unfinished brick walls, black-and-white photographs of the New York Stock Exchange and Wall Street hung as simple accents. It took us a few minutes to scout out our friends at a tall wooden table near the bar. All three of them were present: two with short black hair, and another with dirty blonde, drinks in hand, and their hunter-green and yellow trading coats draped over the backs of their lofted bar chairs. By the noise level of their laughing and joking, in combination with the empty drinks on the table, they had obviously enjoyed a successful day at work. Neither Gavlin nor I spoke Portuguese, which we assumed they were speaking, leaving us without a clue as to what they were saying.

"They sure drank a lot in a short time," Gavlin said, bending down to say it near my ear, and I felt my stomach clench from his sudden proximity.

"Not at all," I said with a nervous laugh.

"You will slip a jacket and then scram without me. I'll follow with the other," he said, reviewing the plan briefly.

"Good luck."

The moment Falon commented on the three men outside of Bovespa, it was not them that I noticed, but the small identification on their jackets. I quickly figured that if we could grab the trading jackets, there should be at least one with an electronic key card and identification for the building. The odds were in our favor. Buildings such as stock exchanges were guarded by multiple sets of security guards and card readers, to assure everyone only had access only to what they were permitted, when they are permitted. It was simple for a person to keep his identification clipped to his trading jacket so he'd identifiable and always with the proper card access. These were the conclusions I came to, based on a lot of assumptions from my experiences with the Chicago Board Options Exchange.

Gavlin walked to the other side of the bar, while I walked around the backside of the table. With the currently packed state of the bar, there was nothing suspicious about me slightly bumping the back of the chair as I swiped a green jacket. It was just my luck that the jacket slipped effortlessly off the curvature of the bar chair and into my arms. The instant after I snatched the jacket, the three men all turned in my direction. I caught only a glance of their faces before my head flew in the other direction to lock sights on the most direct route out of the bar. I crumbled the jacket into a little ball and dove into the crowds of people. My short stature had its perks, as I darted and wove my way through the maze of people and tables to the door and out of sight from the table. Emerging from the masses of people next to the door, I could not resist the paranoid voice in my head. I took one glance back. No one. I briskly jogged up the concrete steps two at a time until I burst out into fresh air. The cool evening air gave me a boost as I took one last look back and let my body carry my mind where it wanted to be. I sprinted down the block with the jacket clenched to my chest. I nervously watched every detail around me, concerned not only with the men in the bar, but the fact that I was in an unknown city, at night, and by myself.

The abrupt sound of the feet against the pavement kicked my pace into a higher gear until I gained the nerve to look behind me. Barely a block away from the bar myself, Gavlin came pounding down the concrete only a few steps behind me. My poor night vision was straining to make out more than his figure in the dim street. Then my eyes locked onto something. At first, I figured my eyes might have been playing tricks on me, but within striking distance I could see a green jacket similar to the one clutched in my shaking hands. His longer stride caught up with me and then slowed to a gentle lope. Both of us wore a devilish grin. At our current pace, we would probably make the mile run back to Bovespa in around eight minutes, which would be a personal best for me. If only my gym teacher could have seen me now. Slow and steady has always been my mentality when it comes to any form of running. I do not do sprinting. When we returned, the others would hopefully still be there. We figured it was best to keep as many people as possible out of the line of fire. Also, keeping in mind the suspicious amount of luggage we were carrying, we needed to keep any unusual activity to a minimum. With the brisk air pumping through our lungs and adrenaline through our veins, Gavlin looked over with a smirk. I caught his eye and returned the gesture, accepting the challenge. Then we took off running. Once running, I did not want to stop. It was just the wind and my lungs attempting to take in air as fast as I could before it rushed by. I would regret this later. My body was not conditioned for running. Abruptly, the feeling of invincibility wore off to a cramp in my side and not enough air in my lungs. My stride was nothing compared to Gavlin's longer legs. He won. I slowed down and he followed suit, though we were both gasping for air when we arrived back at Bovespa. Between it all, we were still wearing the same grins from earlier.

We caught sight of three other familiar faces waiting, or in Riley's case, walking along the sidewalk cracks. After coming to a halt next to them, I unfolded the jacket for the first time since I'd left the bar. There was only one thing I was looking for—the only thing that would get us in the building and make this worth the last hours. From the left pocket I pulled out slips of crumpled paper, written on in chicken scratch. I pulled out a heavy blue pen. I hastily moved to the next pocket and found nothing. Finally, I looked in the most obvious place. There they were; attached securely with a plastic loop and a small metal clip to the front breast pocket were a badge and an electronic card.

I looked up to see Riley holding the other jacket while Gavlin was bent over, rummaging through the two jacket pockets. "Gavlin?" I called out, hoping he'd had luck with his jacket as well.

I received a thumbs-up from Riley and a set of matching cards from Gavlin, which meant we were winning on two accounts. I was still not relieved. This was not a complete win on our part, not until I was physically holding onto the documents from my father.

I took control of the situation. "We have two sets to get in, and they are both men, which means we really do not have any choices. Rowan and Gavlin, you're up. Here, take this, Rowan," I said and handed him the jacket. "You guys need to make your way to the balcony on top of the actual trading floor. I do not believe there will be direct access to it from the floor, and these cards may not get you there, but at least they should get you into the building. From there, get creative and aim for a couple of stories up. On the balcony, there should be a podium with a bell or a button that would make the electronic bell go off. I have never seen any bell except for New York, so I don't know. Look around the podium for the key, unlock it, grab the documents, and go."

After I finished the debriefing, I pulled the gold chain out from around my neck. I unclasped the back, slipped off the skeleton key, and handed it over to Rowan next to me. Strangely, the fact I was standing next to him had nothing to do with why my instincts told me to hand it over to him instead of Gavlin.

"I make this jacket look good," Gavlin joked, with the jacket loosely fitting on his very slim frame.

It was killing me to watch them jog across the street knowing that on my own mission I was on the sidelines. Starting from the time they entered the building, everything went in slow motion. We girls started by just staring at the narrow glass doors; we thought that maybe our thoughts would bring them out faster. Staring lasted all of about twenty seconds for me before I pulled out my computer, and opened a Word document. Thank goodness I had charged it the hotel and, Macs have the best battery life. Riley noticed what I was doing and looked over when I started to type.

"Hi Riley =)" I wrote.

"Much faster than writing," she replied.

"Yep. I am not good at lipreading or gesturing. Sorry I cannot sign. I couldn't just sit there. I don't do the whole 'doing nothing' thing well. Haha."

"It is good. I can tell. You remind me of my brother. He likes to be busy."

"Can't help but ask. What is he so uptight about all the time? Is he always like this?"

"Usually not. I think he is really stressed."

"I try to talk with him, but he just ignores me. I have no plans to talk to a wall. Are you OK?"

"I'm fine. He listens. Trust me. He's a little quiet. I do most of the talking at my house."

"I bet it's hard none of us understand you."

"It happens. Not with my friends. Most are Deaf. I like when people want to learn sign."

"You're a freshman. Right?"

"Yes."

"You said your friends are deaf. Do you go to school with all deaf people?"

"Before high school my school was deaf. I liked it because everyone could sign. There was no language barrier. Now I go to the deaf school for part of the day and the public high school for part. It is harder. I have an interpreter. School is school. Lol."

"You don't have to tell me. It's scary to think my senior year is almost done. You play sports?"

"Cross country."

"That would not be my idea of fun. I'd barely make it a mile."

"People say that lots. You could if you wanted."

"I think not. Plus, I need a distraction, like music. Loud music gets me through working out."

"I like cross-country because with new places to run it's pretty to look around, and think. The silence is nice. But I do like music."

"?"

"I can hear it if it's really loud, with my hearing aids. Drives my brother insane. Good thing we do not have any neighbors nearby. Two days before we left, my friend pushed me in a pool, and my hearing aids drowned."

"That's no good! What type of music?"

"No rap."

"I grew up with country music. No judging."

91

"No comment. ;)"

"Funny. It's OK. I get that reaction more than not. How long do you think they're going to be? We should place bets."

"My brother and Gavlin will be there until they find it."

"Your brother is stubborn, and Gavlin cannot back down from a challenge."

"He likes you."

"Who?"

"Gavlin."

"That was not blunt at all."

"His yellow eyes are unbelievable. They look through you."

"They are scary how almost golden yellow they are, right?"

"You like him."

"Jumping the gun a little."

"Whatever you say…" She caught on to my little white lie and continued our little chitchat.

Thirty minutes later, both of us were still on the computer, with Falon occasionally peeking in. Suddenly, I caught a quick movement at the Bovespa entrance. Initially, I dismissed it as a passing car or person, but it was late at night, and anything could have been cause for concern. I knew it was a real issue when Riley stopped typing in mid-thought, slammed the computer shut while I was still looking, and shoved it into the nearest bag. I looked up in time to see the boys tear out of the building like a mythical, six-headed, fire-breathing dragon was chasing them. They ran straight past us with only the slightest glance. From our view, it looked like Gavlin had something of fairly decent, rectangular size clenched in his left hand. I could only hope it was the documents. Before we could determine what the three of us were supposed to do, a silver metal case came flying toward my head. Luckily, my reflexes were high on adrenaline and saved me. I ducked and the box whizzed over the top of my head and the back of the bench. When I got a hold of Gavlin later, he was going to die for almost nailing me in the head again. I heard Riley grab the case off the sidewalk before I dared sit up straight following the aerial assault. Falon, Riley, and I rapidly began work on collecting the bags in order to move locations quickly within the next few seconds. I had not the slightest clue where we would be going. Both of the boys were stripping off the green jackets and throwing them on the sidewalk as they keep up their spring down the block. Moments passed before the doors of Bovespa flew open for the second time, and the two-headed dragon appeared. The dragon actually resembled two large-set security guards who were screaming out orders in another language and clambering like elephants after gazelle. Their beady black eyes did not even look over to the three of us, frozen like stone across from the door. After all four disappeared around the corner of the building on the right, the three of us looked at each other. Someone needed to make a decision.

Falon's eyes were bulging like a frog's, and I could tell that it was taking every ounce of self restraint, and my convincing, to detain her from running in circles, screaming at the top of her lungs, with hands flailing in front of her face. "What are we going to do?" she spat out without breathing.

"We're gonna grab all the bags and get out of here before they see us," I said calmly, with authority.

Riley must have agreed because she took her and her brother's rolling bags, slung her shoulder bag on the top of her rolling bag, and took off. Falon followed suit. When she picked up her purse, I could tell she was shaking. I lugged Gavlin's inconvenient boxy suitcase on top of my rolling bag. Who buys a thirty-pound suitcase without wheels? I almost forgot the metal briefcase hidden behind my bag that was the cause of all our problems. I snatched it up in my spare left hand and headed after Riley at a jog. We continued a brisk walking pace at Riley's lead until we were three blocks away from the building. She hailed us one of the few cabs wandering the streets at this hour. In the cab, she pulled out the plane tickets, and pointed at Falon and the driver. Falon, hands still shaking and looking pale white, got the clue and told the cab driver we needed to get to the airport, quickly. From the time printed on the tickets, it appeared we had a plane to catch in an hour and a half. I had no clue how far the airport was. At least it would not be rush hour.

I was bewildered at how we could leave behind the guys, though intuitively, I knew Riley would not leave her brother. With all of us rapidly breathing in the back seat of a cab with ripped plastic seats and trash littering the floor, I turned toward Riley. "Where are Gavlin and Rowan?" I said, signing their names. Riley had given us each a sign name: a mixture of the first letter in our name in some distinctive location. Gavlin's was the letter "G" sweeping from the right shoulder forward; Rowan was a "R" on the left shoulder; Falon was an "F" near the chin; and mine was a "D" on the left shoulder.

She repeated the whole question in sign and mouthed each word slowly without making a sound, which was her attempt to teach me. I was always up for learning sign, but at this instant, I wanted answers, now.

"Rowan and you. Meet. Airplane? Money and something. Both of us," I said while repeating her gestures and probably only getting about half of them correct.

"*Close.*" She smiled. "*Airplane. Split.*"

"Oh, you two split everything when you were waiting for us. You are *amazing,*" I complimented, using both palms open in front of me for the sign "amazing." We might make it through this after all.

94

The short taxi ride to the airport involved me nervously picking at my nails, Riley folding the paper tickets into tiny squares before realizing what she was doing and unfolding them neatly, and Falon staring out the window. Falon had regained some of her color, though we were all clearly distracted. None of us knew where Gavlin or Rowan was at this moment in time. For all we knew, they were already being dragged down to a Brazilian prison. If they got caught, we would only know if they did not show up at the airport. And then, the only way to spring them out would be to turn ourselves in, summing up the mission to a complete nothing. If it reached that point, we would all be crisped and served like pigs on a platter. My mind kept getting away from me and conjuring up every possible horrible outcome.

chapter 9

The security line was an entire hour-long wait. Last time I checked, it was almost 9:00 p.m. In the hour we spent moving an inch every couple of minutes, we panned the crowds, though it was hard to see farther than the few people surrounding us, especially with my vertically challenged stature. We had no choice other than to wait in line and hopefully make it to our plane on time. Somehow, we managed to sneak all five of the suitcases, backpacks, and Falon's oversized purse through the detectors. Security must have been leaving bag counting to the bag-Nazis patrolling the gates, because the rule of two bags per person, with one that could stow under the seat, was not being enforced. It significantly helped the situation that we loaded the bags on the conveyer quickly, slipped off our shoes, and jetted through the scanners in a nonchalant and efficient manner, like seasoned pros. We had perfected the art of pretending. The São Paulo Airport proved more challenging to navigate than a corn maze without a map. The signs hanging sporadically throughout the airport were more of a hindrance than help. When we followed one, we would find ourselves in the wrong location. Left, right, back the same direction, stand, wonder about signs, go back in the same direction we came, turn around, left, left, spin in a circle, and stop.

By the time we found our gate, we were running on borrowed time. As we weaved through stop-and-go traffic, we were only about thirty feet away from our destination, when Riley dropped her rolling bag and took off running. Falon and I looked at each other, wondering if we were being chased again, and looked behind us. My legs were tensed and slightly crouched for immediate takeoff. Other than the hum of suitcases rolling against the floor and the varied beat of footsteps, none of which were running, there was nothing behind us. The traffic ahead then parted, and I caught a glimpse of Riley throwing herself at someone. There were very few options for whom it could be, and there was a collective sigh. The rolling suitcase Riley had cast aside still lay abandoned on the floor. Falon made no immediate move to heft it off the floor. I was already dragging two rolling suitcases, so I shrugged my shoulders in a bit of a hint. With an over exaggerated sigh, I watched Falon reluctantly struggle to upright the small bag, throw her shoulder bag up again, and trudge off. Riley was just releasing her brother from her vice as we closed the last couple of feet to the gate.

"What took so long? You didn't even have to run here." I heard that irresistible, characteristic laugh I longed to hear, from behind Rowan and Riley.

"We were worried you would be in prison, ashamed at yourself that a bunch of fat security guards outran an Olympian. Oh, and next time you buy luggage, wheels work great," I said back, dropping the bags, with a heavy thud to the ground, in a heap.

"Careful now, there are valuable things in there," Gavlin joked.

"Does it look like I care?"

"For that, I shouldn't share any of this," he taunted, with a bowl of what appeared to be vanilla cream.

"For everyone's safety, I would hand that over," I said and snatched up the vanilla ice cream in his hand before he could pull it out of reach. Ice cream was my weakness, but what girl doesn't have a soft spot for ice cream after a long day? And this had most definitely been a long day.

"I decided we could fit that in the budget, considering this cash will not work at the next location," Rowan said from behind me, causing me to jump into three suitcases, and almost impale my mouth with the spoon of ice cream.

I regained my composure and swallowed the melting ice cream. "Can you try not to sneak up on me?"

"I have been standing here the whole time."

"But not right behind me."

"Yes, I have." He glared back stubbornly. I had never met anyone with such an irritating effect on me.

"Enough, you two," Gavlin said and jumped in between the two of us, making it uncomfortable so that we both jumped back. "They are boarding the plane, unless no one wants to join me for some sick boarding in Switzerland."

"I'm coming," I replied quickly, shoving the melted ice cream in my mouth. It was good while it lasted. Rowan just turned around, picked out his bag from the mound of luggage, and headed toward the gate with Falon and Riley.

"I am not sitting next to him," I whispered to Gavlin.

"It would be great entertainment for like nine hours."

I sneered at him, and he just fake tackled me, but grabbed my arms at the same time so I could not hit him back. I am sure the airport did not appreciate our rowdy behavior. Nonetheless, we boarded the plane and took our expensive seats in international business class. I am not sure whose money we spent on the seats, but no one was complaining. Following a smoother takeoff than the last jet I was privileged to be aboard, we were cruising over the Atlantic Ocean. After reaching our soaring altitude of thirty thousand feet above the crashing waves and fish life below, the seat belt sign was turned off. I made my way over to Gavlin's seat and pulled the headphone bud out of his ear.

"Hey," I said. "I want to know what happened in that building."

He smiled. "You always have to know everything?"

"Yes," I said, sitting down on the arm of the chair.

He unlocked his black iPhone, turned off the music, and pulled out his headphones. His eyes were the color of Felix Felicis's from *Harry Potter*, and had the same effect on me when he looked up and started to talk. "When we walked up to the building, a security person asked for our IDs, and we just flashed them like we belonged there. I think he had a hard time believing he had never seen us. Rowan is some flaming ginger. But he waved us through. In the main hallway, there was another security checkpoint. We threw our jackets on the conveyer for the scanning machine and successfully made it through the metal detectors. We didn't talk with each other, which was hard because we had no clue what we were doing. I did a quick scan around, and I could see the floor thing you were talking about. I remembered how you'd said the stage area was maybe upstairs. When the elevators opened on the second floor, we walked into the hallway and only had to open a few doors. I think it was the third unlocked door. We were looking at the entire stock market area. There were a couple of custodians and people working, so we carefully snuck out toward the podium. It took us the most time to search around for the keyhole. We looked ridiculous crawling around on our hands and knees and considered just smashing into the wooden podium or pulling apart the bell button. It would have been fun. I think it could've caused some problems. After we had looked in every corner, Rowan found a hole in the tile near the bottom of the podium. It looked like someone had just dropped something and banged the tile. The key actually fit. When we turned it, something clicked, and the entire tile came out. Pretty cool. Under it was the case. I really wanted to go kinda crazy when I saw it, but I didn't. It was all good until, boom! There were security guards below us, pointing up. We made a break for it. I grabbed the case, and we hit the stairs. The guards must have taken the elevators as we flew down the stairs because at the bottom they came hurtling out of the elevator. It was ridiculous how both tried to get out of the elevator at the same time. When we busted through the doors like bats out of hell, that is where I threw the case at you guys."

"That metal case almost smacked me in the head! What is it with you and trying to knock me out?" I asked jokingly.

"Think of it like a game."

"You live for games like that. Not me. Next time, it's gonna be you."

"Not cool. Not cool at all."

It only took me an hour to become bored of my music, and Gavlin was sleeping. I could see from across the aisle that Falon was crashed out as well, with her black sweater thrown over the top of her head. I am not sure how she managed to breathe under it. Rowan was looking out the window in the seat in front of Falon, so I approached him, really just looking to get my key back. My neck was feeling vulnerable without it.

"What's up?"

He turned around. "Thinking it would be more interesting to be flying this thing than sitting here."

"True. Imagine me trying to fly it."

"We would die."

"Thanks. You have no confidence in me?"

"Nope," he said plainly.

"Can I have my key back?"

Rowan reached into his pocket, fished out the antique key, and held it up for me to grab. "Thanks," I said.

End of conversation. This kid was impossible. Every time I started a conversation with Rowan, he drove me insane. He either ignored me, or refused to hold a conversation for more than ten seconds. Yet, I kept trying. I felt this connection to him that the both of us were repressing all that had happened in the past couple days, and sooner than later the floodgates were going to break. In our own isolation, maybe we could find a little company. Regardless, today it would be a losing battle, so I turned around and walked to where his little sister was doing something on her computer.

"Hi," I said after she looked up at me.

She finger-spelled out very slowly "*B...o...r...e...d?*" It took me a few seconds to process, but I was very proud of myself for figuring it out.

"Yesss."

"*Sign?*"

"*OK.*" I signed the two letters I knew best next to those that were associated with the first letter in our names.

For the next few hours, there was a lot of laughing at my inability to retain half of what I was taught or figure out what Riley was saying, and my knack for signing some really interesting and often bad things. I do not remember French ever being this difficult. She looked pleased with my slow progress, but I think she just kept me around because it was entertaining. On one occasion, I fell off the edge of the chair laughing into the aisle between her and Rowan. He quickly turned his head and, seeing nothing, looked down. I was still laughing when I waved at him from the ground. He looked at me in disapproval and turned back around. We were making way too much noise for a language that is not spoken. Considering it was midnight, without any time changes taken into account, we received a fair share of glares from the other passengers and a little blonde flight attendant with penciled-on eyebrows. By the end, I could pretty much say a lot of basic things, though my signs looked like a hippopotamus doing ballet compared to Riley's fluid movement. My favorite sign at this point had to either be "again" or "I don't know" to emphasize my lack of ASL knowledge. I eventually returned to my seat and turned on my music until I feel asleep.

I woke up to Gavlin shaking my shoulder. "Good afternoon. Isn't it nice to wake up to this handsome face?"

"Uh-huh," I mumbled, sitting up and cracking my stiff neck down every vertebra.

"It's one-seventeen local time, and you might want a sweater."

I stood up and stretched like a cat before opening the compartment above my head for my luggage. "Thanks for the warning. Any plans yet?"

"I've taken the train to get to Zermatt before," he said, while leading the way down the aisle a couple of minutes later.

"We could do that. Would we have to show an ID?" I asking, trying to be realistic.

"It might be more fun to invite our friends," he said, with a laugh.

"Because I *love* being shot at."

"Sense of adventure and a challenge."

"It's personally too much running," Falon said from behind us, looking like she had woken up from a long winter nap. Her once straight hair was frizzed, and her shirt remained wrinkled even after she pulled on it in an attempt to straight it out.

We both turned around. "You run like a girl," Gavlin said, while mimicking Falon's hand-flailing run.

"You will be happy to hear we are planning a train ride and not a run to Zermatt," I said to an unpleasant-looking Falon.

She did not reply as we all made our way out of the plane's door and to the extendable walkway toward the airport.

"You remember how far the train station is?" I asked Gavlin.

"Me? I travel way too much to remember."

"Guess we don't need you," I joked.

"You're going to want me once we get to the mountain."

"Whatever you say. Personally, I don't look forward to beating off a hoard of fan girls."

"I have never understood such immature and starstuck behavior," Falon chimed in.

"I could not agree with you more, Falon," I said.

"It's funny. Doesn't bother me," Gavin replied.

"If I could roll my eyes, I would," I remarked.

"Although, I am sure the good-looking ones do not hopelessly chase celebrities," Falon said.

"They are a little obsessed, but you'd be surprised," Gavlin added.

I turned back to look at Falon and shook my head. I received a grin with a halfhearted eye roll, which was nice to see.

When all five of us had come to a halt on the side of the hallway in the airport, I threw out the possible plan. "Gavlin says we can take a train to Zermatt. It could work, except we may be on the radar too much."

Rowan thought about it and then replied, "I am not thrilled about that idea."

"Surprise, surprise. Well, why don't you think of a better plan?"

"Taxi."

"Not going to work that far, man," Gavlin replied, while Rowan and I were in a locked stare.

"We take a train, and we'd be telling them exactly where we are,'" Rowan said.

"We will be in more trouble if we just wait around here," I snapped back.

Riley must have gotten some type of wireless Internet on her computer because, out of the corner of my eye, I saw her sit down on the ground and intently begin scanning something on the screen.

"Riley said our names are not in the system from the plane," I said in a raised voice.

"There is no guarantee they do not have some other way to track us," Rowan replied.

"Do you have a secret tracker in your arm that I am not aware of, because I sure don't!" I yelled in frustration.

"Enough!" Falon interrupted. "You two are causing a scene."

"Do I hear silence?" Gavlin mocked. Both Rowan and I stared at him. "You two are pleasant. Now, when *this* was going on," he said, indicating Rowan and me, "Riley was doing something. There is a train to Zermatt we can take. There is also a pretty cool twist." Those are words you never want to hear come out of the mouth of an adrenaline junkie.

Riley held up the computer with a map of Switzerland and a couple hundred multi-color lines running across—a map of almost all the train routes in the country. She pointed her finger to the city of Zurich, where we were at the time, and then traced it along a purple line to Visp. From Visp, she then traced a light-blue line to Zermatt. We all looked at the map for the "twist" Gavlin had mentioned. It still only looked like two trains on our way to the mountain. Subsequently, Riley pointed to the colored key and matched the light-blue line to a line that said: "Freight Line Only." Falon, Rowan, and I looked up at Gavlin and Riley. They both smiled mischievously.

"That is one way to not be tracked," I said optimistically.

"What does this mean?" Falon asked.

"It means we're going to sneak onto a train," Gavlin replied with excitement.

Falon was still confused. "Freight means no people?"

"Yes, it means boxes," I said.

"¡Ustedes están corriéndose las tejas!" Falon exclaimed.

"Huh?" Gavlin said.

"You are all *loco*." We all knew what that meant.

chapter 10

The train station was conveniently located just outside the airport. The brisk afternoon air bit through my thin jacket and burned me as it worked its frosty fingers across my skin. I pulled my fingers into my sleeves to escape the numbing sensation. Even though Switzerland is a small country and it would still be physically a quick trip, mentally, a trip in this cold would feel more like an eternity, and require a couple of more layers of clothing and a mug of hot apple cider. The second was probably not going to happen in the near future, but a girl could wish. Upon arriving in the warmth of the train station, Riley pulled out a small, flat, black bag with a zipper, from her shoulder bag, and rifled through it before pulling out a stack of euros. If anyone saw our cash pile, there would be a whole lot more questions that we did not need. Even split into about three piles at this point, each set amounted to a large worth of cash, credit cards, and a handful of falsified passports. Waiting in line, the electronic boards above the ticket booths read in green blocky lettering, numbering the train times and their respective destinations from

Zurich. When Visp flashed on the board, the times read 14:06 and 20:19. It took me a second to sort out that they were in military time, which is standard for Europe. It was 13:57 now.

"Falon, you are going to hate me," I said, still looking at the board. Hopefully, the others were thinking along the same lines.

"One does not even need to ask in order to guess your implications," Falon replied.

"Well, I don't have plans to sit around and wait," I said. Falon offered up a long and dramatic sigh. Thankfully, I received an affirmative from Gavlin and Riley when they stepped up to the glass window of the ticket counter. We waited tensely, shoes tied and bags at the ready.

"Five passengers to Visp, at fourteen oh six," Gavlin said.

"You have only a few minutes until departure," the lady behind the booth replied.

Gavlin took our five passports from Riley and slid them onto the counter. "We can run."

Run we did. As soon as the printed tickets were slid across the counter, Gavlin snatched them up and dashed off in the direction of the ticket attendant's pointed finger. Everyone else follow in quick pursuit. None of us bothered to pick up our rolling bags as we dragged them behind us down the cement stairs to the platform. They collided with the walls, legs, and other luggage in their general vicinity. When we hit a straight hallway leading directly to the platform below, it became the homestretch sprint. Our bags' wheels could not keep up half of the time and instead were forcibly bounced instead of rolled cross the floor. The sound of scraping plastic against the floor filled the space between our pounding feet. Gavlin instantly had an advantage carrying his awkwardly shaped, box-like suitcase without any contact with the ground to impede his movement. It was a mad dash with arms, bags, and people clobbering anything in the way of the train and us. I kept glancing back to ensure Falon was still keeping up. Trailing the group, she was still managing a decent speed. I could only allow my gaze to shift back for a second before needing to focus on the quickly changing scene in front of me. We finally clattered down a set of stairs to reach the train platform; the doors were already closing. In the best running shape, Riley sprinted ahead of Gavlin, her suitcase chattering across the uneven ground. She reached the doors just as they were closing the last few inches. Her presence was enough for the conductor, a younger gentleman with blonde hair, to take notice of the stampede of four other wildebeest narrowing the gap to the train door.

When we first came to a screeching halt at the now open door, he looked at us like we were carrying one hundred pounds of bombs in our bags. He had clearly missed our performance earlier because if they had been bombs, they would have exploded within the first few collisions with the ground and walls of the train station. Gavlin thrust the five tickets, mashed in his hand, at the young man. It took him a couple of seconds to flatten them out on the side of the door, while looking slightly annoyed. The look on his face rapidly changed when he saw that the time our tickets said 14:00. The clock on the wall read 14:07.

"You were fast," he said with a comical smile on his face. Personally, I am not sure how comical it was running across a train station in order to be on a train in a record seven minutes. Though, I am sure it was great entertainment to anyone watching. I wanted a gold medal.

We all shuffled onto the train, still gulping air like goldfish. Gavlin and Riley were obviously in better shape than our heavy breathing demonstrated, and I liked to think I was as well. I think we had been holding our breath the entire time until our feet were firmly on the train. The train was fairly crowed, though we finally found one empty table with four seats across the way from two other empty seats. The other two seats were occupied by two well-dressed businessmen, laptops humming away on the table, and various file folders stacked next them. They did not look pleased when Gavlin and Rowan took up residence at their table, one next to each of them. Luckily for them, there would not be too much talking as we all settled down from our train station dash. Those of us with music and computers were ecstatic to find power outlets to charge everything. There would be no Internet access, unless Riley could indiscreetly hack us into the system. I am not sure if I even wanted to know what the headlines had to say about us. It was even more thrilling when Riley and Falon went to the restroom and came back with news of food. I did not even realize I was hungry until the mention of food. It tended to happen when I became so caught up in something. While the food was nothing spectacular, it was food: a few oddly branded candy bags and sandwiches. I took note that the candy had nothing on a Ghirardelli Chocolate Square.

After inhaling every last morsel like a pack of starving hyenas, everyone was content to settle down and enter into a food coma. I handed my royal-purple iPod nano to Falon, and I think she managed to find something between Taylor Swift, Mayday Parade, and Brad Paisley to listen to, while I plugged my extra headset into my computer. Riley messed around on her computer. She was probably hacking into some international database, for all I knew. As Gavlin had pointed out earlier, I am way too nosy, so I asked her what she was always doing. She never struck me as a computer person, between her very outward personality and adorable sense of fashion. But I soon learned her idea of "fun" was writing computer programs. At least, that was my very general interpretation of what she attempted to explain. From the look at all the crazy notations and endless lines of text, numbers, dashes, and whatnot, it looked more like work than fun. Returning from somewhere, Rowan surprised us all with a magazine that had Gavlin's face plastered across the front cover. There was a four-page spread all about our celebrity friend, written in English. We all took turns passing it around and enjoyably asking Gavlin what the interviewer's reactions were when he had answered a couple of the questions. Rowan talked more than I had ever heard him do before, which was still not saying much.

"Is there a question in there about what I did after winning gold?" Gavlin curiously asked.

"Um, no," I responded after scanning the questions again. "Should there be?"

Gavlin stared back at me, holding us all in suspense. Riley grew impatient and waved her hand in a motion that indicated, "continue." Falon pretended not to be interested, but leaned forward to catch the next comment.

"Maybe," he replied in a coy tone.

"And…?" I said.

"I plead the fifth. But, if any of the locals ask, I was at the hotel knitting sweaters with my grandmother."

"You cannot just not finish the story," I demanded.

"Bad decisions make for fun times," he said.

"I can only imagine. You were in Russia, after all," Falon said judgingly.

We all eventually dropped the idea when we could pry no more details out of him, and the conversation puttered to an appropriate end. Through the glassy view of the passing countryside, the sun set with beautiful hews of dark oranges and purple against the ragged mountaintops.

"Thanks," Falon said, breaking my unfocused stare out the fin-gerprinted window, at the vague shapes among a black background.

"Yeah. No problem." I took back my iPod from her French-tipped fingers. "So, I never asked, what's in the box from your dad? I looked at mine on the plane. Just a stack of papers and two flash drives."

"Is a flash drive the same as a jump drive?" She searched for the right word to describe the memory device in her box.

"Yep. You have a couple?"

"There's a plastic sleeve of papers with signatures, in addition to a flash drive."

"Makes me feel like we're getting somewhere. Piecing together the scissors to cut down all the invisible guide wires holding the Langer gang suspended above their stage."

There was a distant look in her eyes with a polite "uh-huh" in return.

"I wish we could just pop them in a computer and have Riley take a look at them. I'm just worried they might have a special self-destruction security. Everything is just going to be in limbo until our dads get a hold of them."

"Whose fathers?"

"Yours and mine are the only ones. I thought," I said, questioning my information.

"If that's what you heard, I will take your word for it. Yet, it is dif-ficult to take anyone's word after seeing my grandfather and being told my father exists. To me, he was dead and still is dead. Nothing can be done to remedy every part of my life he was not in. By the time I was five, I had pushed the idea of his existence far from my mind and knew that while my real father would not ever be there to see me, I had my aunt and uncle, and they were my parents. Now, I must contend with the idea that I have a father, and not only does he appear to be alive, but now I am sent to clean his mess. How could he think that I owe him any debt worthy of risking my life, to obtain a box full of information with value I do not understand." She exhaled a strained breath.

"Well, then. Someone is in for a talk."

"On the contrary, no such thing will be happening. I never want to talk with the man who abandoned me while the rest of your parents raised you, despite being in the exact same situation," she defied.

"You will never know unless you talk with him," I suggested lightly.

"I have no desire to hear his excuses. If he wanted to be a part of my life, he could have tried before I unsuspectingly found out from someone who turns out to be my grandfather. Oh, and that. All this time mamá, papa, and my grandfather have been covering for him. What else are they capable of lying about? It is never going to be possible to return to my life now, and there is no reason why I should have been placed in this position."

"Yep," I acknowledged. "You're not the only one. At least you lost something you never knew existed."

Arriving in Visp there was a definite drop in temperature due to the disappearance of the sun and the increased altitude. My whole body was violently shaking only moments after exiting the train and being assaulted by the frosty air on the train platform. Reaching the interior of the station to regroup, I pried my numb fingers off my suitcase handle. Likewise, Falon attempted to warm her hands up by energetically rubbing them together.

"I vote we all change into some really warm clothes before we jump on a train without any heat," I suggested, with my teeth still chattering.

"Too bad we aren't near Zermatt. We could have gotten a bunch of gear," Gavlin said.

"Too bad," I said, sarcastically, bent over my suitcase with intentions of wearing every layer of clothing in my possession that could possibly fit.

Gavlin, on his return from Japan, had brought some of his winter gear and threw on an insulated black coat while the rest of us looked like rainbow marshmallows. Clearly the least prepared, Falon was reluctant to take the sweater I offered. As a consequence, I resorted to stealing Gavlin's black zip-up sweater. We could see from the back of the station the freight trains parked a distance behind the passenger cars. From the train map, we understood there were a couple of tracks leading out of Visp. If we were to catch the wrong one, we would have illegally snuck onto a train only to be going a few hundred miles in the wrong direction. In order to keep Rowan and me from cutting out each other's throats in an argument, Riley opened up the map on her computer. Upon consultation, it was determined if we walked toward a track headed southbound, we would be good. If it had not been a dark night with thick cloud cover over the sliver moon, we would have stuck out like the five kids on the run that we were. After a trek south of the station by about a half a mile, the fence gave way to thick brush lining the tracks.

"Who wants to go through the bushes first?" I said in an overly enthusiastic tone.

Through the dark light, I could see four sets of eyes staring at me.

"Buddy system. Let's go, buddy!" Gavlin grabbed my arm and dragged me into the dark, overgrown brush. The brush itself was much thinner than I had initially thought, and the other side was only about ten feet away. The worn silver of the track reflected off the minimal light cast from the moon. Gavlin's eyes were nothing short of freaky in the dusky light. They were the same color of an animal hunter at night; only the whites kept them from looking completely animalistic.

"What?" he asked.

I broke my stare on him. "Your eyes are scaring me."

"Scaring?"

"They just look...catlike, in a creepy way. The black outfit and hair does not help your situation," I stammered, taking note how his black snowboarding jacket had replaced his typical black jacket with a pair of black jeans.

He hissed at me, which instinctively made me jolt back a couple of feet into a tree trunk. He laughed at my jumpiness, which also made me laugh a little at myself.

"We better go get the others," I said.

He flashed a devilish grin. "Don't want them getting any ideas."

"The things you say sometimes," I said while I walked back through the way we had come, not checking to make sure he was behind me.

When I emerged on the other side, Rowan was on guard, with Riley and Falon sitting on the suitcases. "The tracks are only a few feet on the other side, and I see our ride," I said.

Gavlin came bounding through the bushes a little faster than he should have and smashed into Rowan.

"What!" Falon and I screamed at the same time.

Gavlin picked himself off of Rowan, and they both resettled their feet. "Sorry about that. I probably shouldn't have come that fast. But I think our train is leaving."

Immediately, we were off on our second dash of the day toward the train we were supposed to be riding. There was no telling when the next one would be coming through. Missing this one was out of the question. We were all a little clumsier in our layered clothing, but the suitcases were a little lighter. I almost fell on my face over a branch in the brush I managed to miss earlier and a let out a human-sized mouse squeak. Thankfully, this time there were no stairs because every muscle in my legs was still complaining from earlier. If anything, I was going to be in pretty decent shape after this trip. We successfully managed to jump over the tracks, metal ringing through the air upon contact with the suitcases, while praying that no other trains would be on the tracks at the same time. Rowan reached the train first, with his suitcase held off the ground in his hand. The train was only moving a couple of miles per hour as it just started to gain momentum on the track toward Zermatt. I came trailing in with Falon, who was beyond raged about running for the second time in one day. If I had known Spanish, I am sure I would have made out a large selection of unsavory words under her breath. At least she had removed her fancy sandals from the beginning of the trip and was sporting a pair of knee-high brown leather boots. They did not look terribly comfortable to me, but she had assured me they were water-proof and made for working at the horse barns, not that I believed her boots had ever seen a day of physical work in their lives.

Realizing the train was pulling various barrels and stacked loads, we halted and waited patiently for those train cars to pass through. After about ten cars, we noticed what I assumed we were looking for: our luxury wooden cargo box, rusted in places, on a train track to Zermatt. Personally, I thought these wooden crates on wheels died with the *Boxcar Children* books from the 1940s. Rowan and Riley both dropped their things and jogged alongside the train. Gavlin dropped his suitcase as well and joined them as they attempted to heave open the door. With the forward momentum of the train help-ing, they grabbed onto the door. I heard a screech as the door rolled along its rusted door rail. It moved only about five feet, which would suffice for human-sized cargo. At this point, they were about two hundred feet away, and the train was picking up its pace.

"We have got to grab this stuff and run!" I ordered Falon.

She gave out an exasperated sigh, but surprisingly grabbed her bag and Riley's backpack, and ran toward the train car. It was nearly impossible to roll the suitcases along the gravel of the tracks, and I was forced to resort to using my weight to bounce them off the ground behind me. If our suitcases were still alive after this, they were pretty worthy of any type of travel. Rowan was nowhere in sight when Gavlin and Riley sprinted back in our direction to pick up the last two suitcases. When we finally reached the train car, I found Rowan. He was inside the car, his red hair whipping wildly across his face from the increasing speed of the train car. To keep up, we maintained a progressive jog.

"Get in front of the car, and toss the bags in!" he screamed above the engine of the train and the wheels on the metal tracks. We followed his instructions and ran ahead, picked up the bags and heaved them into the moving car. I refused to throw my and Riley's backpack with both of our computers. Instead, I kept mine on my back and planned to hand hers to Gavlin to bring aboard. Once Falon and I had the first three bags in, Riley and Gavlin were jogging next to us and followed suit with the last couple of bags.

Rowan must have felt assured he would be safe from flying luggage and appeared in the doorframe once again. For a moment, I almost wished I had one more lightweight bag, though I think Gavlin might have been a more appropriate target as revenge for all his hits to my head.

"Falon first, and then the rest of you!"

I gave a thumbs-up to save my breath for the increasingly faster run alongside the train. Falon picked up her pace to get close to the door where Rowan had his hand down to grab her. She looked down at the fast-moving ground, then at Rowan's outstretched hand, and fought that little voice in her head that told her not to jump. Since she was not the running type, we hoped that exhaustion would overtake her instincts before the fear kept her going. Finally, she took a large jump up while Rowan pulled her in. She landed flat on her stomach, mostly in the train, and then wiggled her way into the train car. I looked at Gavlin next to me, and he indicated with a wave of his hand that I would jump in next. We were now running at a decent pace. I sped up next to the train, grabbed Rowan's outstretched hand above his wrist and jumped. I am pretty fearless, but it took every ounce of the adrenaline pumping through my veins to make a jump like that. If I had missed, I would have hit gravel and possibly been knocked unconscious by the side of the train. As my body went up and forward into the train, Rowan pulled me hard enough to force my body almost in. There was a hard thunk on the wooden floor where my left elbow made contact first. I wiggled my feet and rolled across the floor until I was safely inside. My first instinct was to jump to my feet and move out of the way. I was glad I did because immediately afterward, Riley came launching inside where I had been before. Her landing was slightly more graceful, and she scampered to the side with me. I decided not to move from my location pressed along the door of the railcar, body rattling with the loose door and listening to the whirring sound of the wind. The last member of our train-jumping brigade came crashing through the door as I felt the train's acceleration significantly increase. Gavlin made no effort to remove himself from the floor as he rolled over on his back and waited to catch his breath.

Since I was standing against the door, I immediately came to my senses and helped Rowan push it closed, battling the weight of the wind and the rust binding the sliding rail on top of the door. The wood felt surprisingly smooth from years of push and pull under my bare hands as I threw my entire weight against it. It was amazing that the three of them had been able to previously open it. With the door coming to a close, we stopped when slightly less than a foot of night was streaming in. The cold air would have been nice to trap outside, yet the dim light of the night sky was much better compared to the shadow-infested railcar. After my eyes adjusted, I turned around to see the railcar empty except for our bags tossed carelessly on the other side. The only sounds echoing through the still night were the clinking of the tracks and our heavy breathing.

"I refuse to run after *any* more trains today," Falon angrily spat.

Gavlin sat up and looked over at Falon. "Aren't you having fun?"

"Additionally, if I ever meet my father, he's going to hear an earful about it," she said with a lighter mood.

"Maybe if you get lucky, we'll find you a car to chase. Change it up," I joked.

"That would be worth watching," Rowan surprisingly said.

"He talks," I said in reference to the shadow sitting against the wall next to me. There was no reply.

"Hey guys, I don't know about you, but I'm gonna catch some sleep," Gavlin said.

A few minutes later, everyone was bundled up on the cold wooden floor. Gavlin, with his ability to fall asleep anywhere, at any time, was out before Riley came to sit next to me. Riley fell sound asleep next to me, with her head rested on a pile of clothes from her suitcase, the both of us close to stay warm. Falon curled up nearby, and soon my eyes could not resist the urge to close.

chapter 11

Sleeping on a train that creaks and moves is by far the worst sleeping condition I have experienced. I probably only dozed off for an hour when a raging headache rudely awakened me. Every muscle in my body was tense from the frigid air as I slowly sat up. I rolled my neck until every inch cracked, which relieved my neck, but by no means the headache. Near the slightly cracked door was a shadow sitting against the wall and looking out into the night. I half stood up and, on sea legs, made my way toward the door, trying to keep my balance against the movement of the train.

I sat down next to him, with my back against the wall and my knees pulled to my chest. "Hi," I said, gazing out the open door. He never turned his head.

I continued, "It's beautiful." Outside, the sky dusted snow across the countryside like a sprinkle of powdered sugar. It was the kind of snow with elegant flakes that blanket everything in a fluffy cover, their fine little crystals distinct and delicately perfect when they float down to a gentle landing. The beauty in snow is how it makes everything look perfect. It covers up the little imperfections in the world and lends itself to a silent elegance, uniform with only the dulled, curved outline of hidden features. With the countryside free of the lights of a city, the stars were out in full force against the black sky. Even the dullest stars were visible to the naked eye. It reminded me of camping out west with my father. For the few times he did not work, we would escape to the open west, and at night we could stare up at the stars with nothing in the way. I knew nothing of the constellations, and yet I would connect them together in my own little storybook puzzle. The moon shone as a thick crescent far in the distance. The nippy air bit my soon frosty cheeks, and I kept my hands jammed safely in the protection of my coat pockets.

"You should live in the mountains," Rowan replied without turning around.

"If only."

"At home, we're up in the mountains. On nights like this, I go out on the deck and watch the snow fall. There is something about sitting there."

"Nature is magnificent," I replied. "What you just said is the only thing I have ever heard you say that tells me anything about you."

"Why do you care?"

"I don't know. Maybe because we are going to be together for the next I-do-not-know-how-many-days, and it is not like the whole experience will just disappear when we drop the documents off."

"It doesn't mean afterward we are going to stay in contact with each other," he snapped.

"Why are you so angry with me?"

"Why do you ask so many questions?"

"If you would actually talk, I wouldn't have to," I said as my anger increased. I knew I should douse the smoldering flame inside me.

After all, he had reason to be bitter at a world that had taken every-one from him. Yet, I could not, because at some point it is no longer possible to hide.

He readjusted his position, still looking out the open door with no intention of partaking in the conversation any farther.

"Seriously? This is not going to just disappear," I said in an effort to make him talk.

"If you want to talk, go find your friend Gavlin."

Although Gavlin and Rowan talked often enough, I could tell by the tone in Rowan's voice that he was not keen on my relationship with Gavlin, so I chose to ignore his statement.

"I'm talking to you," I said venomously. The temptation to walk away from him and not waste any more of my time was almost too great, but then he would win and the two of us would have had it out for each other. Plus, sleep was not an option. I had no phone, and there would probably be no service if I did. I needed a distraction from a computer without power, and a raging headache.

For the first time since I had sat down next to Rowan, he turned his head to look at me. His face was only a foot away from mine. His green eyes locked onto me with a stare that was challenging and guarded. Normally, I would have averted my eyes. Instead, I looked straight back into his.

"You have my attention," he said.

"Good," I said quickly and turned down my eyes.

"Now, what do you want?"

"Nothing in particular. Any reason you're not sleeping?"

"Can't."

There. He did it again. I was finding it impossible to reply to words that deserved no response. "This train is not for sleeping.

My head feels as if someone is driving a railroad stake through the front of my skull," I replied.

"The other's don't seem to have a problem."

I followed his gaze behind my shoulder and to the others sleeping as black masses on the floor. "I will never understand. Your little sister is one of the nicest people I have met."

"She really likes people," he said with the slightest smile.

"Are people not your thing?"

"You are kind," he said trying to sound defensive.

"Just an observation. I would say you are just one of those introverted people. Regardless, you two never seem to disagree, which last time I checked is not normal sibling behavior."

"How would you know, only child?"

"Touché. Observations."

"We do. I usually just go along with what she wants unless it will get her hurt."

"Sounds like a big brother." With no desire to sleep and needing to stay out of my own thoughts I had been working so hard to keep hidden, I kept talking. "What do you do when not on these world-saving missions?"

"Flying and school."

"Let me get this straight. You get to fly jets and live on some of the nicest mountains in the world?" I said slightly jealous.

He nodded in agreement. "Can't think of a better place to live. You flew in from Chicago, or was it just a connection to Denver?"

"Chicago is home. Actually, Chicagoland, which is a legitimate term used for the surrounding suburbia. To be specific, I live in a suburb called Naperville, with my Dad and my dogs, Poseidon and Zeus. I wanted a Hades to finish my Greek Gods theme, but Dad said two German Shepherds was already two too many. Your turn."

He surprisingly took the bait and said, "We live in Colorado Springs. Close enough to Denver for my father to drive for work at the airport. Besides dealing with Riley, there is her monstrous living stuffed animal, Bear. He's a black, one hundred thirty-pound Newfoundland she convinced my dad into a few years back. He's quite a character. Loves the snow, plays hide and seek, and listens well enough.

"She could convince anyone into acquiring a one hundred-thirty-pound shedding, drooling fur ball with those eyelashes. Those are the mountain dogs they use for search and rescue a lot. They are black and white as well, right?" I thought about how little my dogs would look in comparison to a Newfoundland.

"Yes, those ones. He only agreed because she started staying home alone before I came home from school. If she doesn't notice, he informs her someone is at the house. His size is the only deterrent. He would rather play fetch than be a guard dog."

"Playing with strangers. Always good."

"Always." He seemed to not find my statement offensive.

"Are you looking forward to skiing in Switzerland?"

"Colorado is better. Still, it'll be like home a bit."

There was a brief silence as both of us were tempted by the little devil to relive our lives back at home—the ones torn apart. I could not go there now, and if Rowan did I would lose him. "Speaking of home, I could really do for my old leather couch, a marathon of *House, M.D.,* and a mug of hot cider."

"*House, M.D.?* Please do not tell me you are one of those kids."

"What kids?" I challenged.

"The ones who have already decided they're gonna be doctors. They already have their lives planned. Even high school is just about doing more activities for the college resume."

He pretty much pinned me.

"And if I was?" I refused to openly admit it in front of him.

"It explains a lot."

"Like what?" I added a little too defensively.

"We need people to be doctors, but you all are just too intense. Won't do anything that does not benefit the goal."

"Sorry I have plans."

"You have more than plans. If it doesn't work out, you'll have missed too much."

"What am I missing?"

"I can't answer that."

"Why? If you ask me, I am content, happy, and I happen to do most of the stuff because I like it, not because it is another requirement for me to get into a good school, so I can get into another good school to be a doctor. To think that this all started over the brief mention of a television show."

"Hmm. When is the last time you did nothing?"

"By nothing, you mean mindlessly staring into space? I have none of the patience for that type of sitting around. My mind does not do 'nothing.' I have to be constantly thinking or something. Even if it's just pacing around directionless," I rambled.

"You are a thinker. You're more introverted than you think."

"Okay. But honestly, is this topic going to continue?"

"What were you thinking, then?"

With his comment, I knew I had locked him into some form of conversation. There was something still holding him back, though he was tolerating me, which was good enough in my book. By the end of our conversation, it was no different. In his opinion, there was no need to divulge more information than needed, and I could not help but feel judged. Judged in a different way, as if he was still juggling the idea of trusting me. Regardless, I managed to discover he has a genuine smile, subtle in the same way Gavlin's goofy one puts a whole room at ease, including me. He loves Italian food. He plays guitar. Secretly, I was completely crushing on the guitar part because what girl does not wish to be serenaded? He catches the smallest nuances in conversation. My lying skills were going to need to take a dramatic change for the better if I was going to slip anything by him. He lacked Gavlin's animation when he talked. Even against the dark of the shadows, he reminded me of his sister with the way his emotions read clearly across his face. His fluency in ASL, starting, I assume, when Riley was born, must have been one of the reasons. For anyone who has not seen sign language, it is the most beautifully expressive language, and I could see it carried through in his mannerisms. Finally, he was simple. Everything had a simple answer, yet they were only simple because they had underlying complex ideas and theses behind them. I explained things with details. It was refreshing to get a glimpse into concepts more thought out than my own, but articulated as if sifting through a strainer.

Our conversation was cut short when we had to wake everyone up and begin scuffling around to put our things together. The train yard at the mountain town of Zermatt was in plain sight, and we needed to make a quick ninja exit before someone found us out. Fortunately, the train actually came to a stop. Our departure was exceptionally easier than our entrance. We simply threw our bags out and followed them with a short jump onto the rocky gravel. Like raccoons sneaking away from a ransacked trashcan, staying out of a searching spotlight, we snuck across the vacant tracks and through the gaps in other trains. We threaded our way across through the thick lining of trees surrounding the station and found ourselves in the small town of Zermatt.

The town resembled a Christmas storybook that had sprung from its bindings and manifested into a three-dimensional replication. The town itself was small, the main street extending only an eye's distance, and with minimal side streets venturing off to the mountain. The stores were closed, yet some kept their glass fronts lit with small lamps while others slumbered away until their owners arrived for the day and the tourists flooded in. The snow had stopped falling and left behind a few fresh inches of powder. The dim streetlights glowed every few feet, with snow piled on the tops of the black lampposts. The streets lacked the littered tracks of cars that crushed the snow and turned it black, necessitating road salt. Gavlin informed us that cars are not allowed in Zermatt. In front of us loomed the mountain, watching over her child like an overprotective mother. Her jagged tops reaching into the clouds, and her rough outlines were covered in snow that glistened a brilliant white against the early morning sky. With Gavlin slightly clueless, we wandered closer toward the mountain until we came to what looked like another train station. Train stations at this point were our worst nightmare. We expelled a collective sigh of relief when we found a shuttle car waiting for passengers. We boarded the vehicle bound for the mountain. This time it was in a completely legal manner. Our driver, an older gentleman, was in no rush and felt no need to push the snow-tracking capabilities of the shuttle as we made our way across the unplowed roads at a pace no faster than a walk. At least we had heat. My fingers pickled painfully when I put them next to the heating vent.

The little shuttle that could climbed for twenty minutes after taking a right-hand turn on a mountain path, the actual road invisible to a foreign eye. Falon was completely wonderstruck, glued to the scene outside the windows, fogging up the glass with every fresh breath. Unlike the rest of us, she had never seen such a sight. Actually, I am not sure if she had seen snow. For the Colorado kids and our snowboarder, it was home. The mountain tips reached high into the heavens, breaking the fogging mist of the clouds, the sharp edges forming steep, flat declines and layered levels. There were only few sections too sharp for the snow to successfully grab hold of the mountain, while the rest was undoubtedly holding up many feet of variably packed fluffy snow. The sun's rays from the east reflected drastically off the colorless snow, bouncing back to illuminate the sky. At the top of the road's incline, and nestled at a flat base of the mountain, we could make out the outline of a wooden caramel-brown building, with balconies extending off each of the upper rooms. The building was about five stories and gave off the aura of timeworn mountain wisdom. It looked like a private lodge meant to be a celebrity's unspoken escape and not just a hotel available for traveling tourists to casually reside.

Exiting our shuttle on the main driveway, my feet crunched the snow left behind by the plow. Looking ahead, the hotel had not yet managed to shovel any of the snow off the sidewalks to the building. It was well before any guests would be leaving their snug beds, with skis in tow for the day. It was questionable at best to determine where we were expected to walk in order to reach the centrally located front doors from the driveway. The suitcases refused to roll as the snow bound up the wheels. Honestly, it was a surprise the luggage had any wheels left. Hence, we simply resorted to picking them up, my ears mute to the usual complaints by our one comrade. Gavlin took the first steps into the seven inches of fresh snow, stepping with high knees enthusiastically on his own path to the front door. Riley literally jumped into the snow, unconcerned about the condition of her leather boots—a small child delightfully released into the first real snow of the year. My first few steps were a calculated attempt to place my feet into the marks that Gavlin, Rowan, and Riley had made. Unsuccessful by the third step, and after nearly losing my balance due to the unequal distribution of weight from my rolling suitcase, my left foot planted into seven inches of wet, cold snow that snuck its way into my shoes and burned my skin. It was a lost cause now. I would soon be inside to heat and dry clothes. I figured I might as well make the most of the experience, and maybe even have fun. I playfully skipped through the snow, arriving at the door, stomping my feet to remove the excess snow, and noting how *not* waterproof my chucks were.

A welcoming wave of heat from the crackling fireplace in the central lobby confronted us, upon piling through the simple front door. The ceilings reflected exposed beams of wood and the lobby breathed the crispness of minimal homey decorations. There was a set of progressing pictures that told the story of the building in her earlier days on the mountain and her continued service as a much beloved family heirloom. A couple of old-fashioned wooden skis were mounted to the wall next to an original black-and-white print of the building we were standing in. When I walked up to the desk with Gavlin, the look on the young woman's face was unmistakable. Considering we were at the finest hotel in Zermatt, she obviously had seen her share of famous people check in, but she was having a very difficult time containing her excitement over the newest guest.

"Good evening, Mr. Fleet," she said with a huge smile before Gavlin even introduced himself.

"Good evening," he said, playing up his genuine smile.

"It is great...um...very nice to meet you," she stammered.

"And you too, Clara," he said, reading her name badge. "Now, I don't have a reservation, but would you be able to find me and my friends a room tonight?" he asked.

She looked down to the computer and started clicking around the screen. "Let me see. You have been here before, I see, which should not surprise me. I am sure you have been to almost all of the famous mountains at this point."

"There are still a few left. Yeah, I was here before the Olympics."

"There are two rooms down the hall from each other. Will that work for you? I can look and see if there are any others closer to each other. I wish I could offer the executive suite or a similar room, though each is currently occupied."

"Cool. That works great. Thanks." He handed over his own credit card to the receptionist. I elbowed him hard in the side, and he looked over at me and waved away my concern for the credit card.

"Here are your cards. Have a good night," the receptionist said while handing over the key cards. We could tell that she really had something to say, though she was undecided if she should say it before we disappeared to our rooms for the night. "Would you autograph something for me? Only if you want to, of course, but I would really appreciate it."

"Sure." Gavlin responded.

Her face lit up. "That would be wonderful!" she exclaimed, and then immediately returned to a forced, much calmer state. She took out her phone and, along with the autograph, I snapped a picture of them. When we rounded up the group and headed to the rooms, I finally felt we were out of earshot from the receptionist.

"You used the credit card. What were you thinking?"

"The paparazzi will know I'm here by tomorrow. No use trying to hide. We sleep, we get the documents, and head back," he said nonchalantly. For the first time on this trip, we had run into a situation where our celebrity was going to be the burden, not that I didn't see it coming. I was surprised we had lasted this long. There was no way to bring a snowboarding superstar to the snow and not attract some attention. If I knew him like I thought, it was going to be darn near impossible to keep him from showing off tomorrow.

"Okay, fine. What time is wake-up call tomorrow?" I asked, hoping that it would not be some ridiculous hour.

Riley started signing fast to Rowan, and he interpreted. "Riley says early. She wants to board before people catch us and we need to leave."

"Do I have to actually ski or board or whatever you do tomorrow?" Falon said.

"Where is your sense of adventure? It's fun. Well, I suppose you can just ride the gondola up and down with us," Gavlin suggested.

"I can manage such a thing. Where I am from, we do not do snow or cold. I do fruity drinks on a sunny, ninety-degree beach, in a bikini, tanning. Also, if I am going to be in this arctic weather for any length of time, I need something to wear."

"And that's what your surprise is tomorrow," Gavlin said, smiling mischievously.

chapter 12

The next morning I rolled out of bed to find sunlight pouring through the open curtains to reveal the chestnut-colored wood that covered the walls and ceilings. There were some unique Swiss touches of fabric choices, but nothing beat the view out the sliding glass doors. With only the occasional harsh edge not covered in snow, the highest peak of the mountain jutted way above the earth, its speared tip toward the ceiling of the world, untouched by human society. Below the balcony, the terrain surrounding our hotel had at least a foot of fresh snow piled upon the rest that had been accumulating all winter season. Slightly beyond the hotel were these creatures. They were some type of ram that resembled something like snowballs, plowing their way through the tundra. They were entertaining to watch as they moved toward each other for warmth and continued snuffling around the ground for a nonexistent food source, leaving narrow, crossing paths in the snow.

I was dressed in my usual jeans and multiple layers of shirts and sweaters by the time Falon emerged from her beautification in the bathroom we three girls were sharing. Shockingly, the amount of makeup she was wearing had been significantly reduced, and her hair was pulled back on her head. Her outfit was no less "designer," but there was a noticeable change from runway model to runway model on her day off or, in our case, on the run.

"I feel absolutely disgusting, though the way I look at it, none of you seem to care. If I am going to be with all of you, there is nothing I can do to change the way we are all going to be looked at," she blurted.

"Uh, thanks? Are we bringing our bags with us when we go to the guys' room?" I said.

Riley shrugged and continued packing away her things.

"I do not believe we will be very safe in this room later, and while I am unsure who will watch all of our things, we should bring them with us," Falon replied while folding a shirt and delicately placing it in her open suitcase on the bed.

I nodded in agreement. "Let's blow this popsicle stand."

When we reached the guys' room, Rowan opened the door and ushered us in silently. Gavlin was busy on the room phone, which I considered to be another not-too-brilliant idea on his behalf. Originally, it might have been one inch, yet now he was racking up the miles when it came to drawing attention to us. He seemed relaxed and was joking around with whomever was on the other line before wishing them the best and hanging up.

He looked over in our direction. "Good morning! Who's ready to hit the moun—HEY!"

I had chucked a pillow at his head before he could finish. "What were you doing on the phone, you moron?"

He threw the pillow back at me, but it hit Riley standing next to me, who grabbed it and whacked me with it.

"Chill. Everyone already knows we're at this hotel. I just hooked us up with gear. I talked to the guys down at the shop so we can do a hit and run. Easier and less attention. You're gonna be thanking me later. We need to get down there before all the craziness starts at the shop," Gavlin said while grabbing his bag and heading toward the door.

"How do you sign, 'I am going to beat him over the head'?" I asked Riley.

In the lobby, guests were already dressed in their mountain attire with a few of them dragging skis and the occasional snowboard behind them. The skiers were primarily dressed in subtle shades of blacks, whites, solid navy blue and the occasional red. The snowboarders, a culture of their own, were sporting brightly printed neon colors and dizzying patterns, boards well branded in stickers and designs. We did our best to sneak up to the front counter and check out of the rooms. Our receptionist friend, tired from her long night, was waiting.

"Good morning, Mr. Fleet!" she practically shouted before we were in striking range of the desk. With that, anyone who had been in doubt or was ignorant that a celebrity was in proximity now knew very well that we were here. We checked out with a couple of clicks of the computer mouse. The four of us, especially Rowan, were looking to keep walking through the throng of people and make it out as fast as we could manage. Gavlin, on the other hand, loved his fans too much. He insisted on stopping for pictures and autographs, smiling his quirky smile. Yet again, he appeared to have forgotten about the whole "we are a bunch of teenagers on the run" thing. It was all too much for me and way too much for Rowan as he made a beeline out the door, away from the commotion and the crowds. Falon followed him in eager pursuit. Riley and I were still following Gavlin around the lobby until I finally reached over, grabbed his hand, and physically dragged him out the door. I was going to pay for that later if the news caught wind of how I was holding hands with him. Thank goodness we were out of the country, otherwise I would have been his girlfriend by tomorrow's tabloids. Not the way I wanted to achieve my fifteen seconds of lifetime fame, but we needed out.

"I know you were enjoying your fans and being back at what you do best, but we really need to get going," I barked at him.

For a brief second, he looked upset as his eyes cast down at the ground. "Sorry. I just don't want to disappoint them."

"Riley says that's nice of you," Rowan mumbled, while his sister looked at Gavlin with a huge grin.

"Least I can do," he replied.

"Least you can do is help keep us all alive until this is over," I added.

The ride down from the hotel to the city was even more spectacular during the day. The snow glittered in the sun, and the defined ridges of the mountain were carved in a delicate, yet rugged way from the terrain. The town, at only 8:00 in the morning, was buzzing. It was, after all, a ski town, where early starts were the norm. Without cars, people walked at their own pace to their destinations. There were the older couples on a peaceful mountain trip, the young group looking for a good time, the natives walking with a distinctive direction and purpose, and the general tourists snapping away pictures on their digital cameras. For the most part, I was definitely not hearing English, and hoping our lack of a translator would not cause any unforeseen issues. Still, with luggage in tow, we found our way to a large ski and board store offering rentals, lessons, and general equipment. Inside, people were flying around with coats and hats, trying on one thing or another and admiring themselves in the mirrors placed at various places long the walls. Employees behind the counter were busily signing papers and measuring customers for rentals prior to dashing into the back room for the appropriate gear. For the most part, the guests looked ecstatic. They would continue to be until the older ones awoke tomorrow to every muscle, including those they did not know they had, screaming in pain.

Gavlin marched up to the counter. "Hello, I talked with Nico this morning."

"Nico?" he said in a heavy German accent. Gavlin nodded his head in agreement.

"One minute." The young man hurried off to the back of the store.

While we were waiting, we had a couple of young guys walk up and introduce themselves to Gavlin, take a picture, and receive an autograph. Then, a young guy with blond hair, who was probably only twenty, walked up to us.

"Nice to finally meet you, Gavlin. I'm Nico."

Gavlin shook his hand. "Thanks for everything, man."

"For you, no problem."

Gavlin turned toward us. "These are my friends, Rowan, Falon, Riley, and Devon."

"How did you guys get lucky enough to travel with this guy?" Nico said.

"You have no idea," I said sarcastically.

Nico motioned us to follow him toward the rear of the store. "Your board is set, and I have the other sets of skis and boards aside."

"Cool. For you guys," Gavlin said, motioning toward us, "enjoy shopping on me. The store is free range. Be quick," he said, eyeing Falon.

"I need to have you try on boots first, so I can set them. Then, you are free," Nico said, standing next to a couple of wooden chairs with boots piled high next to them.

"I'm going to go look around, because we all know I am not ski-ing," Falon said before she turned around and headed into a forest of winter coats.

"She comes to Zermatt and does not get on the mountain? Whoever has the board, you're first," Nico said.

"Not worth it with that one," Gavlin added, as the two of them watched her waltz off in search of the perfect Eskimo wear.

Riley walked over to Nico and sat down next to Gavlin, who was picking up boots and casually examining them, mostly out of curiosity.

"You board much?" Nico asked Riley, bent over and examining the boots on her feet.

Rowan interpreted for her. "We live in Colorado on the moun-tain, so it's every day we can," he interpreted for Nico.

"Nice," Nico replied, slightly confused when he looked up to see Rowan talking while he handed Riley another pair of boots. "How do these fit?"

Riley gave him two thumbs up, with a smile. "Great. These are nice," Nico replied.

Riley took off the boots, jumped up, signed something quick to her brother, and bounded off into the forest of black snow pants and ski parkas. Rowan sat down next and tried on about eight pairs of boots multiple times before he finally found ones he was satisfied with. It was one-word answers and questions to figure out a differ-ent size or a different model. Instead, Gavlin had started a conversa-tion with Nico about snowboarding and the season currently finish-ing up on the mountain. Nico was thoroughly enjoying a friendly conversation with the one guy everyone was lining up to interview. Gavlin was pleased to be in his own realm, talking to someone with the same interests and nearly the same age. Some of his answers were intentionally short, and it was obvious how much information he was allowed to divulge for one reason or another. Regardless, after being with him for a few days, I concluded that he was an open book. He lives in the spotlight, and the person you see in the interviews is the same person you get while traveling on a life-or-death mission with him: down to earth and carefree. It was refreshing and added a little hope to the idea that my celebrity crushes might be all the gentlemen they appear to be on television.

"Your turn, Devon?" Nico said.

"Yes. Good memory."

"You know that if you expect to be my friend after this trip, you're going to have to board," Gavlin joked.

"I could give it a try, after I make it down this mountain on something I can actually slightly manage," I replied in reference to the skis I planned to use. "I personally also prefer to not spend most of the day sitting in a foot of snow on my ass because I have no concept of how to maneuver a snowboard."

"Where's the fun in that?" Gavlin said.

"Yeah, because going to the hospital is just what we need at this point."

"What are you here for?" Nico asked curiously.

Gavlin and I looked at each other with no idea which of us was going to craft our newest little white lie.

"Get away from everything," Gavlin replied.

"Not easy, but you might be able to. You are all done, Devon. Go spend this guy's money. Come to the front, and everything will be ready for you," Nico said.

"Thank you," I replied.

Gavlin and I both grabbed our things and went headfirst into the central part of the store, buzzing with people and crowded by puffy down-filled coats. A few seconds later, we found Falon right where she loves to be: in front of a mirror. Riley was next to her admiring a purple and white coat she currently modeled.

"Looks good," I said to Falon in reference to her slightly puffy, fitted maroon coat and gave a thumbs-up to Riley as well. Next to them was a pile of coats Falon had obviously tried on and discarded in her achievement of the perfect outfit for the snow.

"Go figure she would go for purple. It's her favorite color," Rowan said from directly behind me.

I jumped around in shock. "Could you try not to sneak up on me? We have been over this."

"I only walked over toward everyone," he said plainly.

"Well, next time please walk around me before you just start talking."

He simply smiled and set down a pile of black clothing on his suitcase.

"Ninja look, or something?" I asked Rowan.

"Or something," he replied with a rare, but genuine smile.

Just then, Gavlin came tearing into the open area we were standing in, with a red and black plaid coat on and goggles already on his head. "I'm ready!"

Riley signed "nice," and Gavlin replied with a "thank you" before he turned and dashed off yelling, "I forgot something!"

"*Forgot*," I managed to sign to inform Riley of the meaning of his dashing off and yelling. "I thought he had a coat? Oh well. I'm gonna go look around and grab some things quickly," I said.

I came back about ten minutes later with a black-and-white coat, black pants to match, gloves, and a really nice, expensive pair of Oakley goggles. I felt guilty, but figured Gavlin was not concerned at this point about the few hundred I was about to spend compared to what he would be making this year with the sponsorships and competitions. I am sure he had a deal with the company anyway. I had never treated myself in this manner and just avoided looking at any of the price tags.

"Whose idea was it to wear helmets…because I approve. I think it might be the only logical thing we have done this entire trip to ensure that we are going to make it in one piece to The Hague," I said.

"Stupid to be without," Gavlin said, smiling, and threw me a black helmet.

I pulled my hair down from a messy bun, letting it wildly fall loose before reining it into a low ponytail, and stuck the helmet on. "Fits great! We ready to go?"

"I finally found a coat," Falon said while wearing a sleek-fitting, slightly puffy white coat, "so we shall go."

"We have royal approval. Let's roll," Gavlin remarked.

At the front desk, Nico waved us forward in the crowd of waiting people and started to scan all of our gear and lift tickets through the register: snowboards, skis, boots, coats, helmets, goggles, gloves, hats, scarves, and snow pants. I am unsure what the total actually summed to, but Gavlin was undeterred and handed over his credit card to charge our little shopping spree without considering any of the dollar amounts. I could only hope this would be the last swipe for that card while on this adventure. If not, it was going to meet a nice pair of shiny, sharp scissors and a trashcan. We thanked Nico again for all the help, Gavlin signed a couple of things, and we lugged everything out the front door with a considerable amount of coordination and brute strength. Although we had eaten breakfast a few hours earlier and we lugging around all the gear, we decided it would be best to grab a bite to eat before the ski day officially began. We ventured down a couple of blocks and found a small restaurant for breakfast.

When I had stopped shoving food in my mouth, the guys were still downing everything in sight. Gavlin was double fisting a roll of some form and a fork stuck into a breakfast omelet. I deemed it an appropriate time to bring up the idea of what the actual plan for the day was, not that we did plans well.

"In all honesty, I find it much more thrilling to just play it by ear, but do we have any ideas what we do once we get on the mountain?"

"You mean besides board?" Gavlin said.

"Very funny. Do you know where your package is?" I asked.

"Yeah. The top."

"Where on the top?" I prodded.

"Um. Not sure. Figure off to the side somewhere," Gavlin said before taking a bite. "Haven't thought about it."

"*Let us know when you do. That would be helpful,*" Riley said.

"We should give a prize to whoever finds the special snowflake in eight feet of snow," I added.

"A little positivity. At least it'll be an adventure," Gavlin remarked.

"I am unsure who will be having the fun, though it will not be me. Speaking of such, where am I going to be?" Falon asked.

"We will probably have you ride the gondola and then wait around for us," I said.

"With these mountains it's short hits down. There are no giant lifts, so we'll stick you on with a ticket," Gavlin verified.

"That is going to be horribly dull. Still, it'll be better than falling down in the snow every ten seconds in my attempt to ski."

"*You could if you wanted,*" Riley happily included.

"Learning is much harder when you did not pick it up naturally at the age of two," Rowan told his sister, to give her a hard time in good fun. She looked at him mockingly and signed something.

"We're settled. If we find what we need quickly enough, we may buy ourselves a little time to have fun. Deal?" I summed up.

There were a couple of head nods in agreement. Riley then picked up the shopping bags next to her, held them up for me, and indicated toward the restrooms.

chapter 13

A half hour later we emerged from the restaurant fully out-fitted to battle the mountain: parkas, gloves, scarves, hats, goggles, snowboarding boots, ski boots attached to bags, helmets, and the high-end clumsy boards and skis. We looked like pack mules making our way to the mountain. If it were not for the slick, shiny appearance of the gear we had just bought, we would have looked like a collection of vagabonds. Considering our suitcases were a bit on the suspicious side, we found a hidden spot in the base camp lodge near the ticket sales, where we hoped they would not be found. For safekeeping, Falon and I grabbed the documents and their complementary electronic memory devices and put them inside our coats. There was not a chance they were going to be lost, stolen, or left behind in a potential mad rush out of Zermatt.

We waited only a short time at the gondola lift on the southeast-ern side of the mountain before piling in for a climb through the sky. At a point on the mountain named Furi, we vacated our gondola for another ride up to Trockener Steg, which would put us slightly short of ten thousand feet in elevation. From the view inside the gondola, we could see a multitude of people below buzzing down the mountain and carving paths as their edges cut quickly through the powder. Their snaking trails wove across the mountain. Coming from the Midwest, the snow here was gorgeous in all its non-icy fluffiness. Skiing in the Midwest subjects a person to manmade "hills" forcibly carved from flat cornfields and machine-driven snowstorms shot into an icy skating sheet. Midwest skiing is not real skiing; it is learning how to properly grind your edges against frozen water to keep from spinning out of control. The pain associated with falling on one's ass on ice has always kept me from strapping on a snowboard to crash down the hill in my attempt to learn. I could feel the pressure in my ears, popping every couple of feet, as we climbed vertically to the top along the thin metal wire holding us above the ground. Three thousand vertical feet later, we arrived.

Upon reaching the top, Falon remained in the cozy lodge in front of a roaring fire, with a cup of hot chocolate. We promised that whatever happened, we would be back, and told her not to go anywhere, under any circumstances. There would be no way to contact Falon if all hell broke loose. In any normal circumstance, we would all be toting iPhones and using Facebook, texting, and Twitter. While everyone had encouraged Falon to strap on a pair of skis and take on the mountain, without any experience, looking at the runs we needed to venture down, it would have been a dangerous idea. They were short, sharp runs with deep snow to catch your skis on and drop-offs close enough to the edge to make my stomach flip. It was going to be challenging enough for me.

Although the documents were the priority, we decided to take a lift that would release us up a little higher than our intended search area so we could move past all the bundled-up antics that came with strapping skis and snowboards to everyone's feet. We all understood that if we were deprived of all fun, it was going to be difficult for everyone to concentrate. We jumped on one of the few chair lifts to ascend up a couple hundred feet. It worked out to where I ended up next to Gavlin on the chair lift. Between his helmet, goggles, and a black neck warmer pulled to his goggles, not an inch of him was exposed.

"If I didn't know any better, I would think you were hiding," I said to Gavlin.

"This is how I normally look. All of the admiring fans don't usually have the honor. You've been lucky enough to admire my handsome face for the past couple of days," he said, laughing. If we were not on a chair lift, I would have pushed him jokingly, though I have to admit there had been some major admiring at times.

At the top, Gavlin and Riley clipped into their snowboards. Riley finished seconds after Gavlin and I lent her a hand and a helpful tug to her feet. Then, without the slightest inclination, Gavlin jumped his board in the air to get going, adding a chirping and gleeful holler as he took off. It took a couple of moments for us to gather ourselves before taking off in his wake. I was a little rusty, yet it came back to me fairly fast. Skiing on ice most of my life, I experienced the thick powder trying to force apart my skis with every turn. Instead of grinding edges with a cutting noise, my skis eventually found their place next to each other and glided down the mountain. While I managed to stay in control with my larger turns, the three ahead of me looked at home on the snow. Rowan had put on some heavy speed. Despite the fairly thick snow, he was finding his way down like a skier doing the Super G. Riley slid along, throwing in the occasional spin of her board on the way down. There was no doubt this was Gavin's life. With little effort he created the perfect movement and found his own creative ways to not just simply go down. It was as if everything he did was pure instinct, and the tricks were just his natural way of goofing off. It reminded me of my dogs after they had been cooped up all day, and then finally being let out to play, with an explosion of energy. Gavlin rode with the board in one direction, then the next, and then riding close to the edge of the pathway to catch enough air for a spin. For the first time in days, it was just the mountain and me, with only a light breeze and the sunshine overhead. One could not have asked for a better day. At the bottom of the run, I slid to a stop next to Riley and Gavlin. It seemed strange that Rowan was behind us considering his initial speed and the fact that I could not remember passing him. Before I could ask where he was, I heard a pair of skis behind me with the edges grabbing hold of the snow in a sideways slide and was promptly covered in snow. I turned around to find Rowan enjoying the fact that I looked like Frosty the Snowman, and me, smiling, as I wiped the snow off the side of my helmet and goggles.

"Riley says let's do it again!" Rowan shocked me with his enthusiasm.

"Agreed, but not until we find what we came looking for. There is no use having to leave early and not actually get what we came for," I said, not thrilled about being the ruiner of fun. But someone had to be, and I was accustomed to it.

"Why are you always the practical one? No fun. I want to go on the half-pipe," Gavlin mockingly whined.

"Later, superstar. Where are we going?" I asked.

"Lift to the top. I was told to look in the woods, and I guess I would know. My guess is that it will be a short way down and near a tree marked with red. Go seventeen steps around the tree," Gavlin said.

"That is quite a guess," Rowan stated.

"Red has always been my color, and it is always for love. After I finally made some money boarding, I sent my parents here for an anniversary gift, and it was their seventeenth. Best I can do," he explained to our shock at his inferring abilities.

"Let's go!" I said and popped my skis off in order to enter the gondola.

The trip up was slightly longer than before, and to the right we could see the sharp point of Matterhorn. Gavlin informed us that Matterhorn was a couple thousand feet higher and resided in Italy. There were no skiing paths on the Italian side, but from the looks of it, there was not a chance I would want to tango with the sharp rock outcrops. At the top it did not take long to decide Gavlin and I would be together on one side of the trail, while Rowan and Riley would be responsible for the other side. Our newest task would involve slowly making our way along the tree line of the open ski path, looking for any traces of red—a long shot at best.

For a majority of the time, the two groups remained even across from each other on the path, slowly sliding down in the thick snow. Gavlin definitely had the entertaining partner. I would often not balance my skis properly and find myself sprawled in the snow. With snowboard boots, Gavlin had the easier task of simply taking off his board and walking the way down. By the looks of it, it was going to take all day to make it down, if we were lucky. I could only hope the instructions Gavlin gave us were true and we would find it somewhere near the top. After an eternity of looking at monotonous, identical fir trees, my legs were burning from manipulating my skis, and I finally fell down. There was no getting me up. Skis jammed into the snow, perpendicular to the mountain, I remained sprawled uphill in the snow. Eventually, I sat up and made myself useful by momentarily looking through the woods. At first glance I thought my mind was manipulating my eyes into seeing red just so I would be done with this torture we were forced to partake in, until Gavlin threw a snowball at my head.

"I have another if you don't get up," he said, holding up a snowball and looking down at me.

"I think I see something red in the woods. Look a little to my left," I said. When he turned around, I reached into the snow and carved out a huge snowball. The snowball made contact with the back of his head, without a helmet, perfectly on target.

He turned around quickly while reaching his hands down into the snow. "You asked for it!"

We both proceeded to grab as much snow as possible without real care as to whether they looked like snowballs or not. I was immobile with my skis, and with my body jammed in the snow, there was not much I could do to evade the attack. When we finally ceased, I was buried in snow like a snow mermaid. We were red-faced and laughing so hard that Gavlin collapsed next to me in the snow. I found it impossible to sit up with my snow blanket and without a place to prop my hands and push myself up because of Gavlin's proximity. When Gavlin finally stopped laughing, he sat up and bent over the top of me. He pushed away the snow and snapped the binding off my skis so I could pull my feet up from their awkward position wedged between the snow and bound by skis. When I sat, up my face was only inches away from his. For the first time since I'd seen him on television, I didn't feel like the only one staring. His eyes were so bright in the sun that they could have been considered yellow, which, in my mind, was even more captivating than the sharp, ice blue. His hair fell shaggy around his face, without any defining shape, still not disrupting our intent stare. All breath felt stagnant in my lungs, and the tension around my ribcage could not be overcome. Then he leaned in, and our lips met. It would not have felt any different if we had known each other for more than a few days and were not sitting waist deep in snow, on a mountain in Switzerland. I was waiting for the sparks to fly. We both held on, my hand wrapped around his shoulder and his hands planted in the snow next to my shoulders. When we slowly pulled away, it was only a couple of inches and we, once again, kept our eyes fixed. We needed no words to describe how it felt. Nothing.

"Can we pretend that didn't happen?" I asked sheepishly.

"Yeah," Gavlin replied without moving away and a smile coming to his face.

"It felt like the right idea," I said, with a smile growing on my face. There was still some force that lit me up inside whenever he smiled.

"Yeah, but it might be better this way," he said and continued to tackle me into the snow until we were both laughing. Peter Pan would never grow up, and Wendy always needed someone to keep her feet off the ground.

I got to my feet and then turned toward the woods where the red band around the tree still existed. "I was serious when I said there is red on the tree. Look there," I said, pointing.

"Awesome!"

I ditched my skis and walked over to the tree a couple of feet off the trail, where I touched the red around the tree. "It's a metal band they put on there. Clever, and only noticeable to those who really looked. Even then, it looks like it's there on purpose. You said your parents went when you were what, around sixteen?"

"That's right," he said, starting to count off seventeen paces into the woods.

I mimicked him and walked seventeen steps up and parallel to the trail. "That would mean they only put this here about two years ago."

"Yeah. They moved it because they thought someone might have found it. Don't know where it was before then." He stopped and began pushing the snow away from around him.

I walked back toward the tree and back out seventeen steps in the opposite direction. This gave me a general idea about how to draw a seventeen-foot semi-circle around the tree for the general location. Gavlin had given up on his first location and was slowly moving toward his left, digging away the snow with his board as a shovel. My search through the snow was not going much better, and my hands were getting cold despite my thick waterproof gloves, from digging through more than a foot of crystallized water. On the one hundred and first dig and a good few minutes later, my hand jammed into something, and I let out a squeal of surprise and pain from the contact between my hand and the edge of a metal box.

"Ya good?" Gavlin asked, looking up from the snow.

"Other than the fact my hand just smashed into a metal box, wonderful!"

He threw down his snowboard and came running, the best one could in the snowy conditions, toward me. "You found it!"

"I think...," I said while uncovering a metal container only slightly above ground level and about the size of small file box.

Gavlin crouched down next to me as we worked to expose the box. With the ground frozen solid, it showed no signs of coming out, but thankfully the lock was on the side close to the top. Gavlin fished around his pockets and found a plain-looking house key with a jagged and complicated key mechanism. We both held our breath. A little wiggling and reversing the key half a dozen times later, we finally heard the locking mechanism in the box give way. Why there would have been more than one box buried on a Swiss mountain in Zermatt was beyond my anxious brain at the moment. Inside, there was a sealed plastic container, and inside that was a plastic bag with just what we needed—a stack of paper documents and their corresponding electronic copy in the form of a small, black, unmarked flash drive. We both stared at it for a few seconds until Gavlin pulled them out of the box gently, leaving them safely enveloped in their plastic covering and turning them slowly in his bare hands.

"You want me to put them in my backpack with the others?" I offered, pulling my backpack off that I opted to ski with in order to keep my valuable documents in my possession. "Gavlin? Do you want me to hold them?"

He handed them to me without looking up and wiped a sleeve across his face. "Uh, yeah, thanks."

"I'm sorry," I whispered. Then I was stuck in that horrible moment when I was not sure if I should say something else or just sit there, or force myself to give the other person a hug. It's hard to comprehend how such a silly little bit of affection comforts people when I see open arms and proceed to duck down and dart in the other direction. I reached over and crouched in the snow, his arms open before I was fully committed to the idea; it lasted for a few seconds. I could feel his head rest against my helmet head hair and my deep breaths filling in for his, abrupt and taking in only enough of the crisp air to keep his body physically alive. Beyond that he had sunken beneath the snow. I pulled my body back enough so that my voice would trod softly though the air. "We can sit here a little longer."

"Naw. We should go." My body stayed stationary while he used both hands to take away the frozen bits of pain on his face, leaving behind watery eyes. "Okay, let's enjoy this for them. Should we cover this thing up?"

This elicited a toothless smile. "Yeah. Definitely. We better go find the other two."

After the documents were safely stored with me, and we trampled through all the snow around the area to make it exceedingly difficult in case someone came looking, we appeared back out on the path. I was breathing hard and running a mild sweat under my layers of clothing. Trampling through thick snow was hard enough, and the stiff plastic ski boots were not helping. It was a relief to know when I popped my skis back on that I would not be straining every muscle in my body just to slowly slide down the mountain.

"Come on, slow poke!" I yelled to Gavlin while he was latching on his board and putting his helmet and goggles back on.

I started to ski my way down and, before I knew it, Gavlin had raced in front of me and attempted to cut me off. I had to come to a grinding halt to avoid careening into him, which involved my lack of coordination and almost falling down. By the time my skis were stopped and rearranged in the proper positions, I pushed off hard and raced down the mountain. It was an unbelievable ride down as the terrain became easier, and I picked up even more speed. I figured he would be down near the lodge where we had left Falon, so I headed in that direction. Once close to the lodge, I began to slow down to avoid a collision with other skiers waiting at the bottom. I eventually slowed to a stop and leaned forward to prop all my weight onto my poles as I looked around for a sign of anyone. With my back toward the top of the mountain, I was eyeing the lodge when someone grabbed me from behind. The militiamen had me in their vice. Every nerve fiber in my being shot off. Fight-or-flight mode was initiated, and I went into survival mode. My mind started racing to configure the quickest escape, and my heart skipped a couple of beats.

"Hello!" came a familiar voice from my capturer.

"Gavlin! I'm going to kill you!"

"Hey there," he said, laughing.

I could not even muster a smile because my whole body was straining to not follow the shaking pattern of my hands. "I thought you were one of those militia guys and that we were all captured, and who knows what was going to happen, and we would never get the documents there, and they were going to kill us!" I blurted before finally stopping for a couple of seconds and telling myself to breathe. I was still going to kill him.

"Good, now?"

"Yes. I am still going to kill you," I sighed, just pleased he was back to enjoying being here. "Look, there's Rowan and Riley."

Both of them came out of the lodge, looking warmed and ready for another trip. Riley came running over first and starting gesturing something to me, which I half understood.

"Find them?" I said. She nodded in agreement. "Yes," I said pointing to my backpack.

She was thrilled and immediately told her brother about our find.

"Good. We checked on Falon and other than whining about being bored, she is good," Rowan said in his matter-of-fact fashion.

"Why did you come down here?" I asked.

"Ski patrol saw us. We skied down and back up. You were in the woods when we reached you and hoped you'd both found it."

"Time for some fun?" Gavlin broke the silence.

"We'll follow you," I said.

Riley and Rowan both grabbed their respective gear, and we followed Gavlin over to the half-pipe. This area was more crowded than other parts of the mountain had been, but there was still plenty of room for me to find a nice spot to sit near the bottom and watch. A couple of people came through with some amazing tricks, flipping, spinning, and finding airspace eight feet off the edge before landing gracefully, or not so gracefully in some situations. I still had no idea how someone would even start to learn how to launch off the side of an almost vertical wall into the air and flip around in an orderly fashion. In my case, it would be a matter of finding the guts to risk bodily injury. Before Gavlin or Riley came down, Rowan skied next to me and took off his skis to sit down. It was strange he had not tried to cover me in snow, considering I was a sitting duck on the ground. I could tell he was not just being quiet. There was something weighing on him that had occurred since I'd departed from him and his sister to look for the documents. There would be no use in asking because he would just ignore me or avoid the question entirely.

"So, is Riley gonna show us some tricks?" I asked, avoiding what I really wanted to know.

"Yeah, she's up there," Rowan said.

I watched for a couple of more seconds until I saw someone launch a little over twenty feet in the air, which was much higher than I had been seeing. After a couple of more hits of insane flipping and spinning, it was obviously no other than the Olympic gold medalist himself. He continued to make his way down with some impressive tricks, but nothing like I was sure he could do. When he landed at the end, he steered off to the side near Rowan and me, and stopped in front of me.

"Impressive. I have seen you on TV and videos, but it doesn't compare to actually sitting here and watching," I said, looking up.

"That was fine. It's too dangerous to show you the real tricks with all the people."

I followed his gaze back up the pipe to see Riley coming down. I was impressed by her abilities to board grab out of the pipe and perform a basic rotation. There were a couple of wobbly moments, but she never fell, which is better than I could have ever managed. She saw us watching her from the bottom and steered her way over.

Gavlin gave her two thumbs up, and she mirrored him with a smile.

I noticed she was breathing pretty hard, which was unusual for a runner who lived at a high altitude.

"You hold your breath the whole way down?" I joked.

She nodded while laughing between breaths.

Gavlin took off his snowboard and picked it up. "Since we have no snowmobiles, I guess we're gonna have to walk," he said and waited for Riley before trudging back up the exterior of the half-pipe.

"Guess we are waiting around, unless you want to ski down and back up," I told Rowan.

"Whatever. Don't you want to watch your boyfriend?" Rowan said.

And then it dawned on me. Rowan and Riley saw us off in the woods, and instead of coming to help or confirm their assumptions, they kept skiing down. Clearly, Rowan saw more than just us digging gopher holes in the snow. The one thing that still puzzled me was why he even cared. It was not like he ever wanted to talk to me, and every time we were near each other it was either complete silence or a venomous argument. There was another reason, other than him having a crush on me.

"It was nothing," I told him.

"What?" he replied, like he had no clue.

"You know exactly what I'm talking about."

"No."

"Fine. I know you do. Just know that it meant nothing."

"Whatever you say," he said, making no eye contact with me.

"Why do you always try to aggravate me?"

"I don't."

"You know exactly what you are doing! We are either not talking, arguing, or you just refuse to answer me beyond one muttered word," I said angrily.

"Maybe it's you."

"Me? I am the one trying to get along with you, and all you do is make it worse. I know I have a tendency to be stubborn, but at least I am willing to give other ideas a try. You, on the other hand, are still trapped in what happened to get us into this mess. All of us hurt. Don't you understand that?"

"Nice to hear your real opinion of me," he said without raising his voice.

"If we're gonna play that game, tell me what you think of me. I really want to hear this."

"You don't."

"I insist."

All I received was silence. I waited for a couple of seconds, but he was intentionally ignoring me. "This is what I am talking about! Every time you have to actually have feelings, you just shut down."

"You're not going to give up, are you?"

"Giving up is not in my nature."

"It's gonna be a long few days for you then," he replied.

"Arg!" I said, looking back up the mountain. There was no use talking to him anymore if it was only going to ruin my wonderful day.

chapter 14

For the next hour, I watched Gavlin teach Riley a handful of new things, which involved her falling down most of the runs. A couple of young snowboarders took notice of Gavlin after witnessing a couple too many huge airs and flips not done by the average amateur. People with cameras and phones videotaped the scene from all angles, as well as others who had stopped just to watch the spectacle. The crowds were starting to make me slightly nervous as the number of people grew, each person adding greater interest to those that were skiing past. A couple of times before Gavlin and Riley unstrapped their boards and walked back up the hill, I caught a couple of words with them. There were numerous spectators who were probably wondering who the three of us tagging along with Gavlin were, although none of them approached Rowan or me. A couple of girls waited anxiously nearby, taking a few steps toward us, but continuously retreating back. I wanted nothing more than to ski, yet I did not think it would be the greatest idea to be off by myself on a foreign mountain without a cell phone. And there was no chance

I was taking Rowan with me. Instead, I unzipped my warm jacket, propped my feet in the snow in front of me, with my knees bent, and leaned back with my gloved hands in the snow. After another one of his immaculate runs, Gavlin pulled up next to me and sat down to watch Riley descend the half pipe, not even looking at his boots while unclipping them.

"You done?" I asked.

"I'm not gonna push my luck today. That was good. A little bit like the old times when my buddies and I would come out and do this. Back then, it was for home videos," he said while watching the pipe. Despite what he said, I knew how much he enjoyed watching his face across a big-screen television. Everyone wants to see all his or her hard work recognized or if nothing else than to have bragging rights.

"Riley looks like she's a quick study."

"She's a natural. I never really taught anyone before. Normally we give each other tips and whatnot. I was sitting up there gesturing and not really knowing how to explain how I moved the board to do what it does," he said, laughing.

Riley made it the entire way down without any crashing and, from my inexperienced eyes, minimal mistakes. "*Awesome!*" I signed to her.

She started talking excitedly to Rowan, although I could tell she was crushed from the combination of walking, just to come back down, and the consistent impacts with the hard packed snow of the half-pipe.

"I agree with Riley. She says we should go check on Falon," Rowan said.

"We can take the lift down further to the lodge," Gavlin said, strapping his board back on.

The lift was a comparatively short trip back to the lodge compared to all our other gondola rides on this day. I thankfully was with Gavlin again so that Riley could continue talking to her brother at Mach-10 speed about what she had been working on all day.

"You guys should've skied," Gavlin said, referring to Rowan and me.

"I wanted to, but I was not going with him. Not to mention, we talked for a couple of minutes, and after arguing and his angry mood, I could not guarantee he would be alive if we had gone together."

He started laughing at how ridiculous I must have sounded. "Hmm. I won't leave you two alone."

"Good choice. Wouldn't want to have to clean up the mess."

"I don't need the media."

"If you really wanted to, I could send a picture message to the tabloids of us together, and send them all into a head spin over our "relationship." I used air quotes for emphasis.

"Don't even try," he said with a serious, threatening face before returning to his smiling self.

"I would like to see that."

"That'd be ugly. I actually want to keep you around," he said as we came off the chair lift and waited for the other two.

"Aw, gee thanks." I only hoped he was not just saying that to be polite.

We decided to venture into the lodge and find Falon so we could determine if we would stay around a little longer or jet out before anyone was on our track. It was obvious that it would only be a matter of time before our visit was abruptly ended because, with Gavlin, we could not hide. Even if we had been trying, he was not assisting the situation any. Although it might have been safer to not act like a herd of deer in an open field, it was liberating to just pretend we were not being hunted down. We were just five teenagers, with unlimited cash, and one of the most beautiful mountains in the world. It could have been the dream vacation.

Riley was the first one to notice something suspicious inside when we heaved open the wooden doors to a wave of heat from the lodge. Five men dressed in street clothes, as opposed to parkas, and watching the room like hawks waiting for an unsuspecting mouse to dart out of its safe burrow and into open talons. Riley immediately stopped short three steps through the door and turned around, grabbing Rowan and me by the arms before pushing us back outside. Once forcing everyone out, she dashed off to the side of the building void of windows. We followed in quick pursuit. My first concern was for Falon, but we needed a plan. My heart started racing a hundred miles per hour; I thought it would have adjusted to all this action and near-death peril by now.

"*See Falon?*" I asked Riley.

She nodded her head no with a look of fear for where our friend may be. One thing was for sure—they were not using her as bait to lure us into a trap because none of us had seen her in plain sight.

Huddled on the side of the building in a tight circle, compulsively looking over our shoulders, we were all waiting on each other to reach a solution to another one of our roadblocks.

"It's possible she's hiding inside. Too bad we don't have a way to talk with her. Should we split up and see if she returned to the bottom when they arrived?" I whispered.

An idea suddenly sparked Riley's thoughts from what I mentioned, her eyes lighting up and giving us a glimmer of hope. "Riley says *bathroom*," Rowan said, trying to cooperate in the situation, although I could tell it was driving him insane that I was taking control.

162

"Let's go with it. Okay. Riley and I will sneak in, ninja our way to the bathroom and hopefully find her. If we are not back in ten, get out of here. Gavlin, take these," I said, removing my backpack full with two of the four sets of documents and shoving it into his hands. "It's at least half. No recognizance missions if we're not out. Get those there. Got it?"

"I can't agree to that," Gavlin opposed. I responded with the best stubborn face I could manage.

"I'm still not agreeing," he replied.

"Just get them there. There are already too many bodies in the ground for this to not mean anything." I did not intent to sound insensitive, though at this moment, he needed a heavy dose of the horrible truth.

"It will happen," he halfheartedly agreed. I was not convinced. Still, there was no time for me to take up an argument.

"See you in a few," I said, taking Riley and heading around the opposite side of the building to gain access to where we deemed would be the closest door to the women's bathroom, not that I expected the picture of a stick figure wearing a skirt, on the door, to stop our dark friends. We both tried to calm down and act like nothing was going on, but it was hard to cover up the intense fear pounding through our veins. Edging around the corner, I spotted no one and walked forward at a slow pace toward the single wooden door. The creak of the hinges made me cringe slightly for some reason as I pushed open the door and slid through. Riley was directly behind me, hopefully looking out in the opposite direction while I scanned the narrow hallway. I found no signs of anyone. The narrow corridor took an abrupt turn after a couple of steps to my left. A few steps to the right, a slight right-hand turn, and about ten steps across completely open space, and we would be in the safety of the restroom. I gingerly made my way down the hall, if one could consider walking in locked ski boots to have any delicate connotations. We both paused briefly to peer around the corner and into the open space lit by two large windows and an exterior door that opened and closed as people came to use the bathrooms. With enough people there would be some cover, though the small confines could be deadly. A man standing off to the side, acting suspicious, had my heart racing. About half a dozen people were mulling around the space between the bathroom and us. To make the straightest path would have involved bypassing a family with two young children on the right, a middle-aged couple dressed in matching red parkas, and a group of snowboarders looking at a mountain map and the screens of a couple of iPhones. It took me twelve steps before I literally slammed into the swinging door of the bathroom, crashing in on the other side.

"Falon," I whispered to ensure anyone on the outside would not be able to hear us.

"Coming out," I heard from the stall on my left, with the door shut and locked. Falon emerged terrified and immediately hugged me. Normally, hugging is not my thing, but she was obviously happy to see me, so I returned the gesture. Her slightly puffy eyes gave away the no longer present tears. She looked as frightened as a baby raccoon.

"All of a sudden, a group of guys in black entered from a couple of the doors, and I just did not know what to do. I finished drinking my drink, but I was sitting by myself, which might have helped because they went to the groups first. Then I needed to leave, but you told me not to, and I did not want to lose any of you, so I just hid, but the only place I could think of was the bathroom, which is why I am here. They really are repulsive. I had to tell myself it was the only way. How did you find me?" Falcon blurted, on the edge of tears, once again.

"Riley's idea. Good choice to be in here. I'm sure you're ready to get out of here."

"Yes, please," she said, trying to hold back all the tears and fear pulsing through her. Our lifestyle was affecting her most, and I could only hope she would make it through the entire venture without a massive grabber. Her poor little heart was luckily young enough to withstand the constant spike in blood pressure from this type of stress.

While I tried to calm down Falon, Riley walked over to the door and opened it a crack to look into the hall. The look on her face was not promising when she motioned for me to come over to the door. She opened it slightly, and I peered into the hallway. I pulled back from the door in horror. One of them stood with his broad back toward us only a few feet from the door that was our only escape. He could not have showed up at a more perfect time. I scanned the tops of the bathroom walls. As I suspected, we were boxed into the interior of the building. While our lives sure were shaping up to be the next action movie, there was no possible escape through the ventilation system.

"Wonderful," I sarcastically remarked.

"What?" Falon said, sniffling, her voice shaking while she examined herself in the mirror, recomposing her look.

I did not want to upset her any more than necessary, but we needed her cooperation to make it out without drawing attention.

"They have posted a watch on the door outside of here."

"How did you get in?" Falon asked.

"He was not here before," I said, feeling like a mouse trapped in its hole with a cat sitting on the exterior, ready to pounce.

We all sat there for about a minute. A couple of ladies walked in and out, but did not seem overly concerned with our presence. One asked if there was anything she could do in heavily accented English after we stared blankly at her first foreign comment. We pleasantly declined. Falon was propped near the edge of the sink, subconsciously twirling a long strand of loose hair around her finger, with Riley sitting, feet dangling, on the counter. I was concentrating hard on the dirty tiles of the floor from a full day of foot traffic and randomly started to count how many were in the bathroom. No ideas came to my mind other than to just sit and wait. Even then, it could have been hours, and who knows what would have happened to Gavlin and Rowan. Maybe Rowan would be the sacrificial lamb for our escape; I would be good with that. Suddenly, Riley jumped down from the sink, and my head popped up in shock. She took my helmet, which was dangling in my loose grip, and handed it to Falon. The goggles inside of it she gave to me. She snatched her white-rimmed, gold-tinted goggles from the counter, put them on, and buttoned up her coat. After being covered head to toe, she held out her hands in a "ta-da" gesture. Her idea was good, because if they could not identify us, they could not grab us without us making a huge commotion. No one wanted attention, especially if it meant they would look like they were kidnapping three innocent girls.

"Falon, hand me your hat," I said, eyeing her white and maroon hat with earflaps. I took my ratty brown hair, tied it in a low ponytail, and jammed all my hair on top of my head, with the hat to cover it. I then put the goggles on top of my head and buttoned my coat up a hair higher than necessary. Falon looked like she knew exactly how to wrangle all of her dark hair into my ski helmet. I figured the art of doing it might have been related to her knowledge of horse-riding helmets because her extensive amount of thick hair couldn't have been an easy beast to tame. It looked a bit odd for her to be carrying a purse, with no ski boots, and to be wearing helmet.

"Give me your purse," I suggested. "It's too bad none of our boots would fit you, but at least you're wearing snow pants. Thank goodness you're a wimp about the cold." I tried to lighten her mood. "Let's go in two groups. You two should go together because Riley knows where the guys are. I'll follow. I don't want to give them any reason to think it's us. You said they were checking people in groups earlier."

I received two nods before Falon and Riley hugged me, unexpectedly, and I shoved them out the door. I had no clock to determine how long I had been waiting. I gave them at least a minute before I was too jittery to stand there any longer. There was a group of four girls in their mid-twenties touching up their makeup in the bathroom. They were my opportunity. One of them looked a bit like Riley—two platinum blondes and a very heavyset lady. For the most part, they wore nothing on their faces and had nearly not enough resemblance to us to be stopped. I followed them closely as they left the bathroom, hoping that they would walk outside. They did not. Instead, I had to make a quick decision to either follow them near another exit, or break away. The guard was still propped near the door. With his normal dark-colored street clothes, the only thing giving him away was the gun he packed along his waist and the ear bud in his right ear. My flight instincts were screaming in my head to run. I mentally yelled back at myself to just walk casually out the door. No attention. Breathing and casually walking. Breathing. Walking. The hair on my neck stood up when I passed only three feet away from him, and I could feel his stare trying to examine my face for any similarity. I glued my eyes to a small, knotted imperfection in the wood on the wall and resisted every urge to catch a better look at one of the men who was following us.

When I reached the door, I grabbed the icy metal handle, gave it a forcible swing inward, and walked out into the brisk mountain air.

I kept looking straight ahead, but when I did not hear the door behind me click shut, my pace quickened. I took a sharp left around the side the building, maintaining a walking pace. When I turned, I saw that I was not alone. I saw that man placing his wrist near his moving mouth, out of the corner of my eye. He had just signaled someone. My mind was now screaming to run like crazy. My movement became more jittery as I attempted to contain my pace to a mere walk. As I neared where we had left our gear, I saw the others nervously glancing around for me. I made eye contact with Rowan first. With a slight twist of my head toward the gondola, I indicated for them to go. I watched as he snatched up Riley's snowboard and hurriedly told the others, who instantly grabbed only the other snowboard and booked it toward the gondola that would take us down, if we made it that far. I veered slightly to the left to make a straight line with the gondola. I was praying that if they managed to grab me, at least it would be obvious to everyone else waiting in line. It was my only hope. I was only a couple hundred feet from the end of the gondola line, but I was not stopping any time soon. I had no plans to wait at the end of a fifty-person line because the men chasing us would not be patiently waiting three people behind me for their turn. *Where were the others?* Suddenly, I saw them. As much as I disagreed with treating celebrities differently, right now, we needed it. Gavlin was leading the group toward the front and obviously using his presence as an excuse to get to the front of the line.

I obeyed the gut feeling to take off running. I shot forward as best as I could, in horribly awkward ski boots, and dodged around all the people in line. I received a lot of angry looks and yelling. I just ignored them as I literally pushed my way to the front, knocking over boards, skis, and people along the way. The others had loaded their things, and the gondola was preparing to leave when I pushed aside the operator and dove inside before we was able to finish closing the door. By the time my pursuers had reached the loading area, we were already bouncing down the mountain. I could see from the window of the gondola that my favorite friend in the front had pulled out his handgun, demanding the lift attendants to bow to his muscle, and presumably turn off our moving ride. The main operator was a tall and muscular young gentleman under his fitted yellow and black winter jacket. For all he knew, that man might have been an assassin out to destroy the world's snowboarding poster child. Around these parts there were probably enough celebrities and billionaires to take this as a serious threat, so he held his ground. The man stood directly in front of our militia friend, the gun aimed directly at his chest, refusing to move. With his unmoving presence, the gondolas continued to file past them, buying us more precious time. This was all contingent on the fact no one was waiting at the bottom to throw us into the back of an unmarked van. The last image I could clearly distinguish before the bodies at the top became blob shapes was our savior standing there and the militiaman being joined by an additional two men. The third gondola after us was just passing them. All of us were glued to the window, watching things unfold. Even when we could no longer see, we kept staring into the muddled background of the action unfolding a few hundred feet above us.

"Sorry guys," I apologized, feeling guilty about having a tail on us. I was more deeply sorry for involving an innocent bystander brave enough to save us.

"Don't worry about it," Gavlin said reassuringly. "I thought it added some excitement; it was getting boring."

"I hope the guy at the top will be fine."

"With the attention firing off a gun would cause, I am quite sure he will be unharmed," Falon said, surprisingly, trying to ease my concerns.

"Yeah, it should be fine," Gavlin added.

"How are we getting out of this infested town now?"

"I think we only have trains," Rowan said.

"Yeah," Gavlin agreed. "I think we can get one back to Zurich."

"There are a few train paths from here, and we could easily take a different one," Riley pointed out.

"We only did the freight last time because we didn't want anyone to know where we were, but Mr. Famous here couldn't help but get us noticed," Rowan snarled.

Gavlin looked slightly offended and hurt by the statement, and sat in silence. No one knew what to say. The only sound was the delicate and occasional creaking of the gondola for the next couple of minutes. When we switched gondolas halfway down, the look of shock on many people's faces when we exited the first gondola was priceless. Some people in line looked frightened to be in the same vicinity as the target for a couple of hired guns, while others were just shocked to see us alive and running. The gondola staff must not have known Gavlin's face from one of the numerous magazines or television appearances, though with everyone pointing it out and whispering to themselves, we made it to the front of the next gondola line without any pushing or squeezing to the front. A few long minutes passed. Stop one was a success, and now we were heading directly to the bottom. There was absolutely no telling whom we would have the privilege of meeting at the bottom. It was not shocking when we reached the bottom to find a swarm of local police spread out among the base. Of the nearly fifteen law enforcement officers there, each could be seen performing a respective job; some stood watch, others scanned the area, some directed foot traffic, and others were busy chatting over radios. No other people were being allowed up the mountain from where once we had just come. It would have been nice to be able to trust the people who were upholding the law, but we could not trust anyone. We knew as soon we eyed the police officers that we needed to hide Gavlin. He would be the only recognizable one of us and, as the presumed target, he was likely the only one the police would be keeping an eye out for. The five of us shoved on our helmets and goggles, which had managed to stay with us this whole time.

Right before we were preparing to land at the bottom, Riley spoke up. "*Gavlin, Rowan, switch.*"

Gavlin inquired to as what she was talking about.

"*Coats,*" she indicated.

"*Uh, why?*" Gavlin said.

"*They will stop Rowan before you if they have a description,*" she reasoned.

"Brilliant!" Gavlin said, throwing off his gloves and unzipping his coat.

A rapid coat change later, we quickly exited the gondola at the bottom. Rowan, without commenting, intentionally left his helmet off. It never dawned on me until we were dodging people that the red hair was a definite giveaway. There were no doubts the person wearing Gavlin's coat was indeed not Gavlin. Instead, he was someone covered head to toe as if the mildly cold weather were too much for him to handle, and wedged inside our group. Once we snuck past the hoards of people angrily waiting to go up the mountain, their day absolutely ruined, we reached the crowded interior of the lodge overflowing from those not wishing to wait in the cold. No one even made a move to take off a layer of clothing disguises as we quickly sought out our hidden bags. If stomping around in full mountain clothing indoors and lugging rolling suitcases was not suspicious, I am not sure what these people were accustomed to. Regardless, unstopped, we continued in tense silence out the front doors and down toward the city of Zermatt.

The uncomfortable silence continued as we walked on. I was sweating profusely in a bulky helmet and fully zipped parka. Eventually, out of earshot and eyesight, other than those few people in passing cars, I broke the cloud of silence following us. "You don't know how upset I am to leave all of our amazing gear here, and these are going to have to go soon, too," I said, looking down at the ski boots I was still painstakingly walking in. "We used it for less than a day. It feels like a waste, though I am planning to drag this coat all the way home if I can," I said to Gavlin.

"I'll get you new stuff if you're that upset," he replied happily.

"And that's why I keep you around," I said to him.

"Who wouldn't?"

"Don't push it. How far do we have to go? When can we stop to regroup so I can remove my oven-like coat and these boots not clearly made for walking?"

"Don't know. Hey Riley, how far?" he said, turning around to face her.

She gave us the "huh?" look. "How far to the train?" Gavlin repeated. She held up both hands for ten minutes. Gavlin told her thank you, and turned back to me.

"In ten minutes. Those are like two hundred-dollar boots," he said.

"Yes, and they are beautiful ski boots, not walking boots. You are in a pair of cushiony snow boots," I replied while ripping my helmet off. I instantly felt a few degrees cooler. My hair was static in every direction, and I did not have a spare hand to fix it. At this point, I honestly didn't care.

"This is what you get for being a skier," Gavlin mocked.

Winding our way down through the mountain and on streets without sidewalks, it remained a peaceful walk. Thankfully, there were enough signs to point us in the direction of the central train station, allowing for a direct and brisk walk without a GPS system or map. I prayed that we were not being followed, that none of the goonies were waiting at the train station, that the Swiss police would not desire our presence, and that we would not be found once we took a plane from the Zurich Airport to Ireland. With any luck, we would be alone in the Irish countryside twenty-four hours from now. There was no efficient way to make it to Ireland without taking a plane across Europe. This time we would have no access to a computer to manipulate the system as we had in Brazil. Also, whoever was chasing us across the world probably had access to any place our names could electronically appear. They probably had MI6 clearance.

At the train station, Falon looked too mentally exhausted to be concerned with any threats, and within seconds of our arrival, she was sitting on her suitcase, fixing her hair halfheartedly. Riley was her normal upbeat self. My first survival and comfort concern was clearly how fast I could remove the ski boots I walked over a mile in. They were forcefully removed and cast aside in exchange for my well-loved chucks. The entire time I was seated on the ground, my head swiveled back and forth, nerves on edge, ready to run at any second. Rowan did not look much better, pacing a couple of steps around the group, eyeing every person in our general vicinity. Thankfully, our train would leave in the next ten minutes, leaving barely any time for either the police or the secret operatives to realize where we were. Our rapid mountain descent might have had them still believing we were careening across the powdery slopes into Italy. Gavlin, being the teenage guy he was, and given ten minutes of spare time, dragged Riley along to find a couple of bags of snacks and sports drinks from the train station vendors. Regardless, I could not manage to eat as I constantly eyed the station.

Rowan had still not spoken a word to Gavlin after the one comment on the gondola earlier. His continued frustration was very clear by the occasional glare in Gavlin's direction. Gavlin appeared undeterred and had already reverted to his usual self, throwing and catching Cheese Puffs in his mouth. The whirr of a humming engine and the whooshing wind tunnel announced the arrival of our next mode of transportation. I was the last one on the train, dragging behind my trusty, poor little roller suitcase. I found an empty seat next to Gavlin, with the others seated across the aisle in the well-cushioned, standard gray fabric accommodations. A completely exhausting day starting more than sixteen hours ago was finally coming to an end. I flung my suitcase, a pathetic effort, under the seat and flopped down into the seat next to the foggy window, lines from busy fingers visible against the unclean glass. With the icy window out of the question, I rested my head against Gavlin's shoulder, not concerned with what anyone wanted to think, and curled my stockinged feet underneath me. His relaxed breathing and presence lulled me into a feeling of safety, and I closed my heavy eyes before the train even blew its whistle to leave the station.

chapter 15

"You were crashed out," Gavlin said when I lifted my head up a couple of hours later. Our train was still jetting across Switzerland in a northern direction toward Zurich, under the cover of a deep blue night.

"I can't believe I fell asleep like that," I said, cracking my crooked neck to realign it. I felt as if this type of sleeping was becoming an all too common occurrence on this little adventure.

"You must've needed it."

"Definitely." I looked over to see the three across the aisle flopped over in slumber. Rowan had his coat jammed against the window as a pillow. Riley and Falon were propped against each other in a pile of coats and tired limbs. "I see everyone else is asleep. I am surprised you aren't."

"Someone needed to watch and make sure we would not have to run and make a quick exit."

"That could have been interesting," I said, resting my head against Gavlin again.

"Well, it's gettin' a little boring."

"Boring is okay right now. You should catch some sleep." I looked up at him, catching the side of his face.

"What's up?"

"What do you mean?"

He looked back at me waiting for a reply.

"Nothing."

"You're preoccupied."

"Why would you say that?" I asked curiously. "I have been awake for thirty seconds, and all I was doing was using you as a pillow."

"Because you're good at the act that everything is fine."

"And why would it not be?"

"'Cause you have been distracted. We are on a train with no one chasing us, and you are just too quiet. You are thinking about something."

I curled my stockinged feet up on the seat and shifted my body, with my back leaning against the window so I was facing Gavlin. "You say a word and you will never hear the end of it, comprenez?"

"Comprenez," he repeated.

"You and Rowan talk, right? Clearly you two are not talking right now after what was said on the gondola, but before that, I am sure that you did."

"I see where this is going. You're upset because you can't have a decent conversation without like killing each other," he joked.

"It's not 'like killing each other'; it's more like 'coming seriously close,'" I lightly corrected. "I mean, I try, and I want to get along with him, but he just won't let me. He refuses to answer when I talk, and if we do talk, it turns into an argument. He is a selfish jerk, isolating himself from everything in the world. We are all going through hell here. We are forced to be together, and it would be much more productive if we could just try and solve the issue, instead of creating more problems. It just pisses me off that there is nothing I can do about it. Not that I am a control freak, but we need to think about how we're going to survive this, and if he is one of us, he needs to get on board with the program. I know he lost his father and his life is hell in a hand basket, but we're on his side," I rambled and finished with a sigh.

"That's not your problem," Gavlin said, appearing to be mulling something in his head.

"Huh?"

"Look at it differently," he said, casually slouched in his chair.

"Look for an alternative for which I could just end all my foreseeable problems. Maybe banishing him?" I said, frustrated.

"He didn't start this way with both of us. Maybe you, but not me in all my amazingness. If it was his father, which it could be, then why take it out on you?"

"True. Maybe it's because he's taking his anger out on me, because my father is still alive. Life has not been very fair. Still, why would he be mad at you now? You have done nothing I can think of. The only thing I can contribute it to is jealously over all the attention you get, especially after the time spent in Zermatt," I speculated.

"It's not me. I haven't become more or less of a celebrity than before. He really snapped at Zermatt."

It took me a couple of seconds, but when I realized the true reason, it was exactly what I had been thinking while sitting on the mountain with Rowan at the half-pipe. Now, there was someone else confirming my thoughts.

"Yeah." Gavlin responded to my silence.

"Are we..." I faded out.

"I thought it was way clear 'we' were not."

"Okay, good. Glad it was not just the cold and altitude getting to me. We are all too emotionally messed up at this point to think straight. I would rather have a friend any day; otherwise, you would probably turn into a Taylor Swift song, with your name included in the title, preferably. I am thinking something along the lines of 'Picture to Burn.'" I started laughing, and he obviously got my hint about the horrible fate of any relationship we could have at this point. When I caught my breath, my curiosity was too much for me to not confront. "So, the whole reason he is treating us both—but mostly me—like shit is because he thinks we are together? He obviously does not have feelings for me, so why would it be a problem?"

Gavlin returned my rant with an "it's not my problem" look.

"Not helpful. Not at all. Could you just say something to him?"

"It'd be better from you," he replied.

"Arg! We do not need any more complications." I leaned my head on Gavlin, mentally exhausted, and he put his arm around me in a cocooning embrace. "Is it still okay for me to fall asleep on you?"

"Of course. Don't worry, I'll wake you up if we have any guests."

"Thanks."

"You're welcome. Any time."

A couple of hours later, at about 2:00 in the morning, the screeching sound of the train breaks grinding on the track reverberated up through the floor as we entered the city of Zurich. It was only a quick train change, and we were on the way to the airport. It had been determined that without sufficient funds for a private plane and no access to the Internet, we would be boarding a plane last minute. It was a Hail Mary plan, though it would hopefully give the systems less time to track down our names. The way I wished to think about the situation was that Ireland is slightly closer to Zurich than the government buildings in Washington, D.C. are to Ireland.

If the government goonies intended to launch a fresh group of minions, we had the advantage. Except we would be on a commercial flight, and they would be in military jets, pushing the engines to self-combustion.

Everyone was obviously well rested from the train ride to Zurich. Our conversations on the way to the airport, aside from Rowan's silence, were lively and often involved acting out what we had to say. At one point we had the entire train staring in our direction and wondering why I was on the ground laughing, Riley was standing precariously on top of the side benches, Gavlin was pretending to be cowering in the corner, and Falon was acting her part as a Southern belle. Even Rowan could not help laughing—those crazy, young, American tourists.

Everyone stood clear of the doorway as we piled out, followed by our mangled suitcases. At this point, mine had a tendency to roll with a thunk with every rotation of the wheels, and Riley's now dragged instead of rolled. The few people traveling at this hour glanced conspicuously at us with our on-the-run, disheveled look we were sporting. However, the reception lady was not surprised at our ramshackle appearance.

"Hello. We need to book a flight to Knock, Ireland," Rowan said to the surprisingly perky lady behind the counter. It was 3:00 in the morning, local time.

I looked over to Riley. "*Why Knock?*"

"*Closest city to Boyle with an airport.*"

"Okay, sir. Let me see," the woman at the counter said, pecking away at the keyboard. "How many?"

"Five."

We waited impatiently for her to continue typing in our request. Finally, with her face pressed near the screen, she revealed, "There is a flight leaving at 5:37 this morning for the International Airport in Dublin. It would be a direct flight and land at 1:23 p.m. local time. After that, there is a regional jet from Dublin to Knock, at 2:40 p.m."

"We'll take it," Rowan said, handing her our second of three credit cards from the stash left by our parents.

Given the early morning hours, the security line was a breeze. Slipping off shoes, and pushing coats and backpacks through the x-ray machine, a couple of us were on edge with the possibility that we would be on some type of terrorist flight list, complete with flashing red lights and a police force barging into the airport from every possible escape route. There was nothing. I guess our enemies could not get the international airports to buy that a bunch of teenagers were international, public-enemy-number-one threats without the media attention. Score for us.

We enjoyed a breakfast of Swiss airport food. While the food was not great, there was plenty of strong, slightly burnt coffee to go around. I am not sure how much we truly needed the caffeine because the energy from our early catnaps had carried through to an intense game of poker. We bet candy bought from the airport stores for the very purpose of our favored card game. Through the mayhem, Riley still had all fifty-two playing cards originally from our jet. She still beat all of us, including her brother, by a mile, and Gavlin was still demanding another game for redemption. It was nice to see some things never change, even if it was just cards. I was anxious to leave by the time we boarded the plane. For thirty minutes prior to departure, I had been pacing back and forth, only to be stopped when Riley forcibly grabbed my shoulders, made me breathe, and eventually released me back to my anxious, repetitive motions. At any second, I expected a couple of men in black to appear and kidnap us. It was not a matter of *if* they would be at the airport, but a matter of when. I considered us lucky to be leaving only a couple of hours after scrounging up some of the last remaining seats on the flight.

None of us compared tickets after divvying them up at the counter, so we had no clue who was sitting with whom, or in what aisle of the aircraft. Gavlin peeled off first into the second row behind first class. Falon was back a couple of more rows and across the aisle next to a small child and the mother. A few rows farther back, Riley found her seat and surprised me by throwing her suitcase above her head into the overhead bin. Only a few inches taller than I am, and at about a hundred pounds soaking wet, it was an impressive feat. I was only momentarily pleased to find my seat directly in front of hers until Rowan did not keep walking. Instead, he found a place for his suitcase directly above my seat. I had already taken the vacancy in the window seat when he proceeded to look back at Riley, then look at the seat next to mine, then look at his ticket, then back at the seat, then the ticket, and finally at Riley. In the next two seconds, she obviously conveyed something to him that he was not happy to hear. Reluctantly, he sat down, sulking in the seat next to me. Of all people. Neither of us was thrilled.

The flight crew was obviously looking for a quick turnaround, and the amount of time spent on the runway was not much more than the time it took for the commercial jet to gain enough speed to leave the ground behind.

"You're not sleeping," I said directly in Rowan's direction, after the plane had reached its cruising speed, gliding toward the land of leprechauns and four-leaf clovers. "Don't even try and fake it because you're way too tense to be sleeping, and I know you're avoiding me." When he refused to talk after a minute, I said, "So, here's the deal. You need to cut it out and stop ignoring me whenever there is a problem, which you believe there is with Gavlin and myself. We have at least another eight hours on this flight. If it comes down to it, I will talk to you as if you were a wall."

He opened his eyes. "My ears would be bleeding."

"Just as I have thoroughly planned in my head. Thank you. Now, is there a reason that your sister would not let you switch seats because, trust me, everyone knows that would have been safer for our own lives and all the people on this plane."

"She wants me to talk to you," he said.

"Well, you are talking to me, yes?"

"Uh-huh."

"Can you at least make an effort to tell me why you snapped back in Zermatt?"

"Now, I'm being interrogated," he said.

"It might as well be one because if you look around, there is nowhere for you to go. While torturous, it *is* convenient."

"Let's see if you can crack me, " he said, smiling for a brief second before dropping back to his peeved look.

"You smiled for a second. What was that about?" I asked quickly.

"Thinking of you as an interrogator is ridiculous. Lucky for you, I feel like your continual talking might drive anyone to respond just to shut you up."

"I'm not sure if I should take that as a compliment or an insult. In most circumstances involving you, I would say 'insult'."

"Yeah."

"I'm being sarcastic. Lighten up. Back on topic. In the last couple of days you have gone from being just reserved and opinionated to snarky and avoiding. You had the right in the beginning, I under-stand, though now I feel all of those feelings are being sent in my direction, and toward Gavlin, and Riley, and Falon."

"Ever thought that you might not be so great yourself?" he spat back.

This was good. Anger was fine with me. At least we were getting somewhere. I could not help adding a little bit of lighter fluid to the fire. "Fine with me, but trust me, I am the farthest human from perfect. I have a strong opinion, and I voice it. If that offends you, sorry, but it is not going to change."

"It's your life and your opinions. I only care because I want to make it through this trip for our parents without being killed!"

"I know that if you cannot finish all of this," I said, gesturing to the general space around me, "it would be like saying your father died for no reason. And I am sorry. I truly am, but do not pretend like that is the only thing bothering you. Everyone except you realizes you have changed in the last few days, and not because of this shitty situation we are in. Why would your sister want me to sort out any problems between you and your thoughts?"

"I believe you're over-analyzing the situation, as you always do."

"No. You would have adjusted more than before, not the opposite. You've changed from something I did."

I thought for sure he would have shut down. It was never my intention before we started talking. He looked down at his feet quickly and tensed up. Then, he continued to stare down at the treaded ground of the dirty plane.

In a game of patience, I had nothing on him. I only gave him a couple of seconds until I could no longer handle the immense silence. I continued. "Before we go any farther, I want you to know that there is nothing between Gavlin and me. Turns out all we both needed was someone who would be there in all of this madness."

"Yeah," he said, with a tone of acknowledgment.

"You saw us on the mountain, didn't you?"

"Yeah." He paused for a moment. "Just remember this isn't real life. You keep all your real feelings inside. Trust me, I know how that goes. I don't want to see you hurt later just because he is here right now."

"We are all messed-up right now. Whether it is now or later, how will we ever know?" I turned toward the window, with my back to him. I was not ready to admit he might be right.

I must have fallen asleep again, which was the only real option while stuck in a plane with a dead iPod and a computer with an overplayed game of solitaire. When I woke up, Riley was next to me. It was a disappointment, but a relief at the same time. When she noticed that I was awake, she stopped drawing on the paper on the tray table in front of her and said, "*Hi. Rowan and I switched.*"

"*Why?*" I replied in ASL.

"*He wanted. I'm OK.*"

"*OK.*" I pointed to her drawing.

She held it up, and I could see that it was Falon sitting down. I would never have guessed our little computer whiz was also an artist. The details showed the realism you would capture through a photograph, including the way a breeze was blowing back Falon's long hair as she sat with her serene face. She was set like a model in tight jeans, knee-high boots, and a button-down jacket.

"*That's amazing,*" I commented.

"*Thank you.*"

"I would never have guessed that you could draw like this," I said, thankful she read lips.

She slowly gestured and signed, *"I will draw you later."*

"That would be amazing. It is like I am looking at a photograph. Still, I know she has never worn anything like that on this trip. My artist abilities stop at stick figures and straight-lined shapes."

"Looks like her clothes."

"Totally."

"You talk with Rowan? He looks"—she paused before continuing—*"not as anxious, but a little angry."*

"Slower," I said, and held up my hands in the traditional motion for slow down. "Yep. *I don't know why he'd be angry. He didn't say much.*"

She smiled. *"Rowan's good at that. If he has something to say, he will after a while. I know because he did not talk to me for two weeks."*

"What did you do?" I was a little astonished.

Riley smiled to herself, thinking back before she slowly continued. *"It was a few years ago. I might have let the dog in his room. The dog might have chewed his new guitar into pieces. I was more worried about my dog. I still have the dog, and he has a new guitar. I think it worked out fine. He still has not forgotten about it."*

"It is a dog; what can you expect? I have two, so I would take their side if it came down to it with my siblings. At my house, the dogs are like my two brothers."

"Easier and more fun."

"About your brother, though...I don't know what you can do, but tell him I will talk if he really wants to," I managed with a couple of words in sign, learning more quickly than I initially judged.

"I'll try. No promises. You don't know that word. P-r-o-m-i-s-e. You need to learn, and we have a lot of time," Riley insisted.

For the remaining hours of our flight, we continued signing. Gavlin came back to join us for a little while, standing in the aisle to stretch his legs. We refused to do anything but sign to him for a little while, which made him determined to pick up at least a few words. Languages were not his thing. We would be lucky if he retained anything aside from "food." Falon came to say hello as well. She was awed by the portrait Riley had done of her. There was a lot of thanking and saying how she wished she could look that pretty now. In my opinion, I think she looked beautiful, even on the run and sporting a nice layer of grime. The only indication of her travels was the crumbled look of her once-pressed, beige flowy shirt. Rowan stayed quiet behind us, yet I am sure he was listening to our conversations. When Gavlin came by for the second time, Rowan shocked me by having a brief conversation with him before the flight attendant became insistent that if Gavlin was not in is seat, he should be heading toward his seat. Her piercing dark eyes made the message crystal clear. Gavlin retreated with the look of a reprimanded dog until she turned around, and he proceeded to waltz back to his seat.

We landed in Dublin smoothly, wheels quietly kissing the ground so that we came to a gentle coast. Gavlin was the first one off, with the rest of us not far behind him. After maneuvering my suitcase down the thin airplane aisle, backing up to unlatch my suitcase from the edges of the airplane's chairs only twice, I was on the walkway from the plane to the terminal. I did not see Gavlin or Falon. I waited to the side for the remaining two before we decided it would be best to just head away from the plane. Likely, Falon and Gavlin were in the restroom or waiting at the end of the walkway in a less crowded area at the gate. We wanted to move quickly because we still needed to acquire plane tickets to Knock. For safety, we had only booked one set so there would be a lesser chance of being tracked to our final destination in Ireland. With a few regional airport stops within Ireland, we figured we could get lost in the system easier.

We had only walked about halfway down the ramp leading from the plane to the airport when I saw two heads parting traffic as they traveled in the opposite direction of the departing airplane passengers, at a brisk pace.

"We have company," Gavlin said as he came near us.

"You saw them?" I asked.

"One for each of us, at a minimum."

"Gavlin was able to stop me before I exited into the terminal, and the only place for us to go was back this way," Falon explained. I was ready for her hands to start fanning her face dramatically. She looked pale and about ready to faint from all the apprehension.

The general consensus now was panic. The only way out or in was through that one door at the end of the ramp. If we did not appear, they would be back here as soon as the crowds cleared. We were rats in a cage. "We. Are. Dead," I voiced out loud.

chapter 16

A commercial airplane's emergency doors are much heavier than the stick people make it look on their demonstrations. When flight attendants ask if you are willing and able to open the door in the case of an emergency, it should not be a simple yes or no; a person should have to lift a fifty-pound weight above his head and do a couple of squats before agreeing. It made me genuinely concerned for the actual removal of the door with just any passenger, given a real emergency situation. About ten seconds before this newest revelation, I was directly behind Rowan as we sprinted back onto the plane. It had taken only seconds and pure brute force to heave open the emergency door on the offside of the plane. Almost instantly after the door's removal, a giant slide began to blow up, similar to one at five-year-old child's birthday party. The only difference was that it also set off a string of blinking lights indicating the location of the open exit from every seat on the plane. We wasted no time. With the others standing behind us, the suitcases were chucked out of the plane, with no concern for their value, before the slide had been given the time to properly inflate.

With the last suitcase in my hand prior to its unceremonious exit, the flight attendant, whom I recognized from earlier, and one remaining pilot, realized the emergency door exit lights were not malfunctioning. The older flight attendant was the first to notice and immediately came running back toward us, the thin aisle not conducive to her wide hips. She was yelling something along the lines that we should stop because we were going to get caught. There might also have been something about us being irresponsible and crazy teenagers. It all went in one ear and out the next. In reality, we were just a handful of crazy teenagers, and I know at least Gavlin intended to live up to that stereotype. Despite everything, it did not take her long to close the distance between us, but she could do nothing besides continue to yell. Even if she had caught up to us, there was no chance she could have out-muscled us, and we all knew it.

Rowan wasted no time in grabbing Riley and shoving her out the door onto the giant bouncy slide. It would have been the ultimate waterslide from the window of my bedroom. Definitely what I wanted for my eighteenth birthday. Falon did not pause a second before gracefully sitting down. Once seated though, she looked down at the slide in fear, back at the plane, at the slide, my face, the slide, and finally shoved off, sliding down in the safe feet-first manner. With her out of the way, I followed suit. The parting scene I caught before leaving was the flight attendant crashing into a pilot on her reverse path to the front, in the thin aisleway, while yelling orders to call security so that they could catch us on the runway.

The ride down the slick, shiny, bright-yellow slide was a bit anti-climactic, but thrilling nonetheless. When my feet hit the pavement, my knees bent to absorb all of the momentum I had gained, and I took off running directly under the plane. Riley and Falon were waiting faithfully in the shadows of the landing gear. Only seconds after my own, I heard another two sets of feet hit the ground, pounding at different rhythms close behind me. When I reached Riley and Falon, they had abandoned their luggage and looked around in confusion.

"I have no clue where we're going," I said, breathing hard from the adrenaline.

"There!" Gavlin shouted and continued to run toward the men unloading the luggage of the neighboring plane. The two airport workers carelessly threw the last black suitcase into a trailer so it could be driven over and transferred to luggage claim. They did not hear us approach due to the oversized noise-canceling headphones they wore, designed to muffle the roar of airplane jets. With the last duffel bag aboard, the scruffy-looking men walked around to the cart and jumped into seats behind the wheel of an attached golf cart-like contraption designed for this purpose. We paused for a brief second before we took off sprinting the last couple hundred feet and made a flying leap into the attached trailers, with the luggage.

I jumped through the curtain of the box and collided into a couple of large suitcases, which caused me to fall in a heap between bags now shifted on top of me. Falon came in gracefully, if that is possible, and landed low, but on her feet. The other three thankfully followed.

Even in her sheer panic, she saw me being eaten by suitcases and cracked a smile. "Need some help?"

"What was your first clue?" I said, laughing, and trying to keep her calm, although my mind was screaming at me to get up and run. With a little help from the others, I was freed from the confines of the overstuffed, fifty-pound luggage. Once I was standing along the edge, I looked out between the thick plastic curtains covering the open wall of the cart to see what the others were paying attention to. Back at the plane we abandoned, the pilots, a handful of security people, and a variety of other airport personnel were crowed under the belly of the plane with a combination of dumbfounded and infuriated looks. Our flight attendant expressed only fury, as she pointed wildly around. The pilot seemed caught between, "Darn, I could lose my job for this," rage at how we had been only seconds ahead of him and escaped, and a little bit of shock as to how five kids could have made off so quickly. I could see our abandoned luggage, still lying as wounded soldiers at the base of the slide. It felt wrong to have abandoned them after all their faithfulness to us. Unfortunately, a lot of things on this trip had been sacrificed to make sure we would come out alive. Our clothes were the least of my concerns. Thus, the clothes we wore were going to have to work for a little while longer. Thankfully, the paperwork and stores of cash were split among our personal bags carried by the three girls.

We almost all lost our footing when the cart suddenly jerked forward with our trailer attachment, as it picked up a faster clip to cover the tarmac. Those next to the wall opted to hang on, and the rest of us sat on the floor to avoid being rag-dolled out of the luggage cart and splat onto the cement. The trailer never slowed down as we completed hairpin turns and swerved violently to avoid additional runway obstacles. I thought twice about how pleasant the cab ride in Coast Rica felt compared to the back of this bouncy, jerky, cramped luggage cart. After coming to a screeching halt, tossing us forward and then mercilessly throwing us backward, we scrambled out. The nausea and dizziness were fighting strongly against my deeper instincts to get the hell out of this airport. I just wanted to sit down on the ground and wait for the entire world to stop doing pirouettes. Gavlin led the group around the back of the cart and peered around the side we had come from.

He subsequently leaned in toward Rowan and me first. We followed so that our heads were almost touching, and Gavlin whispered,

"I need one of you to go first. If you look around the other side, there's a space for luggage to go in. Go through. I don't know what's on the other side."

"I'll do it," I blurted out before really thinking about what I had agreed to do.

"Come here," Gavlin said. He led me to edge of the back wall of the cart, turning to peer quickly around the front. As I walked off, I could tell Rowan was not pleased with the decision. He was the one who did everything first, and I believe it was his subtle way of trying to protect the others. Just because I was a girl did not mean I could not handle things on my own. I was not going to wait around for some Prince Charming to save the day. He was going to have to sulk and accept that fact. Plus, now I could check off my bucket list the desire to go through the magical portal that the airplane luggage appears from. Gavlin looked to me and briefly repeated, "They're working on the other side. Make it to the front. When they go back, run and go through. Meet you on the other side."

I took a deep breath to compose myself—something that was coming easier as my tolerance levels unhealthily increased. Next to Gavlin I could see Falon still shaking worse than ever and Riley trying to put on a smile, but her eyes were fretfully scanning our surrounding area. If we did not hear them, she sure was going to see them. Gavlin pointed out around the corner of the cart where I could see the multiple locations for luggage to be put through. The two burly men unloading luggage were focused like machines on their task, on the opposite side of the cart. Luckily, they would be oblivious to any sound I might make. Finally, I nodded to Gavlin and slowly ventured around the side of the cart. I paused near the front. While the men were busy with the opening on my right, there was another available opening twenty feet to my left and ten feet in front of me, meaning

I would be exposed for about twenty-three feet; it was only slightly strange that I could do any form of math at such a time.

Just as both men went back to the cart for another piece of luggage, I sprinted toward my left. I held my breath the entire way and lunged through the opening while ducking over. For once in my life, it was nice to be vertically challenged. In the dim lighting of the inside of the building, I jumped down off the silent conveyer belt. It was clear that the opening I had come through was not going to be a simple in-and-out exit. For safety purposes, the conveyer was not being used and therefore did not open to the inside of the airport. I quietly made my way toward the one conveyer slowly humming as it transported its passengers to their rightful owners. Every few seconds a suitcase was thrown on. Thankfully, I only needed to step up a couple of feet onto the conveyer, ride it for a couple of seconds, duck, and I would be on the outside. I stood along the side of the conveyer, attempting to gain a sense of timing for my next steps. The only predicament was that, unlike jumping rope, there was no set rhythm. This could be epic failure.

There was a large gap coming between a black roller suitcase and a hunter-green duffle bag, and I decided this would be my best chance. I counted under my breath, "Three, two, one." I leaped up and "shoom!" I almost slipped off the moving belt from being startled by a noise behind me of feet hitting the ground. After I had instinctively crouched down to maintain some sense of balance, I looked over to find Falon staring at me. I waved for her to join me and ducked my head as I passed through the other side. When the plastic flaps that divided the airport from the outside had passed over me, I blinked a couple of times to adjust to the bright lighting, sprung up, and dashed off. I could hear the confusion behind me as people stared in shock and talked loudly about what they were seeing. Unfortunately,

I was not Aslan, the talking lion from Narnia—just a dirty teenager from a much less glamorous place.

My sudden appearance had probably served as a good distraction for Falon, as she emerged seconds later. I did not take the time to look back as I darted through the crowd and in the direction of the nearest exit. I could only hope Falon and the others would be following and we could find each other later. There was a customs desk, but I saw another door to the right and headed in that direction. It was only a matter of moments before I threw myself through two sets of doors and was greeted by the cool weather on the outside. My lungs were burning by the time I ran for what felt like a quarter-mile opposite of the airport and collapsed on a bench hidden in a corner. Nearly sixty seconds later, Falon came running with her feet dragging and hands flailing at her sides. When she saw me, she literally crashed down on the bench in relief.

"Nice to see you. I'm impressed," I said, still attempting to regain some pattern of normal breathing.

"I…hate…you," she said, taking a deep breath between each word, with her hands on her side.

I leaned against the back of the bench and looked up. "Did not have much of an option. You see the others?"

"Yes. They were…behind…me. Not sure…why they are…not here. I am not…the fastest…runner."

Her comment made complete sense, and instantly I was concerned. It would not be safe for us to sit here much longer and wait. It would only be a matter of time before the police realized we made a dash past customs. We still needed to make it to Boyle. There was no chance I was going to step foot in that airport again, even if I wanted to. At least we had split up the minimal cash earlier, and at least one bag was with each group, if I could find any source of comfort in that. We both sat on the bench for twenty minutes, and while I should have been scanning for any unwanted persons, I was too exhausted. I was coming off my millionth adrenaline rush and, if I were lucky, might be able to sleep in the near future. I closed my eyes for a couple of seconds, thinking how Falon and I would manage by ourselves.

When I opened my eyes, the world coming into view, I hoped to see three familiar figures. I saw nothing besides a couple of people waiting around for a cab ride. I pushed on Falon's slumped shoulder and then stood up. "We should go," I mumbled.

"They are not here," she stated, preoccupied.

"We need to get out of here," I restated.

"On our own?"

"Unless they suddenly appear, we have no clue what happened. There's no use sacrificing ourselves, too." It came out a little too pessimistic.

"Oh," she said, on the verge of tears.

"It'll be fine. I'm sure we will meet up with them soon. We are all heading to the same place," I said in a slightly quieter voice, unsure what else to say.

"Let's go then," she replied after wiping away a couple of tears and collecting herself.

"Do you need a hug?" I asked. At this point, everyone understood my odd behavior against hugs. I claimed it made them mean more. I then proceeded to give her a big hug, which she gladly reciprocated.

Without speaking, I took a step closer to the curb. The street was no different than any other airport with taxis flying by. I motioned for a taxi and only waited for a couple of seconds before one slowed down.

chapter 17

When I bent down to pick up my backpack, I heard a familiar voice from the stopped cab. "Miss, you need a ride?"

I looked up to see Gavlin open the back door of the taxi, with a huge smile, and step out. I caught him off guard when I tackled him for a hug. I am not a hugely emotional person, except Falon had me in that kind of mood. He hugged me back hard.

Gavlin noticed Falon's sniffling and moist eyes. She initially looked alarmed when Gavlin unexpectedly wrapped her in a hug, but when they pulled away, I could tell she was holding it together, if not for one more take.

I jumped into the cramped back seat next to Riley, who reached over with a relieved smile and hugged both Falon and me. I looked forward to see Rowan. I was frustrated, yet honestly pleased to see we were safe and, once again, together.

"You could at least smile," I said, catching Rowan off guard. "I know you're happy to see us."

His face lightened up a little. "Now that Falon and Devon have managed to draw more attention to themselves, we need to find another method to get to Boyle," Rowan said, trying more than usual to at least be sarcastic.

"And how did you do any better?" I asked.

"Riley noticed another open conveyer, and we went through there. From there, we drifted through the crowds, customs, and out the front. We took a cab, and then we saw you two."

"At least you did not have to run. If I find myself running again, you are going to be carrying me," Falon added, just to complain.

"You'll be fine, Princess," Gavlin joked. Falon gave him a look.

Riley tapped me on the shoulder and pointed at Rowan. "Rowan," I said to catch his attention. While they were talking, she raised her brow with a slight smirk. I caught not a single word, even with all that I thought I knew.

"Excuse me, we need to go to the Weston Executive Airport," Rowan told the driver.

"Dat is private, yer nu? For de military and rich folk," our driver replied in a thick Irish accent.

"We understand. We have a close friend there who is a pilot," Rowan said, which came as a shock to at least three of us in the cab. Either he was making this up due to our delirious state, or maybe it was true.

"Yer choice. 'Tis about thirty minutes away."

"Thank you."

"Rowan, a little explanation would be nice," I demanded.

"Riley remembered that our uncle flies some important customers privately in these parts. We visited a couple years back. It's our mother's brother," Rowan explained.

"Will he be able to do it?" Gavlin asked.

"It's our only bet." Rowan did not sound optimistic or enthusiastic.

"As long as it does not involve me running after our transportation, us being split, or sleeping in some ridiculous hiding place, I am fine with this idea," Falon stated. We all could not help but smile at what should have been a simple request.

The rumble of jets and the unique smell of burning rubber and gas greeted us when we exited the taxi at the Weston Airport. It was a simple, beige three-story building with a control tower at its apex and a runway with chopper landing pads. We walked past a collection of limousines and Bentleys waiting out front for those passengers with the luxury of flying in such a private manner. The interior of the building was a bit dated, but the floors were an expensive light-beige marble. The light fixtures were large wall sconces, and the heavy, pressed curtains hung to the floor from the few windows. There was no doubt we were in the land of the rich and famous. Rowan instructed us to stay put. It must have been confusing to see five scraggly kids without luggage, looking exhausted, parked in the foyer of an elite, private airport. We had fortunately changed clothing before arriving in Ireland; however, we were all still a little on the weathered side. Falon was the only one looking presentable beyond jeans, layered jackets, and hoodies. Even Riley had exchanged her look for a printed, gray baggy sweater with a yellow heart, jeans, and an oversized jacket.

Rowan made his way quietly to the auburn oak front desk. "We need to speak with Mr. Kyle Walsh, please."

"Your name, please?" the receptionist in her neatly pressed suit replied, with slight disdain.

"My name is Rowan. I am his nephew, traveling from out of the country," Rowan said forcefully.

"One moment," she said before daintily making her way toward the back offices.

We waited in the plush lounge watching the passengers come and go. There were a couple of business people busy on their phones, typing and chatting up the newest business deals simultaneously. There was a woman in stiletto heels and a fashionable black dress, dragging along her personal secretary with a BlackBerry in hand and a headset on the ready. With our nerves still on alert and a couple of us with an inability to stay still, I was fidgeting with my signature leather bracelets, and Rowan was pacing back and forth. Riley was standing against a wall. A couple of times she stepped out in front of her brother to interrupt his anxious habit. He paused only briefly, before continuing his brisk pacing back and forth.

Riley was the first one to notice a man walk through the glass doors from the runway and head in our direction down the wide hall. We only realized after we saw her missing from her place on the wall and hugging a man I had never met.

He continued in our direction, and as he neared I noticed the strong features on his weathered face. He shared the same flaming-red hair as Rowan, but with blue eyes set deep below his profound brow that reflected a gentle personality under his solid six-foot-three frame.

"Rowan, it's nice to see yer. I'm sorry about yer father. Is everything all right?" his Uncle Kyle said, stopping in front of us.

"It's great to see you. Thanks. It's a long story, but we need your help. Dad's death was not an accident, and we need to get to Knock to retrieve some things. We don't want to put you in danger, though we have no other options," Rowan stated with little emotion.

"Yer father was too good of a pilot for it to be accidental. Course I'll help yer. Who are dees good looking young people?" He surprisingly did not pry us for any details about our unexpected presence and demands for a flight across the country.

"This is Gavlin, Falon, and Devon. Their parents worked with Dad in the past, so we have been traveling together." We replied politely that is was nice to meet him.

"Call me Kyle. Let me go find a plane an' change some flights. Come with me. I take it yer all would like out of 'ere fast?" he said jokingly.

"As long as I do not have to chase the plane, I would be grateful to leave immediately," Falon voiced again.

"Dat might need to be a story I 'ear," Kyle said, with all of us trailing behind onto the runway. He then proceeded to talk rapidly on his cell phone to a couple of people. Near all of the airplane hangers, we stopped under the shadow from a small, private plane. It was no jet, but it sure could fly the few of us across the country.

"A good friend says we can 'ave his plane fer the day. Nothing special, but she'll do. Yer guys 'ave luggage?" Kyle asked.

"Left it all at the airport, I'm afraid. I believe it never made it past being thrown out the side and splat on to the ground," I remarked lightly, eyeing Rowan, my luggage-throwing partner.

Kyle was busy opening up the door and doing some brief external checks on the plane. "Sounds to me as if yer 'ave had an interesting trip. Rowan, do yer still fly?"

"Yeah."

"This should be easy compared to the jet from Costa Rica. Gulfstream five-fifty or something like that, wasn't it?" Gavlin referenced our previous flying experience.

"Impressive. Who did yer fly her with?" Kyle said.

"No one. I had to takeoff and land it because we lost our pilot and did not want to stay around for a shooting festival," Rowan commented.

"Yer serious?" Kyle paused from his other work.

"As serious as all the other stuff these past days," Rowan replied.

"Well, then I think yer well qualified ter be my copilot," Kyle articulated while holding onto a rolling staircase. He climbed up and opened the door to our newest ride.

Riley lightly bounded up the stairs first, followed by a much quieter Falon, and then me. The interior was nowhere as spacious as our previous planes, but it was hard to compete with the size and luxury of one of the best private jets in the world. Even with my short stature, I felt obligated to duck slightly once in the plane, before sitting in one of four passenger seats. The seats were well-worn leather, molded to many bodies and squished into a space the size of a Volkswagen Beetle. Thank goodness there was no concern with luggage because the only remaining items were my backpack, Falon's oversized black purse, and Riley's shoulder bag.

With the doors closed, the engine came to life with a loud hum, vibrating the entire plane. The front propeller whirred like it was only waiting to be released for a sudden takeoff. In a plane of such size, it was a roller coaster departure as we climbed rapidly into the atmosphere. It was as if my own set of wings carried me into the sky and not some piece of machinery. Commercial flights would never compare. I looked up toward the open cockpit to see Rowan calmly looking forward into the clear blue sky and, for once, I was jealous of him in the front seat. From the small windows, I gazed out on the busiest city in Ireland, Dublin, although not far off were the rough outcroppings and luscious green fields of the countryside.

"It's so beautiful. I cannot wait until we really are able to see the countryside. I have always wished to come here and my parents had promised, but they preferred warm weather vacations. Not that getting a tan, drinking margaritas, and meeting hot guys is bad," Falon said, still gazing down at the green landscape.

"Then why would you want to come here?" I asked, still ever amused with her diva attitude even after days of living with her and watching her completely crack.

"To ride a horse through open fields," she replied, leaning around the back of my seat and into the aisle to look at me in the seat in front of her.

"Maybe we can help you achieve your little dream. I'm not sure though how you are going to get some people in this group on a horse, though."

"It is not the getting them on part. It would be the staying on part," she joked.

"We'll see about that," Gavlin teased.

"*What?*" Riley leaned into the aisle to see what we were talking about.

"*Gavlin horseback riding,*" Falon replied in sign much to our surprise. To our looks she replied, "It is the only thing I can say."

"I could think of some more important words," Gavlin remarked.

"*I would want to see that,*" Riley told us with a humored smile, back on the horse conversation.

"I can arrange that. We still need a way to get to Boyle. Is that correct?" Falon asked.

"Yep. Boyle. I am not sure how far," I added.

"*Twenty,*" Riley said.

"Miles?" I asked, and she nodded in agreement.

"Twenty miles on a horse?" Gavlin said.

"You not want to anymore, cowboy?" Falon flirtatiously mocked.

"Not a chance."

"It's settled. It will be possible to make twenty miles, yet I will not be the one navigating," Falon said.

"I think we can figure it out." I was pleased with our newest mode of travel: trains, planes, automobiles, and now horses. It was going to be interesting trying to convince Rowan to join our newest idea, considering it was not coming from his side of the camp. There was no way I was going to allow Rowan to force Falon out of her grand plan.

A couple of minutes later, when we had all settled down, I was bored out of my mind, so I turned around in my seat to face Falon behind me. "Hello."

"Hi," she replied.

"I want to know more about your horseback riding."

"What would you like to know?"

"Anything."

"Horses are my life. I spend almost every weekend of the year at the horse shows, and every day is spent riding all of my horses. One benefit to living in Ocala is that we have some of the most renowned show grounds, which is ideal with my level of competition," she said. To most people it would have sounded like bragging, but I knew Falon all too well at this point. It was the world she was raised in, and there was no getting around that fact.

"Like every little girl, I asked for a pony, and it never happened. I rode horses for a short time when I was eight, then moved on to other activities. I wish I'd stayed involved," I added.

"I am involved with the "AA" hunter and jumper circuit, so we jump. In the last years, I've competed at nationals for multiple areas on my five horses and a couple I ride for other people."

"Impressive. What type are they?"

"They all came from Europe. One is for my equitation class, which is the class judged on me. His name is Neverland, but I call him Peter. The name fits him because he is a bit childlike: always testing his riders and getting in trouble. Then, there is Devlin. His name means warrior in Irish, which is why I refuse to ride him. He is in training for me because I refuse to ride an animal that actively works to kill me when I put my foot in the stirrup. Nautilus and Sky are my high-level horses, and they are fantastic. Last is Princessa, and while she may be the best one, she has an attitude to match. I have a strong distaste for her, but she wins. In addition, there are horses at my barn and with other trainers, which I ride during the horse shows."

"Princessa sounds a bit like someone I may know. It's all well and dandy as long as it's her idea," I laughed.

Falon smiled at the obvious criticism I had made of her. "Sometimes I feel maybe we just do not understand each other; my horses and I. I compare my horses to athletes. This is at least how many people at my level of riding expect them to be treated. In my world of horses, it is all about who has the best, because otherwise you will not win."

"But they are animals with personalities and quirks."

"I understand them for all the things they do. Still, when they no longer do their jobs, we do not just keep them," she said, offended with the idea that I thought of all animals as pets.

"Is that your voice I'm hearing?"

"What?" she said, confused.

"Who tells you that? I mean, you told me a few minutes ago how they all are. To you they are not just athletes you ride," I questioned, hoping there was more to her than money and a pretty face.

She looked shocked at the statement I made. It was the kind of shock that told me I had hit the nail on the head. There was a human underneath the high-fashion diva from Florida. "You sound like my mamá...I wish I would have told her how right she was," she said, on the verge of tears, again.

I felt horrible for inciting another round of possible tears. In all the days we had been together, I knew the least about her, although Rowan still won the award for most mysterious and guarded.

Falon continued to talk, sniffling to rein back the potential water-works. "She and I always argued about how I had become spoiled. She knew if the horses were gone, I would become a disaster. I would like to believe that is not true. I do it to fit in with everyone, and we all love our horses, but they are not pets. If I wanted to be the best, I had to accept this. I never would have wished for it to funnel into this mindset."

"Sounds like you need some new friends. It may be harder with people. Like most animals, I am sure all it takes with a horse is some food and a little attention," I said, trying to lighten the mood.

She cracked a smile. "Thanks. It might have to be our secret."

"I think I can manage," I said, disappointed she was still not ready to stop playing pretend.

Our dinky plane set down a couple of hours later on a landing strip in Knock, Ireland. Rowan and Riley's uncle was well tuned into our fragile situation and ensured we would not be checking in with anyone. We landed unexpectedly on a secluded landing strip. A couple of calls from Kyle's cell phone ensured a hotel reservation and a car to the hotel. If our names remained off the books for a little while longer, we expected some form of safety until the jump over the pond to the Netherlands.

"I'm sorry for putting you out," Rowan said to his uncle when we were waiting near the plane for our taxi ride.

"That is what family is fer. Jist don't call again," he joked.

"Seriously, be careful. This shouldn't have been your problem," Rowan voiced again.

"Rowan, yer are too much like yer ma. Always looking out for everyone else. Jist do me a favor an' worry about all of yer friends," he said with authentic concern.

We refused to allow the cab to drive away before Uncle Kyle's plane was in the air and on its way back to Dublin. It might have been a pointless deed to ensure his safety, but it was the most we were capable of doing. As the plane disappeared into the east, opposite of the setting sun, I looked over to see Rowan watching as if he were witnessing someone else in his life die.

After passing out of the brightly lit tourist town of Knock, we made our way south into the darkness of a vacant countryside. It was slightly out of our northern route to Boyle; however, Kyle promised a quaint location for us to recover before making the trek to the final document destination. There were only a couple of lights to indicate the presence of a farmhouse occupying a space among the miles of vast and sparsely populated Irish countryside. It was impossible to see the exact outline of the farmhouse, made worse by the ivy covering the house like an intricate spider's web. The smell of livestock carried through the cool, yet humid air along with the occasional sounds of bleating sheep.

Walking up to the plain wooden front door took me back to my own home. For a brief second, it was as if we were just walking into a normal house to crash in someone's basement after a long night of too much fun. The front foyer was nothing more than a cozy sitting room with well-worn furniture passed down through numerous generations, holding the stories of those who had slumped in its cushions. The way the floor creaked and moaned, the scuffs on the floor from years of service, and the small details of the building from a time way past, jolted my mind back to my own quaint home. The home I was yanked from and may never return to.

"*You OK?*" Riley asked.

"*Yeah, fine.* It just reminds me of *home.* That's all."

"Good evening," a petite woman of about seventy said from behind a traditional desk on our right, standing up to greet us.

"Good evening to you, as well. We need to check in," Falon replied, waltzing up to the desk.

"Yer must be the nieces an' nephews of Kyle," she replied happily, putting on her glasses that had previously rested on her dark silver hair. "It pleased me ter be able to help yer on such short notice."

"We are very grateful. It's been a long trip, and with changes to our plans it worked out perfect. Thank you," Falon said, sweetly. You had to give it to her; when she needed to put on the sweet child, she put it on effortlessly and with a genuine, innocent smile. If only she could be like that more often.

"Here are yer room keys. Take de stairs up, an' yer rooms are dere. We have a nice breakfast in de mornin' down in de dinin' room. Have a nice night." She handed two sets of metal keys to Falon.

We all bid her good-night before Riley bounded up the stairs like a rabbit, while four of us trudged our way up the steep, narrow, creaking stairs. At the top, she pointed to the first and second room on the right side of the hallway. Before walking in, we opened up both rooms to find one with a single queen bed and the other with three full-sized beds. The single room was painted a pastel pink with outdated floral patterns while the other embraced a less appealing coral tone on the walls, bedspreads, and curtains.

"Toto, I don't think we're in Zermatt anyone," Gavlin joked.

"You are very right, Dorothy. At least it's quiet, and a place to sleep," I said back as I continued to look in at the rooms from the hallway.

"I'm taking this room," Falon announced, as she strode into the room with the single bed. "Someone may join me as long as I get to take a long bath in peace."

Riley grinned, shrugged her shoulders, and followed Falon into the bedroom.

I looked at both Rowan and Gavlin next to me. "I guess we're sharing a room tonight. At least I get my own bed. Falon and Riley, we are leaving at eight o'clock, so set the alarms accordingly."

Riley signed something to me, but I had not the slightest clue what it was. "She said too early." Rowan helped me out.

"There is a time change. It will feel later. You have more energy than any of us. I'm not worried at all," I said, smiling, noticing that Rowan interpreted for me as he usually did. "*Good-night.*"

I shut and locked the door behind me with Rowan and Gavlin already in the room. Gavlin collapsed on the middle bed, and I had my doubts he would move much more until the next morning. I beelined my way to the bathroom so I could at least take a shower before tomorrow. I sat in the huge bathtub, steaming up the bathroom for thirty minutes, staring off into space, and allowing the heat to wash away everything. Somewhere in my deeper subconscious, I believed the water would just take away all the problems inside of me and wash them down the drain with the soapy water. It was wishful thinking, but it felt wonderful. The only thing that could have made it better was if I actually had clean clothes. Instead, I was forced to put back on my jeans and T-shirt, which smelled repulsive to my clean body after a couple of airplane trips, and the running, and riding on a luggage conveyer belt.

"Clean clothes would be nice about now," I said walking out of the bathroom with a towel wrapped as a modified turban on my head to contain my wet hair.

"Agreed," I heard Rowan reply while I was bent over drying out my hair in front of my face with the damp, white towel. When I looked up, I was shocked to see him looking at me from where he was sitting on the edge of the bed.

"You need something?" I asked. I felt my stomach clench when I made contact with his green eyes. Of all times, why did he choose now to not avoid me?

"No. Good-night," he responded and walked over to turn the lamp off.

chapter 19

"I talked with the lady at the front, and she gave me the number of a person near here with horses," Falon announced at breakfast, with a cup of coffee nestled between her two hands. The five of us were the only ones settled around the eight-person wooden dining room table for a home-cooked breakfast of eggs, sausage, and black pudding on fine blue china. It was 8:30 in the morning, and the food was doing its job as a successful motivator to ensure everyone was awake and moving.

"What do we need horses for?" Rowan asked between bites of food.

"You must not have heard. I have determined our next form of travel will be horseback. You may thank your friend Gavlin for threatening me," Falon said with a mocking smile.

"A car would be faster," Rowan stated.

"I have decided we will be riding horses. I have always wished to see the countryside, and it would be best to take the time to disappear," Falon replied.

"Which gives them more time to look for us." Rowan continued to play the devil's advocate.

"There will be no record of our travel this way," I said, angry at his stubbornness.

"Fine. You guys figure it out," he said, not quite defeated. Now, we just had to ensure there would be no opportunity for him to prove us all wrong and claim he "told us so."

On the way to the horse farm, we took in the sights of luscious greenery, tall grass, and morning dew that soaked our shoes. The wooly sheep and cows bid us hello with their occasional braying and a lift of their heads before plunging back into the thick grass. The unfinished road crunched under our shoes, and not a single car could be heard or seen cruising through our piece of paradise. We chased after each other in brief spurts of childish energy, tempted the animals to come to us, and let the untainted air flow through our lungs. The sun was peeking through the clouds, and the temperature remained at about fifty-five degrees. We were pleased to be dressed only in sweaters after traveling from our previous cold-weather appointment. At one point I found myself yards in front of the others as my quick pace took hold of the welcoming road. I stopped. In the middle of the road I took a deep breath, closed my eyes, and let the peace consume me. The brisk air filled my lungs and refreshed every sense from the days of overload they had faithfully endured. The soft hum of the insects and rustle of livestock in the meadows whispered in my ears. For once in my life, I contently consumed the still of the moment.

An hour of meandering later, we arrived at a white farmhouse with a collection of stone outbuildings. On the phone earlier, a pleasant lady instructed us to walk around the back of the house where we would find her tending to the sheep and horses in one of the barns. Only a few steps onto the driveway, the Abominable Snowman in dog form came flying toward us. It was a bit unsettling, and we all wondered how she had failed to mention a monstrous guard dog during our phone conversation. He came toward us, expressing his opinion with a thunderous bark. Within a dozen feet of us, his tail began wagging uncontrollably, and he barreled into our space, nearly pushing us over in his attempt to be pet. Following our guide, we tagged behind him to a stone building twenty-five squared feet in size. In the nearby fields, horses were spread about, roaming their large pastures and enjoying the mid-morning grass at its richest time of the day.

From an additional small outbuilding on our right-hand side, a woman in rubber work boots and a Mackintosh appeared. Despite the owner of our bed-and-breakfast telling us over coffee that the woman we were to meet had three children around our age, I never would have guessed. Her pale face was sharply defined and accentuated by her black hair messily pulled back.

"Hello! Pleasure to meet yer. My name is Kayla." She extended her hand, callused from years of working on a farm. We all introduced ourselves and shook hands with her.

"Thank you for accommodating us on short notice," Falon said.

She motioned for us to follow her down the dirt driveway toward a large cobblestone barn, talking as she kept up a brisk pace. "Not a problem. I 'ear that yer know horses, and I 'ave a few that need ter go. I jist can't pay fer all of 'em. It seems strange fer a couple of tourists to want to ride horses that far."

Before any of us could cover for our obviously odd behavior, Falon jumped into one of her high-speed rambles. "We were staying at the inn on the way to Devon's uncle's home, and I promised him I would find a suitable group of horses for his young children, considering they just moved here and needed something for enjoyment and to keep them out of trouble. We flew into the airport here, and instead of driving there I figured we could ride our way. It's only a short distance from here, and it is one activity which I could not leave the country without doing."

Kayla looked pleased with the answer and was just as amused as I was with Falon's fast talking and lengthy sentences. In addition, I still needed to accept the news about my long-lost mysterious uncle who now lives in Ireland. We reached the side of the barn, and Kayla grabbed a couple of ropes lying haphazardly on the ground.

"Which ones of yer 'ave horses?"

"That would be me," Falon replied.

She handed over two well-worn and fraying ropes of undistinguishable dark color to Falon and kept another casually gripped in her right hand. "Would yer help me catch yer rides? I 'ave the ones already in mind fer yer in this field. They're in great shape and easy ter ride."

While listening to Kayla, no one noticed that Riley had made her way to the low wooden fence and was affectionately petting a gray pony. The pony resembled a mound of fur whose dark gray mane stuck in every direction as if lighting had come down and given him a good shock. With Riley standing on the second rail of the sagging wooden fence, the little munchkin was the perfect height to nuzzle her sweater pockets, undoubtedly looking for food and convincing her of his intentions with pleading eyes. When her fingers reached the right spot on his face, he leaned his head toward her, sideways, to achieve the optimal scratching angle.

"I think someone found a friend," I commented while keeping my eyes trained on Riley and her newest friend.

With everyone's eyes averted in his direction, the pony went back to sniffling in Riley's pockets, with Riley leaning over the fence to tousle his Afro. Two seconds later, unsatisfied with the lack of food, he pushed his nose forward into Riley's chest with enough force to knock her backward. Not anticipating the backward momentum, she attempted to catch herself on the railing with an outstretched hand, without success. Her feet only reacted fast enough to come under her body slightly as she plopped onto the ground. When she fell down, the pony remained unnerved by her quick movements, with all four charcoal-gray legs planted firmly near the fence line. Riley joined in on our own laughter, not bothering to stand up. Instead, she turned her head upward in the direction of the culprit, who stood over her with a smug look. He shook his head, proud of himself, before blowing air loudly out of his nostrils. When she finally looked over at us, still on the ground, we were in hysterics, with me barely able to catch a breath.

She reached her hands forward with her palms open and then pulled her fingers inward, but not far enough to make a fist, and then pointed to the pony that instinctively reached his head down toward her hand.

Although we all knew what she meant, I verbally interpreted it for Kayla. "I believe she is requesting that one."

"That would be an interesting ride. That there is Comet. He is as tough as they come. Bucked ter many people off. He has taken a likin' to her." She paused and looked out at Riley, who was back on her feet and scratching Comet, except this time from a reduced altitude on the ground. "If she can catch 'im, then she 'as won one fight."

"I don't approve," Rowan quickly interjected.

"He would not 'urt a fly. He will jist run away," Kayla stated.

"I'll be out there with her," Falon offered.

"Fine," he growled.

Kayla and Falon took to rounding up four of the scruffy horses from far out in the field. They dragged them away from their green grass and tied them along the exterior of the wooden fence. With our horses we still needed equipment, so Kayla took the guys with her to retrieve the equipment, handed a worn maroon halter with a rope to Riley, and warned Falon that the most he would do is hightail it up the hill.

Not comfortable around horses, I was relieved Rowan was lugging back tack and not here to sense my uneasiness about sending a young, inexperienced girl into a field with a seven hundred-pound pony known for his devilish ways. Inside the gate Riley slowly walked up to Comet, with the rope hidden behind her back and the other arm outstretched in greeting. Falon remained near the gate with me, insistent that her presence might scare him, which added to my growing dislike for this situation. While Comet made no effort to confront her, he did not take a step in the opposite direction. Holding my breath, I watched her scratch him on the neck and then slowly pull the halter near to his face. Like a large white lamb, he bent down his head toward the halter, and she buckled it around his head. He followed calmly, an oversized puppy ruffling Riley's hair along her back as they walked.

Walking through the gate with him, the others returned burdened with an assortment of equipment.

"Well done," Kayla said, impressed by the docile pony walking alongside Riley.

Four of us stood by, useless, as Kayla and Falon's expert hands set about throwing saddles and bridles onto our mounts. We were set to depart in a matter of thirty minutes.

"Yer going to 'ave Dante," Kayla said to Gavlin, handing him the reins. Attached to the leather straps fastened to the bit in the animal's mouth was a heavyset black horse standing near five-seven at his back, with only one white stocking on his back left leg. In Kayla's other hand was a muddy-brown horse with a short-clipped black mane and only a small white spot in the center of his forehead. Only a couple of inches shorter than Dante, with a slighter build and leaner body, his eyes reflected a curiosity about the world around him.

"This 'ere is Traveler, and he is fer yer," said Kayla. She handed the reins to Rowan, who was unsure what to do with the twelve hundred-pound animal he was now responsible for. "That leaves this little lad fer yer, my dear. Don't yer worry because he is a fast little devil. He will outlast and outrun ther big ones. Mer children call him Willy Wonka," she said laughing and patting the golden rump of a pony behind her. With the color of a Wonka Golden Ticket, Willy, as I was told, was a little Welsh pony with four white socks to his knees and a large, white stripe starting at his forehead and ending under his velvet nose.

Only standing a little over four feet at his back, I figured it would not be far from the ground if I were to fall. Looking up, I saw that Falon had scored herself a finer-boned brown mare with short white socks on her front right leg and back two legs, between the midget ponies and heavyset horses, in size. Falon appeared entirely at ease as she patiently gave instructions to the guys who had no horse experience, continuously walking around with her antsy horse.

"You're going to regret even mentioning this idea in about twenty minutes, and then you will still have another ten hours," she mocked Gavlin.

"Bet's on. I'll be runnin' like a cowboy across the fields by the end of the day," Gavlin challenged, unsuccessfully pulling his reins in various directions to make his beast move. With a couple of hints from Kayla, we bid her good-bye and thanked her for the generous sale of her horses and equipment.

For the next couple of hours, we kept to a walking pace, with the occasional jogging, or trotting speed, in order to keep all the horses and riders in check, and rested before we got ready for a faster pace. More often than not, Falon sustained a slight battle to keep the fire under her little mare, Kina, from erupting and taking off at a hard gallop, which probably would have been ideal for both of them. Unfortunately, one horse running would probably have caused some issues, considering the horses' herd mentality. I vaguely remembered the few riding lessons from my youth, and with Falon's assistance, I slowly eased up. With my mental and physical status relaxed, Willy transformed from a nervous, jolty, and excited walk to a mellow stroll, with his head stretched down. Nicknamed el Diablo, Comet took on the alter ego of his white color as quite the little angel. If he could talk, he would have said the horns were only there to hold up the halo. Gavlin was slightly impatient and felt the need to go faster, but Dante was calm in the face of his impatience and never offered to pick up a pace faster than a slow jog. Dante and Traveler were obviously pals, which worked well as they kept pace and often reached over to touch muzzles. Rowan was silent as usual, and despite his typical stubbornness, listened to our instructions. From the look on his face, there was enough tension to indicate his uneasiness about trusting a sometimes-unpredictable animal with his life.

Walking beside Falon, I noticed how calm she appeared. Her hands rested down on her horse's mane, and the reins were looped with complete trust in her ability to read the horse by acknowledging him as more than just an animal with a piece of metal in its mouth. It was as if, for the first time since I'd met her, she was not putting on an act for the world around her. There was even a genuine glow about her face in the bright sunshine. "I can tell you live in a saddle," I commented to her.

She smiled in my direction, "Yes, it feels wonderful. It feels like it has been forever. On the contrary, I know it has only been days."

"Is this everything you imagined?"

"Riding though the countryside? Yes. It is liberating to have no one yelling instructions at you. There is just all this beautiful land without anything and not an end in sight," she said with actual feeling.

"As if it never has to end?" I asked.

"Exactly, and there is nothing or no one to tell me what I need to do." She picked up her reins, and her horse immediately flicked her ears forward and sped up. "Now, I feel we should actually run. You ready?"

chapter 20

Lacking any formal navigating device, we followed a path parallel to the main roads, which still lacked the breadth of the highways in the United States. The narrow side roads alternated between dirt and asphalt long eroded by Mother Nature and travelers. A constant faint breeze danced across the fields, interrupted by well-established shrubbery and trees along the roadside and fields. The breeze created the gentle rustling sound of leaves shaking in anticipation for a possible flight. Stone walls often started along the roadside as entrances to homes, cottages left in a world long gone and those built in a modern day. Regardless of the modern image of some of the homes, they remained an integrated part of the countryside with a lack of ornate stonework or custom yard decorations, just plain, simple. Despite the cool weather, customary of Ireland in early spring, the sunshine peeked its head out on occasion to look at the land before shyly retreating to the safe cover of the clouds. Considering its short appearances, my body thanked a previous motion among the group to dress warm before landing in Ireland.

We were still in the same clothes and the status of our luggage was now listed as "long gone." The consistent movement of the horses leisurely walking with the soft impact of their hooves on the giving ground relaxed my mind to match the pace of their hooves.

From the antiquated technique of using a paper map spread across the table at breakfast, the determined route to Boyle approximated to eight hours. For the sake of both the chubby ponies and teenage boys, we barley reached the three-hour mark at 1:00 in the afternoon, when it was determined a dire necessity to stop at a quaint pub. With consideration to the horses, Rowan and Gavlin handed their mounts to us, took our meager stash of money, and ventured into the pub insistent on ordering any available dishes. Attempting to pull the bridles off the horses for a break, I became a human scratching post for the monster Gavlin was riding, whose head easily reached a length longer than my own torso. This forced me to exert every ounce of weight to serve as an effective countering force and avoid landing flat on the ground. With the horses' thirst satisfied from a nearby stream, and the muffled sounds of grass being consumed, Falon, Riley and I sat contently under a mature tree.

"We still have another five hours of this, don't we?" I broke the silence.

"Uh-huh. I would very much like some of my mother's cooking right now," Falon replied, while Riley continued to fiddle with a long weed stem in her hands.

"Authentic, I take it."

"She buys fresh meat and produce with nearly every meal and then cooks authentic food her *mamá* taught her from when she lived in Costa Rica. Every recipe is from memory."

"That would be wonderful and a marvelous upgrade from my house, where meals are best when eaten out." I laughed thinking about how both my father's and my greatest culinary work was a toasted peanut butter and jelly sandwich.

"I would be ecstatic to cook for you, or have you at my house for dinner," she offered.

"There is no way I could deny an offer like that. Does your family still have a lot of Costa Rican traditions?"

"I would say in many ways, yes. Regardless, I used to resent it. I felt out of place in my private school where every student was from a rich white family. I wanted to blend in. I stopped speaking Spanish and made every effort to avoid it entirely. Obviously I speak it now, and I understand it is a part of me."

"You have never lived in white suburbia until you've attended my school. I am desperate for some diversity." I tried to make light of the situation.

"I am sure it is easier."

"Eh. That is questionable, between all the smaller cliques and small inefficiencies that come from managing a three thousand-person public high school."

"You attend a public school?"

"Yes. Where I live it's just as good as some of the private schools, although the privates always beat us in math team competitions."

"You're on math team?"

"It's what all the cool kids do," I joked.

"Are you kidding?"

"Dead serious. We have too much fun. It's an excuse to not do any of our schoolwork, and be with friends. Plus, we get food, and with all of the free time between tests we just play games and talk."

"Sure," Falon replied skeptically.

"Don't judge it until you try," I replied sarcastically. "Look! They found food."

Rowan and Gavlin pushed open the wooden door to the pub across the asphalt road and made their way in our direction, each carrying multiple plates piled high with some form of food, though it was unclear and unimportant as to what kind.

"I love these people!" Gavlin exclaimed when he reached earshot of our stationary location.

"You would love anyone who gave you food," I said.

I took two of the plates out of his hands, eyeing roasted chicken, some form of potatoes, and a sandwich overfilled with mystery meat and red onions.

"Well, of course I love them because I got food out of the deal! Everyone around here just loves people. Here, someone take these. I'm gonna get some drinks inside." He moved the plates in Riley's direction for her to take. "Leave some of that sandwich for me. I wanna try it. They told me it's a banger. Some traditional food, I think. Now, it's Guinness time," Gavlin said with a smirk.

"Try again," I replied.

He grabbed my shoulders. "Yes."

"You are bad enough on a horse without the unnecessary alcohol. It could just get ugly."

"I'm of legal age here, and I'm going to take full advantage of that before I am forced back to the States."

"I am sure you uphold that law with the utmost stringency."

"Anyone else want one?" he asked, purposely brushing over my statement.

"Are you really?" I insisted.

"Fine, if you're gonna get that angry. Just know that before I leave this wonderful country, I'm gonna join in with a Guinness," he said, strolling back in the direction of the pub.

"What is this?" Falon said with slight disgust at a plate in her hands.

Rowan bent over. "That is the sausage Gavlin mentioned earlier called 'banger.' There is roasted chicken if that is more your taste."

"Vegetarian, remember?" Falon stated.

"I'm sure there are plenty of non-meat items," I said, examining the potatoes on a plate balanced in my left hand.

With our stockpile of food, we situated ourselves on the thick grass to enjoy a picnic-style meal. Years had passed since I had enjoyed any sort of picnic. It felt like one of those things a traditional family would do. At this point, we might have been the nearest thing to family, with so many losses, but it did not distract from the blissful mood.

"Rowan, pass me the chicken you have in your hand. Would you like to try the fish and chips?" I asked. It had not taken long for us to establish a custom where any food on the table was fair game for everyone to eat.

He switched plates with me over the top of Falon, who sat between us.

Gavlin returned moments later, surprisingly with a lack of alcoholic drinks. Our smorgasbord of food found its way around our semi-circle. The spices of the marinated chicken paired perfectly with a home-cooked taste and tender freshness. The mystery meat of the banger tasted like a typical sausage, evidently combined with some type of breading. Not something I would choose to order again over the chicken or the battered fish, but decent for quick, Irish pub food. With my stomach bloated from the massive amount of food I helped to polish off, I leaned back on the grass with my hands folded under my head to look at the dull blue sky. There was nothing spectacular or cheerful about it. There was just the feeling of a bed of thick grass and silence. I missed the ignorant bliss of my previous life where the largest problem on my plate was three exams forced into a short five-day week.

"I vote we just stay here and never go home." I broke the silence. Everyone's mouths had been too busy during our meal to talk.

"Your choice," Rowan remarked from some direction to my left.

"What do you mean?" I questioned, sitting up to find him lying back in the grass in a similar position to mine.

"Stay here and wait everything out," he said.

"Would you stay?"

"It's not my decision."

"Well, then whose decision is it?"

"Your own."

I was starting to become frustrated with his philosophical mind trip. "What the heck does that mean?"

Silence. While his mind was undoubtedly clear, he had the ability to muddle mine. He asserted himself to keep us all from death, yet between the death scenes, we heard nothing of him aside from the annoying, occasional philosophical question, mostly passed over.

Stopping myself from any further comments before everything spiraled away from my current, idyllic state, I stood up. "We need to get this show on the road! Crickee, pack the bags. Let's move it, heifer," I said in my best Eddie Murphy impression of Mushu, from Disney's *Mulan*.

chapter 21

For the past few hours, we had traveled along on our furry mounts, and to kill some time we all dipped into our pensieves to share a few stories. Rowan started us off.

"With the RV traveling slowly, we wound our way through the turns of Yellowstone. The eastern part of the park was full of the greenery of young trees sprouting after the forest fires that left burnt sticks where trees used to be. With the window open and the camera ready, Riley filmed our excursion and constantly nagged about how she wanted to see a buffalo. We drove along for a while. Without any warning, a buffalo appeared on the right-hand side of the road. His winter coat had partially rubbed off, the remainder hanging in patches across his shoulders. With a head planted low to the ground, he used his horns and powerful hooves to tear chunks out of the earth in front of him. As we passed, he looked up from his mad fury and proceeded to charge at the RV. At this point, our father still had respect for the RV we rented. Later, with all of its problems, including breaking down at the top of the mountain, we would change this opinion. Now, he accelerated away from the charging beast. With the RV gaining speed, the buffalo ran alongside us, breathing heavily from his dilated nostrils. When the buffalo eventually slammed on the brakes alongside the road, he bent his head down once again and took another stab at the ground in our direction." Rowan finished up his edition of a personal narrative upon Riley's begging request. If it had been easier for her to retell the story without his interpretation, he would not have succumbed.

With a huge smile from reminiscing on a family adventure, Riley caught my attention and casually dropped her reins down on the pony's neck. Unconcerned and unaware that he held all of the control, Comet plodded on next to my own pony. She signed *stop,* and then *horse.* Then she signed *drink.* I motioned with a closed fist downward—*yes*—which received a smile of approval.

All five horses were quick to stick their muzzles into the shallow water of a clear stream running along the side of a farmer's unharvested field, only a few meters from the road. My pony's golden ears flicked back with each deep gulp he took to quench his thirst. Shockingly, all the horses, despite Falon's continual judgment, were not suffering from exhaustion and, as long as we remained at a suitable pace, they would be comfortable for the duration of the trip.

With dusk creeping across the country, we arrived on the outskirts of Boyle. A bit of wandering later, we made residence along a line of tall, entangled shrubs that would serve to deter any unwanted attention to our location. With my horse tied to a thick branch, hoping he would not attempt to break its two-inch diameter, I lugged off the saddle. While the saddle only weighed fifteen pounds, my body dropped down from its weight before I half dragged it a few feet to the side and unceremoniously dropped it on the ground. The others were already resting on the other side of the horses in a flat, grassy area. Dragging my heavy legs, I put one foot in front of another until I reached the base of a tree opposite them. It was an old grandfather tree with wrinkled bark and drooping branches overlooking his children tucked safely away in their cottages for the night. My back landed softly on the rough bark as I sat down and pulled my knees in toward my chest. From a slightly higher elevation than the surrounding rolling hills, I gazed out on the land ahead, hoping its serenity would put me to sleep. The acoustics of the insects floated like a gentle lullaby carried by the still of night. I wrapped my hands protectively around my knees, the thick grass cushioning my front row seat to their performance, under the spotlight of the moon. Never before this trip had I spent so many nights with the stars.

Time passed, yet insomnia remained. My body screamed for sleep, but my mind continued to override the need, as it spun in circles and attempted to evaluate all my emotions. In a matter of days, I had been thrown onto a plane with four other kids my father had never mentioned, in search of documents I knew so little about. The hellhounds on our feet were the only clue that it was not all just a hoax. I was given the chance to fall for my celebrity crush. And, for once, it had not ended in complete rejection or regrettable failure. What I thought I was feeling was just not meant to be. And instead of holding on, I was learning to let go of the little things like this. How could teenage love cause so much pain when I did not even know if my father was alive? Yet, it was impossible to just stop thinking "what if?" If we were not here, would it have worked? Did it only seem possible because we were trying so hard to grasp onto a constant in our fractured lives? Gavlin was not old news. I still found myself enchanted with his personality—his particular way of laughing often, cutting me off when I spoke too much, and finding some humor in what I do when I am clearly being a bundle of negative.

And when he smiled, my eyes could see sparks. At the same time, it was impossible to ignore what Rowan said on the plane. As I tried to figure him out, I continuously wondered if this was the same Rowan from one week ago, before I met him, or if that version was forever lost. Is it possible to forgive the world and someone who made it out of the fire while you felt it consume you?

Behind me, I heard the soft snap of a branch, breaking my mind from its dizzying thoughts. I let go of the embrace around my knees and swiveled my head to the right. Expecting it to be a noise from the horses, my body jolted at the appearance of a human shadow.

"Would you stop doing that!" I snap at the intruder.

"Doing what?"

"Sneaking up on me! Did you forget we happen to be on the run from people with guns who want to kidnap us?"

"Cracking under the pressure, I see," Rowan said, as he sat down only inches away from me, with his back against the same tree.

"I am not."

He just turned his head toward me and raised his eyebrows, shadows covering most of his face, questioning my statement without a single world. He picked up a forgotten tree branch on the ground and began to pick it apart while staring out at the open fields.

It was impossible for me to keep my attention focused on any of the thoughts previously consuming me. No longer could I hear the orchestra of crickets. Just an awkward silence. I kept peeking over at Rowan, who appeared content. Minutes passed, and I ended up picking up objects around me to keep my mind preoccupied. When that did not work, I shifted positions to place my chin on my knees, then one knee bent, and then cross-legged. Despite my fidgeting, nothing could keep me from wanting to jump up and find my own place where I was not distracted by the presence next to me.

"So why are you not sleeping with all the others? I thought I was the insomniac who never sleeps," I said, casually trying to start the conversation and hoping we would not retreat back to the uncomfortable silence.

"You aren't the only one preoccupied."

"I just do not like sleeping. If I'm not tired, then I don't sleep. I decided I would find a better view to enjoy, considering I don't have a good book," I lied.

"Worries are the strongest caffeine I know."

"I am not the only one," I threw back at him.

He looked back in my direction and turned his chest toward me. "I would say that's a fair judgment."

"Well, I am not a psychologist, never have and never will be sympathetic or willing to have a mushy conversation about feelings. Just putting it out there."

"No problems there," he said.

"I'm glad you feel that way. Granted, you are not much for any type of emotion. In the words of Harry Potter, 'You have the emotional range of a teaspoon'."

"Thank you. I happen to be a Harry Potter fan. It is a bit of an honor to be graced with such thoughts… One day you will find the key to that part of you."

"How would you know?" I asked with a hope that he would uncover some part of his past.

"Because when your world collapses, a lot of things tend to fall into place."

"For me, I think it's going to take more than circumstances to change the way I have been thinking my whole life. No one has ever betrayed me or given me reason to not have trust. Until now. I trusted people. I accept that everyone is human, but now I do not know what to think. Here we are, all with questions and no answers. Have I been living in ignorance my whole life? After this I can never imagine believing anyone a hundred percent. For goodness sake, our own parents lied to us!" I ranted, not meaning to end up nearly yelling.

"I take it you don't forgive and forget."

"I give people second chances; however, they are hard earned."

"As you said, you're not the only one who has been lied to," he said a bit sarcastically, as a way to cover the sadness in his voice.

I tried to keep the mood light. "Tell me about it."

When a smile lit up my face, I saw his eyes brighten for a second and a smile play across his lips. "I'm going to call it a night. Good-night."

I watched him walk silently away behind the tree and back to where the others were sound asleep. Instead of returning with him, I laid down on the ground with my hands under my head, watching the stars. The last thing I remember was waiting for a shooting star, to make a wish like I used to do when I was young and believed in magic.

chapter 22

"The last time I was this sore was last year when I miscalculated in slope-style practice and crash-landed. They dragged me to a hospital, and I spent the next few hours in an emergency room. I had bruises and a busted rib. This is more like muscles I didn't know existed," Gavlin complained within the first couple seconds of being awake.

I had once again joined the others after a dreamless night under my old tree before being awakened by the rising sun. There was no doubt we needed a plan and, more importantly, I knew there would be demands for breakfast. Among the five of us, we were condensed down to two backpacks, which included valid currency taken from the plane all the way back in Brazil.

"My back hurts from all the knots after sleeping on this ground," Falon chimed in, not the wilderness scout of the bunch.

"Maybe tomorrow we'll have a hotel. Nevertheless, I should probably check the money situation. We still need to get out of the country. I am not sure how we are planning to accomplish such a task or if we will have the money. We only need to make it to The Hague. If I am correct, we are at around T minus thirty-six hours, meaning we need to get out of here tonight, make a puddle jump to England, a puddle jump to The Hague, and then still manage to get into the building with our lives and the documents intact. Sounds like coffee and Red Bull might be our best friend," I summed.

"What did you just say? I thought I finally was able to understand you and Falon's high-speed rants, but that?" Gavlin mocked. "Why don't we just start with food and maybe what we are doing with our steeds?"

I picked up my backpack, which I knew contained a majority of our money. "I had an inkling you were going to say that. Okay, I think I can handle that. Rowan, where is the rest of the money?"

"Your bag and the inside pocket thing on Riley's," he replied from across the clearing, where I knew he would be listening in on our conversation.

"Thanks." I rifled through the bags and set out all of the monetary and travel resources we had left available to us: a couple of useless bills from our trip through Central and South America, about four hundred euros, and a set of fake passports.

"Is that *all* we have?" Falon said in shock over my shoulder.

"Appears to be so," I replied, mentally figuring out how we planned to get across multiple countries with five people. Not to mention, food would be ideal.

"Food first," Gavlin reinforced.

"Of course. No filet, lobster, or fine dining establishments. And especially no alcohol, despite how wonderful I am sure it is for the drinking age to be practically non-existent."

"You always ruin the party. I'm legal here, too," Gavlin teased.

I sat down cross-legged on the ground and spread the money in front of me. A few seconds later, I got the feeling someone was standing right behind me.

"Really?" I demanded, knowing exactly who was responsible.

"What?" Rowan said with a straight face. "Riley noticed that there was a field with horses just down the hill, and she thinks we could just leave ours there."

Falon looked appalled at such a suggestion. "I am not going to abandon five horses we took from a good home. We need to return them to an equally good home. Abandoning them is not helping anyone, unless you lack any soul."

I interjected, "He is a ginger after all. But seriously, there is no option of dragging five horses behind us when we enter into town, and I think if we leave them with others there is a high chance those people will have a spot for a couple more horses. They will either keep them or find them another home. If they have horses now, they must have some respect for animals. We need to get moving."

"I am not agreeing to such a plan," Falon said, glaring back with hands crossed defensively in front of her chest.

I was at a loss, save for the fact that I knew Falon would never stay anywhere without us. "Then stay."

Gavlin stood by watching as if he were munching on popcorn at a movie theater and waiting for the action to start. I did not notice until much later that Rowan had, undetected, slipped into the background. Disappointed in the lack of physical action, despite death glares and a bit of shock on Falon's face, Gavlin inserted himself into the situation.

"You two both have a point. I'm just looking to get out of here alive." He took a step forward to block our view of each other by a couple of inches. Silence continued as both Falon and I burned holes through him. Before I could mouth off a smart comment like "Remind me to pick my partners wiser on stressful missions," Riley came running up to our Mexican standoff with a concerned look.

"*What's up?*" she said.

I shook my head, "Nothing. We are disagreeing on some stuff." I attempted to sign, turning my back to the other two. "*Can you help with the horses?*"

"*Yes!*" she replied with a grin and a little skip, reminding me how young she was. I wondered if I could steal some of her personality. She always acted like everything was fine, without the unnecessary questions.

I could hear Gavlin's voice as Riley and I walked off to the trees where the horses were tied up. "And we have a winner. Sorry, Falon. Try again." Falon stomped off, with her black hair hanging out of her messy hair bun in various places, and the combination of a sigh and a growl as she headed across the open field. I turned around to see Gavlin watching her go, smiling at how she thought she could hide in an open field. There was no escaping this mission.

Thirty minutes later, Gavlin and Rowan forced open a rusty gate attached haphazardly to a couple of wooden posts between wire fencing that ran for a mile dividing one green field in half. There were indeed a couple of grazing furry horses to the far left, spaced only a few feet apart and munching away with lazy content.

"You guys be good. I am sure these wonderful people will take care of you," Falon said, and took the ropes and halters off of her dancing mare and the little brown horse, Traveler, that Rowan had ridden. Before releasing them she grabbed them both by the head and planted a kiss on their velvet muzzles. It took a little convincing with the mare that had her ears perked high from the potential of meeting the horses across the field. Falon held the sides of her halter in both hands and gave her a kiss and pat on the neck. With Traveler hanging out near us and the mare prancing toward her new herd, I gave my little golden ticket a scratch on the neck and up behind his ears, one ear pointed toward the other horses and one trained on me. With a pat on the neck to the towering giant Gavlin had ridden, who was currently nuzzling my pockets for any sign of food, I assured them of good future and thanked them. I took off their ropes and shooed them toward the field. Willy gave a little squeal and buck of joy. The lumbering black giant just pinned his ears at the foolishness of the midget pony. When I turned around, I noticed that Riley had her face buried in Comet's Afro of a mane and her hands wrapped tightly around his neck. He stood patiently, with his rope dangling on the ground, despite his natural heard instinct to run off with the others. She finally released her thin arms from around his neck, and I could see tears rolling down her checks and hitting him. She hugged his face, and his eyes softly closed. With one final kiss, she took off his halter and rope. His feet remained firmly planted next to her, looking toward the field and back in her direction. Quickly, she grabbed him around the neck for one last embrace, one last kiss and shooed him off. He parted with a good headshake and ecstatically galloped to his buddies. Falon walked over and embraced Riley in a hug, walking with her out of the pasture.

After the painful screeching of the gate being forced closed, I said, "We need to walk north into town and find some food because it appears as though it's a requirement to live. We go to Boyle Abbey, we get the paperwork, and eventually figure out a way to arrive in the land of the Brits."

"I heard food, so count me in," Gavlin said, picking up Riley's black leather shoulder bag and taking the lead across the empty field.

About a mile off we could just make out the small homes and quaint town that was Boyle. It probably appeared a bit strange to see five grungy teenagers trekking across an open field. I would be relieved to see a normal road. Gavlin took the lead, with Riley skipping along behind him, to the side and occasionally in front of him, dancing to nothing. Falon fell in line with a proper look of composure, hair braided down her back and clothes looking still supermodel fresh compared to the rest of us. I was behind her, carrying my blue backpack that had never seen the world outside of my car, home, and school. My back was quite discontent with the weight of the documents and the meager hours of sleep I sought on the roots of an old tree that poked through the surface of the ground like varicose veins. Treading a few distances behind me was Rowan quietly making his way through the dense grass. When I stole a glance at him, his hair cast a hue of flaming red in the vivid early afternoon sunlight. I wondered if the population of redheads was indeed greater in Ireland than any other place in the world. His walk was not relaxed or catlike in the way Gavlin snuck around, but pulled tightly together. Not an inch of relaxation. I could tell he was concentrated on the farmhouse that was quickly nearing. Realizing my error of staring, I whipped my head around to see Gavlin motioning everyone into a tighter formation and skirting around the side of a buttercup-yellow two-story home surrounded by multiple layers of trees meant either to keep people out or maybe in.

I sighed in relief when our feet hit the pavement of Upper Marian Road near what appeared to be the single school for this small town. I assumed it was a school because of the stereotypical windows found every few feet in a straight, uniform line to let light into the classrooms. Additionally, a large playground area with basketball hoops resided next to the low, long two-story school building fenced in by a tall chain link fence. The road took a near ninety-degree turn to the right in front of the school and headed north, which we assumed was the way into town. Compact cars driving on the wrong side of the road zoomed by us as we passed the cookie-cutter homes in close proximity to each other. The houses were only vaguely distinguished by the variety of browns, salmons, buttercups, and white stucco on the exterior of the homes.

"I think we should head straight left here," I offered to the group when we came to a "y" shape in the road we had been following for the past ten minutes. On my left, there was a glass building set behind some trees, with a fair number of cars. From our viewpoint, it appeared to be a type of office building. The quaintness of the town continued as we walked down on the side roads and toward the center of town. The cars zipped around hairpin turns as the roads haphazardly intersected and turned at a variety of odd angles. Similar to our earlier impression, homes in various shapes and colors lined the streets with almost no form of backyard space and with no real sense of separate neighborhoods. The neighborhood was the entire town. After a couple more minutes following the straightest path we could manage between roads branching and re-intersecting, we eventually appeared on the stone sidewalks of the most downtown area. Featuring a collection of storefronts with large glass windows, there was a Brogan's Pharmacy in gold lettering below a burgundy and white striped awning and, across the street, a Taylor's Hardware. The road took a split to the right onto Bridge Road, named for the small river running straight through the town, only passable by a couple of narrow bridges. Just before reaching the riverbank, we stumbled upon a gold-colored two-story building with black shutters and "The Royal Hotel" stated above the front windows. When we saw "Coffee Shop" printed in block gold lettering and a sign stating they were now open for food, there was no questioning our brunch location.

I followed Gavlin as he opened the door of the coffee shop. "Well, this is a surprise. Very interesting," I commented.

Riley tapped me on the arm and pointed at the black-and-white-tiled floor, the aged, exposed stone walls and the exposed, deep wood beams on the ceiling with a look of puzzlement.

"I don't have a clue, but it is unique."

"You know what you guys are gettin'?" Gavlin asked us as we approached the front counter behind him.

"You walked in two seconds ago and you have already assured yourself of your order?" Falon said.

"I'm hungry. What can I say?" Gavlin replied, eyeing us as we looked at the menu.

"Give us a second and chill. We're not going to starve you," I commented.

Without asking again to see if we were ready, Gavlin began his order and luckily we all thought fast enough to place ours. For a coffee shop, we were surprised to find a decent variety of potatoes, black-and-white breakfast pudding and some type of sausage. Falon, with her picky and strictly vegetarian diet, opted for some oatmeal, and a cup of coffee loaded with sugar.

Black coffee in hand, I broke the vacant silence filled only by the sound of chewing mouths. "Has anyone been to Boyle Abbey?" I directed the question at the ginger picking his way through some type of black breakfast pudding across the table.

"Riley and I came when we were very young. Been a while and they were doing construction. Could have changed," Rowan replied.

"Regardless, where would the documents be?"

"The tower," he said as he met my eyes only briefly before pretending to be interested in the food he was pushing around his plate. Frustrated with his lack of interest in my attempt to create some type of plan for our reconnaissance mission of *his* papers, I turned to Riley, who made it obvious she had been listening in on the conversation.

"He said you came here when you were young, and the papers would be in the tower," I said while stumbling along with signs that were equivalent to *"Rowan you here before. Papers T-O-W-E-R."*

She smiled at me with a *"Yes,"* and put another bite of food in her mouth.

"Okay. We should probably ask someone for general directions and head over there after everyone has had their fill of food," I said to Riley, but hoped the rest of the table would have picked up on the conversation.

"Are you gonna finish that?" Gavlin said.

"Go for it," I told him. "The black coffee is good for me, although I may need more if I am going to make it through today."

"Would you like more? I'm asking for another cup myself," Falon said, standing up.

I looked into my mug to find it less than a quarter of the way full and considered my lack of sleep in combination with relying on Rowans' knowledge today. "That would be great. Can you ask the gentleman at the counter how we get to Boyle Abbey, as well?"

"I can manage such." She took my mug and headed off.

A minute later, she handed me my full steaming mug. Seated again with all of her thin fingers wrapped around her mug and pulling it close to her chest where her black hair hung in a loose braid over her shoulder she explained, "He told me to follow Bridge Street over the river and turn right on Military Road. You will see it soon after the turn."

"Thanks. Sounds simple enough. I think the biggest issue will be finding the papers once we are there."

"How hard could it possibly be? Nothing can compare with what we just went through."

"Oh, come on. When will you ever have an adventure like this?" I joked.

She raised her eyebrows and gave her customary "you are insane, and I am not amused" look before replying, "If we live through this, someone is going to pay."

chapter 23

"A couple of days ago, the mile-long walk here would have been a stretch when the only attraction awaiting us was an old castle. I can now say I am thankful the walk was only one mile, need I mention through a peaceful and quaint town," Falon rambled on as we reached the intersection of Abbeytown, Old Sligo, and Military Road.

Her comment made me smirk slightly while my eyes admired the green scenery surrounding us. After leaving the downtown storefronts, we found ourselves walking along an old stonewall with vegetation spilling over the top from the yards of wealthy homes set far back from the road. At the intersection, our destination was staring at us from across the road.

Riley caught my attention and pointed at the stone structure hiding behind some trees and extending south along Old Slige Road. Crossing the street, which was less busy than my quaint side street in the historical Naperville suburbs, we could make out various levels of reconstruction on the abbey. Some scaffolding remained erect on one of the exterior walls along with a variety of stones, tools, an idle tractor, and a lift bucket propped on a massive stone for an extended rest. Everything looked as silent and ancient as the abbey, and I had to wonder how long ago the attempt at restoration had been abandoned.

Boyle Abbey. Built in 1142 and still standing proud. The stone structure had deteriorated in places, but the elegant archways and central buildings on the north and south remained, sheltered from the outside world by the surrounding stone wall on the rectangular property. The main entrance opened into a corridor with arch structures between stone support beams. The corridor ended in a three-story stone building that obviously served as a central place of worship during the time Boyle Abbey was a monastery. The stone between my feet showed signs of many shoes; still, grass found its way through the spaces in the stones and filled in the deteriorating parts between the gray stone of the abbey buildings. It was as if I had jumped through a wrinkle in time. Standing there, one could still hear the silent echo of ghost bells from the bell tower.

Looking out to my right at the yard of Boyle Abbey, I could make out a shorter tower structure in the southwest corner. There were a couple of small slits to serve as windows, although the building in front of it covered a majority of the tower. Aside from the tower, the abbey's enclosed yard was home to various stone pathways across a green lawn. A couple of tourists could be found milling around and snapping pictures to bring back a piece of history from their adventures. By the look of one family with two teenage sons, the sons were more interested in anything aside from a history lesson, while the tourist parents were decked out in hiking sandals, large hats, paper maps, and a camcorder on "record."

"This place is like its own world. Whoever built it must not have wanted anyone to enter," Gavlin remarked.

"You make it sound like it was a cult."

"You never know."

"Well, we will never know. Maybe we can hang around and wait for Casper to show up to give us a complete history."

Falon entered the conversation. "A much as I would desire to stay for a ghost encounter, what are we precisely looking for?"

"Rowan and Riley told me earlier that it would be in the tower, which I believe is that round, short structure over there to the right," I said, pointing in its direction. "By the way, where is Rowan? He is supposed to be our tour guide, although right now I would be more pleased to deal with some type of ghost," I snarled.

"That is a possible solution. Unfortunately, I believe they would be put off by your demanding demeanor," Rowan replied from directly behind me.

"Sorry that someone wants to accomplish something," I snapped.

"It's the tower in the corner," Rowan coolly replied and walked off on the path toward the tower.

If not for Riley tapping me on the shoulder, I would have stomped after the figure in the gray sweater. *"Why are you and Rowan arguing?"*

"We are not arguing. We just have some different ideas about the whole trip," I informed her.

"You look angry. It'll all be fine." She reached down, grabbed my hand, and dragged me off toward the tower, taking a couple of skipping steps. Along the way, she showed me the collection of puzzle piece stones that lay on the ground from the existing parts of the abbey. How were these two siblings by blood relation?

Following Rowan under another archway, we were left standing directly in the front of the corner tower. We passed a staff member from Boyle Abbey. As a national monument, Boyle Abbey is obligated to have someone who can act as a friendly tour guide to the eager tourists interested in learning history they will only forget within seconds. Most memories will be of their children complaining about wanting to leave, or of missing their flight later that day. Our on-duty walking Wikipedia for Boyle Abbey was an older gentleman with a kind expression who paid no attention to five teenagers walking around. Trusting us is not a wise decision.

Standing on the opposite side of the small space from Rowan and looking in his direction, I noticed a set of exceptionally steep and shallow stairs winding up the tower starting seven feet off the ground from a minute, solid platform. It would require one of us to nimbly make it off the ground and ascend up the precarious steps to reach where the information was likely stored.

"And why would your father have left it up there?" Gavlin asked, dumbfounded.

"It's going to be between the stones up there." Rowan addressed the group, looking specifically at Riley and me.

She said something rapidly back to him, and a couple of interactions took place before anyone else knew what was going on. I am pretty sure my name was in there; however, I was pleased to have his sister dealing with him.

Rowan finished up his statement and glared directly into my eyes. "Devon, you're up."

"What? When did we talk about this?"

"Since Riley and I decided the girls are the lightest to lift up, we would not be able to yell directions back and forth with her, and

Falon is much more pleased to be on the ground. Plus, you're the anxious one here."

"I am not gonna pretend like this is at all fine in my books." I still walked over to the base of the tower. "Now give me a boost up," I demanded.

Gavlin came over to assist Rowan, and they both cupped their hands so I could use them as stepping blocks to the base of the stairs. At the top, I realized the narrow tower was generously only three feet in diameter. From the small window of the tower, I could peer out onto Old Sligo Road and see a couple of cars whizzing by. My first couple of steps up was an uncoordinated balancing act until I realized the increased ease in standing sideways and moving in a crab-like motion. Once consumed by the tower, the only light streaming in came from the top that was open toward the sky. Suddenly, I heard an elevated voice from below clearly enunciate in her sweet, overly formal manner, "This tower is impressive. The stone work is exquisite considering how long ago it was built."

Something was going on and, from the sound of it, I was not coming down in the near future. I would be stuck in a tower, twenty feet off the ground and balanced unnaturally against a stone jabbing into my shoulder. Nonetheless, I vainly searched the couple of possible gaps in the stonework for any sign of anything—anything aside from a spider.

"Yer would not believe what we'r found ther' just fer weeks ago. A memory device. Put 'er in a computer, and no one could get 'er to work. Even the young lads at some government building had difficulty," declared the voice of the old man who I presumed to be the staff person I eyed earlier.

"Would you know where we could find that memory stick, sir?" Falon asked.

"I sent 'er in the mail to a man who heads this abbey," I heard in response. Even without being there, I could tell everyone was epically failing to cover up the shock on his or her face. If we did not have it, then it was sitting in the wrong hands, probably locked away in a secret compartment of a locked desk in some top-secret organization headquarters behind a dozen additional security checks. I could only wonder if that memory drive was the reason the precariously stable condition of our intertwined lives was sent into a cascade toward Satan's headquarters.

"Of pure curiosity, I thought this monument was a government operated establishment," Falon said, trying to talk our visitor into more information.

"There is a board dat manages ther details of the abbey with a gent by ther name of Peter Boyle," our new friend explained.

"I'm sure it's in safe hands," Rowan said, the first one to respond after an overdrawn pause between the two parties.

"A strange thing to find 'ere, I would say, lad. You folks av'er nice day." The gentleman departed.

After a thirty-second pause, I was relieved to hear Gavlin's voice calling up to my prison tower. With my feet jammed in the small landings and shoulder into a cracked stone, I needed down.

"Rapunzel, Rapunzel, let down your hair," Gavlin voiced in a singsong tune.

"More like heads up. I am coming down. No guarantees the cramps in my feet will allow for complete coordination." I descended to the platform where I unwillingly let Gavlin lift me to the ground instead of using him to balance my weight and jump down. "Put me down now," I said when Gavlin acted as if I were his princess in need of saving before we would ride off on noble stead into the sunset.

In response, he acted like he was going to just drop me, stopping my heart. He gracefully put me down, with a bow. "As you wish, your highness."

"One minute. Let me check if my heart is still beating and the acoustics of the tower were not playing games with my mind." I looked toward the rest of the group. Falon looked unenthusiastic, and both of the others in shock. Rowan's only tell sign was the way his brow was slightly more wrinkled than usual. Fours days ago, I would not have been able to distinguish that.

Riley answered my question with a smile at her own irony. "*I am the deaf one. You heard right.*"

"Wonderful," I groveled. "I should have known by the look on Falon's face while she was thinking about the possibility of adding, yet again, another element to this around-the-world-in-eight-days adventure. In addition, an increased likelihood of men in black suits with sunglasses."

"We need a new challenge. I'd pull out my iPhone and Google that name, but it looks like I lost mine," Gavlin added.

"If your phone was in your possession, I would have previously confiscated it and thrown it in the nearest body of moving water. Does anyone else realize how little time is available to embark on a chase after, what I presume to be, a common name?" Falon said.

Mentally computing the date after not looking at a calendar in days, I stated, "I couldn't agree more. We are on borrowed time. Last time I checked, we had about forty-eight hours to make it to The Hague. We fail, the documents may as well still have been hidden."

The dark silence surrounding Rowan lead me to believe he was not about to call "uncle" on his part of the mission. We had risked too much for ours to give up on his part. While he would never admit it, his father's death was a lead weight chaining him from jumping onto the next plane to mainland Europe.

Against my own personal ego, I could not bring myself to openly invite Rowan to share his personal missive. Gavlin opened the conversation when he said, "But man, it's your choice."

Before Rowan could respond, Riley had already grabbed his attention by practically punching him in the shoulder and going into rapid conversation. As she spoke, Rowan's face took on a stubborn, stone-cold look. By his quick, sharp movement he was rebutting her arguments and gaining momentum. Normally keen to accept our ideas or offer her own creative alternative, Riley was not going to let Rowan prevail. With exaggerated movements filled with concern instead of anger, she continued an exchange of their secret words. Falon was slightly angered that we were not included in their sibling conflict. Gavlin just turned in my direction and shrugged his shoulders, unconcerned and unaware of the significance of their conversation. His guess was a good as mine, I thought, turning back to watch the silent yelling unfold for the next minute.

It was clear Riley emerged the victor when in one quick, last comment Rowan tensely put his hands down by his side. Riley slowed down her pace for a few last thoughts before turning to us with a satisfied look.

"We should figure out how we're getting out of this place," Rowan said.

Indicating to Riley and Rowan standing across from him, Gavlin remarked, "You got any other connections we don't know, so we jump a plane to Britain?"

"*Allow me to call the prime minister,*" Riley remarked, which was completely lost on the three of us until Rowan decided it would be unfair in his sulky mood to exclude his sister.

Between the laughs I was considering the fact that we had no form of money for a plane ticket. On the other hand, we still had the phony passports, which might not set off every red warning light on the international security boards. My name was "Carla Fieldover."

"Unfortunately, walking is not an option. I misplaced my Nimbus two thousand, and the Thestrals are on strike. Any other connections between the five of us?" I remarked.

"*Dumbledore is out on Ministry business today,*" Riley replied, my Harry Potter reference obviously not completely lost.

"Inconvenient. It's too bad not all of us are able to apparate. We will have to resort to Muggle resources and methods," I replied.

With a look of annoyance and slight confusion, Gavlin stopped us before the delusions of Hogwarts and Butterbeer could continue. "I'm pretty sure that was some type of Harry Potter reference. Yeah."

"If I had my wand with me, I would *evanesco* you. Do you happen to have any Muggle connections for us?" I continued in a horrible British accent to further irritate him.

Replying in a British accent, Gavlin said, "How do I bloody know if I can't understand a word you're saying?"

"It is unfortunate you are not versed in the language of witches and wizards," I said in American English. "Do ya know people who can git us out of here?"

"My connections are like finding a half pipe in the Amazon," he remarked.

"*Food?*" Riley asked with no interpretation needed for the word we immediately picked up.

"What? Didn't see," Gavlin asked.

"*Food. Think and eat. Less attention.*"

"Food. Think. Food?" Gavlin repeated out loud, still putting the simple words together.

"She said there would be less attention toward five teenagers if we went and found some food," I offered.

"I could do food. Food any time is good. It's also Guinness time," Gavlin said, smiling.

"Make that a couple Guinness," Falon added, to our shocked faces. "What? It's been a longer few days than three weeks of vacation with my family."

"Is all good. Let's go?" I said.

As I stepped forward, I sidestepped a couple of inches around Rowan, who had remained quiet. Quiet was probably the worst state I could imagine him in; it meant he was mulling over an idea. Reading him was only as simple as he wanted to make it. At this moment, I only caught a stubborn look, but I am sure he had his own ideas about how we were finding a way to England.

chapter 24

Inside the dimly lit pub, we were seated in mismatched wooden chairs at an antique table. If the table could have talked of every dent, ding, and scuff it had endured, I am sure the stories would find their way back fifty years. The building was not looking any younger itself. It smelled of rich, home-cooked food, and stale beer. Authentic. Inside this little hole in the wall, we were guests of the town's warm hospitality and the comfort of a place impervious to the rushing pace of the world. The only inhabitants in the pub were a foreign couple seated at a table to our right and the locals propped up on bar stools conversing over the latest small-town gossip. The pub was in no rush to push their guests out or cook the food, giving us the opportunity to throw around ideas. Regrettably, the ideas were only causing us to talk in circles. Gavlin and Falon were satisfied with a traditional Irish Guinness, which I still could not approve. Once the drinks reached the table, Riley stared in fascination at the way the drink layered itself in a foaming manner upon being poured into a tall glass.

Fidgeting, as usual, with the straw wrappers and any other item I could find on the table, the only options available for the final leg of our journey were, well, nothing. Rowan had mumbled only a couple of brief mutterings since we'd arrived. While he appeared to be uninterested, his green eyes trained somewhere in space, he was still tuned in to every word floating around the pub. Considering I was across from him at the table, it was obvious when he trained his vision on the pub's door behind me. About thirty seconds later, the door opened to quick-speaking voices holding a couple of loud conversations and laughing exuberantly. I turned around briefly to catch the end of what appeared to be a large motor home pulling away from the front of the pub and a family of three responsible for the ruckus. The mother looked to be ready for a party, in her heels, brunette hair twisted into an elegant up-do, black skinny jeans, and a floral top. The daughter, about Riley's age, sported the European punk look with accents of bright colors and layers. The son, similar in age to his sister, had on skinny jeans, with a vest over a white T-shirt. If they were Americans, they would have been sporting T-shirts and jeans with cameras hanging off their necks. I detected a distinct English accent.

I turned back around to remedy my staring, only to find Rowan intently watching the newest visitors. The wheels were turning in his head. I, personally, was more interested in the mound of food that had just arrived at the table. I aggressively grabbed my fork to dig into Gavlin's plate, to reciprocate his love; he was already eating off of mine in the thirty seconds I was turned in the other direction.

The noise of the British family migrated from a table directly behind me, and the conversation changed pace when a man's voice was added into the mix.

"She is parked around the corner in a nice lot…bloody warning lights…before travel east."

254

I could not help but ask Rowan, *"You are staring. Idea?"*

It took him a couple of seconds to register that I was signing to him before he responded, in what I translated to be, *"You ride car home before?"*

"Car home?"

"M-o-t-o-r home."

"No."

He nodded in acknowledgment before holding up the universal sign for "one minute," standing up, and walking around the back of me.

"Where is Rowan off to?" Falon asked.

"I think he is getting us a ride. Honestly though, not sure."

Walking straight to the end of the English family's table, Rowan paused prior to warmly saying, "Hello. I'm sorry to interrupt your lunch or intrude. I heard you might be having problems with your RV. I saw you drive it to the front; it looks like quite the rig. I'm sure you want to be on the road again quickly."

Not wanting to stare, I could only hear the conversation behind me. The father replied enthusiastically. "Dave. Nice to meet ye. I bought her only a couple of months past and took her on the ferry from Liverpool to Ireland. This is our first trip, and we're heading into Dublin this afternoon. My wife has been concerned about the engine's warning light for the last hour."

"My family had an RV a couple years back with a warning light issue. A mechanic showed us how it sometimes can be a simple loose electrical connection in the dash. I could give it a look and maybe reconnect the part after you finish your lunch."

"It might be difficult to find anyone with experience until we reach Dublin. Such would be much appreciated."

"We've already ordered our food. If you would let me know when you're ready, I can look at it for you."

"Thank you," the father replied, sounding satisfied with the possible, simple solution to his travel predicament.

Riley looked apprehensive about what had been said at the table behind us. When Rowan returned, he explained to her, and Riley was shocked and confused. Her eyes opened wide in astonishment, and she was silent for a minute. From my perspective, it looked as is if Rowan had done a bit more manipulation than we were all aware of with the unsuspecting family. Something lead me to believe an "engine warning light" was not a simple connection malfunction. No one was about to question his methods.

"Do you actually know what you're doing?" I whispered to Rowan as everyone stood outside and watched him bend under the giant wheel of the bus while I stood, as he instructed, as a shield between the eyes outside and himself.

Ripping out a small incandescent bulb from under the dash and shoving it into his sweater, he popped his head up and exclaimed, "You're all set there. It was a loose connection in your light system. I reconnected it."

My eyes bulged in amazement. His answer to my question was obviously "no."

"Thank ye. Can I pay ye for yer time?" the husband offered once Rowan descended the stairs from the RV to the ground.

Rowan waited a couple of seconds and responded nonchalantly, "Well, we're actually looking to travel to Dublin. My aunt, who was supposed to pick us up for a family wedding in Dublin, has come down with a case of pneumonia. We cousins flew into Boyle to sight-see a little, though we're now stranded until another relative can pick us up. Hopefully, it'll be before the rehearsal dinner tonight; two of us are in the wedding party. All our luggage was lost at the airport and will meet us in Dublin," Rowan eloquently lied through his teeth.

The wife finally spoke. "Dear, we are only driving three hours. We could take 'em to Dublin. Weddings are stressful, and I would hate to have another family member drive six hours for these generous young adults. Would that grant for the five of ye?" she graciously offered without waiting for approval from her family.

"That would be wonderful, ma'am," Falon said in a slightly higher-pitched, sweet voice.

"It should be on the tight side. It is only a few hours. Climb on in!" The father beckoned us into the thirty-five-foot black and tan RV.

The two children entered first, to claim stake to their territory inside. Despite having nine people crammed inside, the two beige couches and small dining table provided plenty of room for everyone to take some type of seat before the engine roared to life. Rowan seated himself across from the boy at the dining room table, whose name was Elijah. Elijah was not pleased with our presence, or maybe even the whole family road trip. He inserted his earbuds into his ears and continued to play some violent, dragon-slaying game on his computer. Falon, Gavlin, and Riley settled into the longer beige leather couch along the left-hand wall of the motor home and across from the dining table. Since we'd left, Gavlin had been maintaining his most calm behavior and welcoming grin. Across from them, on a shorter couch, sat fifteen-year-old Haley and me. She pulled back her wavy brunette and blonde-highlighted hair into a bun and set her laptop carefully on the ledge to her right before folding her legs underneath her.

"You are all cousins?" she asked, curious to learn about the band of five travelers her family had picked up in a quaint Irish town. When one put it like that, it did sound a bit on the odd side.

"You mean we don't look alike?" Gavlin joked as he pointed to the pale-skinned, dirty-blonde-haired Riley next to him and his olive skin and jet back hair.

"Quite truthfully, no. The two of ye," she indicated to Riley and me, "look like cousins."

"Rowan," I said, pointing toward the dining table, "and Riley," I continued, pointing across the couch to help with names, "are siblings. Otherwise, we are all first cousins." I had some fun adding to the lies. Hopefully, they would not strangle us before the end of the next three hours.

While I had been talking, Haley stood up and walked toward the back of the RV to fetch something. Moments later, she returned with an iPad. With the flat screen held in front of her face, she intently waited for something to load. The conversation came to a brief halt while we waited and watched to see what the dire emergency was that required an iPad.

"Your name is Gavlin?" she asked, without raising her head and simultaneously adjusting the iPad screen with her left hand.

"Um, yeah. Should I change it?" he replied, as puzzled as the rest of us.

"You are Gavlin Fleet. The American snowboarder who won gold at Olympics in Scochi this year," she said, completely shocked. I glanced over to see his picture on the iPad screen; the gold metal adorned his neck with an American flag draped on his shoulders while he stood on the Olympic podium. She then looked over the top of the screen to make eye contact with the live version only three feet away from her.

My first thought was, "Oh great, this is not what we need." His name was undoubtedly linked with ours on the international fugitives list, and if these people mumbled a word of our existence, our names would be back on the radar.

Unable to deny the accusation and probably unaware it was a real issue, Gavlin responded, "Glad it took you this long to notice. I've been tryin' to lay low."

"Mum? Pop? Do ye remember watching that snowboarder on the tele at the Olympics, who beat everyone? This is him!" she excitedly said, pointing to Gavlin.

"What would be the chances?" the mother replied and turned around in her La-Z-Boy recliner-like passenger seat. "They allowed an Olympic medalist with yer status to travel alone?" She sounded less confused and more concerned with the abnormal situation.

"I've been working really hard the past few years, and I just needed to take a break. Lay low and hang out with these normal people. We decided if I got out of the country, it would be hard for anyone to find me. The family knows to keep it quiet," he again added to our story. I hoped she would buy it.

The mother skeptically bought the story. Her husband, on the other hand, was too concentrated on maneuvering this vehicle that he was obviously not comfortable driving down a desolate Irish highway, to be concerned. Haley wasted no time and snatched her Nikon camera, plus a permanent maker, notebook, and blue athletic bag in one frantic trip to the back of the RV.

"Can you sign these, and can I have a picture with you? My mates are never going to believe I met you. I wish I had a picture for you to sign or a Olympic poster or anything else," she rattled off without taking a breath.

"Give the camera to Devon," he said standing up to switch places with me and sat down next to Haley, who practically started to hyperventilate. He first took the marker from her and signed her bag and notebook with a couple of pages of signatures to her friends. He seemed pleased to be at the center of the attention, which was not a surprise to me.

"Picture time!" he exclaimed, setting down the other things on the ground and wrapping his arm around her shoulder.

In shock, she managed a huge smile for the camera.

Before I could ready the large photography camera, Falon said, "Would you like to take your hair down as you had it earlier? It looks nice now, though I figure you will be showing these pictures to everyone, and it looks beautiful down."

"Oh, thank you. I woulda forgotten, and then I woulda looked at the pictures and been disappointed. Thank yeh." She pulled her hair down and arranged the waves down her shoulders.

"Smile." I focused the camera and took a couple of photographs. After looking through them to make sure there was a decent one, I handed the camera back to Haley. She promptly set it in a camera case next to her feet.

"Where is yer gold medal? Do ye get to keep it?" Haley asked.

"At my house where my parents, um, live." To those of us who understood his hesitation, I could see his gaze drop down as he tried to push away the recent tragedies plaguing all of our lives.

"Was it…I mean were ye really nervous standing there the second time because yeh had fallen the first time? Everyone said ye were never going to do it and…" Haley continued to throw questions at Gavlin, who sat slouched back on the couch as if he had been asked these questions a million times. Just another interview.

"Everyone knew me before the Olympics as the kid with some recent wins, and I know people expected the guys with more experience to win. I got off that first run, and my parents were at the bottom with a disappointed look but tryin' to pretend it was fine. I was pissed because I'd worked years to get there, and they'd given up a lot to get me there. I knew I'd have to land the run I planned to use only if scores were runnin' high. I don't remember ever being so angry with myself. I remember ignoring everyone at the top before ı dropped in. The rest you saw."

"Uh-huh," Haley said. She had run out of obvious questions, but the look on her face indicated there were a few more lingering in her mind.

"You can ask me anything," he prompted her.

"Ask if he has a girlfriend. That is all I want to know about celebrity guys," Falon chimed in coyly, causing Haley to turn bright red.

Laughing it off and loving the attention, Gavlin continued with, "Are you sure you don't work for the tabloids, Falon? No, not enough time. For the right girl, I'd work it out," he said, smirking, a look I knew was for me. I could not help looking at Rowan. He never missed nuances, much like his sister. His jaw line tightened as his green eyes burrowed into Gavlin relaxing on the coach.

"It is not really what I wanted to know," Haley said, and then tried to move away from the slightly uncomfortable situation. "Do you have friends who are not famous?"

"Yeah. Couple guys from back home. They keep me normal, and I knew them before, so it's nice to chill with them."

Waving her hand to catch his attention, Riley signed very slowly for Gavlin, "*Gavlin, I bet lots of girls want to be your girlfriend because you're a celebrity.*"

"I caught my name and "girls" because those are clearly important things in the world. Oh, and *food* and *snow*," he joked while signing the last two words.

"She said girls want to be your girlfriend because you are famous." I was starting to get good at filling in the blanks when I could.

"How do you sign 'Only a couple hundred'?" Gavlin asked Riley, who giggled at the statement.

"How does she understand if ye are not motioning with yer hands?" Haley asked.

"Riley reads lips, if you just talk normal and face her."

"That is cool." She looked toward Riley to talk.

"*Thanks. Where is your family from?*"

"Where is your family from?" Rowan interpreted, speaking for the first time since we'd left over an hour ago.

"We just moved to Liverpool for my pop's job transfer. I don't 'ave a clue to how long we'll be there before another move."

"Hell, fer all we know, he will drag us to the middle of bloody Africa into a civil war," Elijah snarled without turning around.

"He is just angry he is on this trip with the family instead of going to a concert," Haley commented.

"At least the trip back to your old house to see friends is short and not a return from Zimbabwe. That would be quite an RV trip," I said, trying to lighten the mood.

"I would burn this bloody thingamajig to the ground before going anywhere in it again," Elijah said, eyes glazed over, staring at the computer screen, concentrating on the game before him.

"What are you playing?" I asked.

"Ye would have not an idea. It is the only game I can play that's wireless."

"He has been playing it since we left our home," said Haley.

"What have you been up to in this motor home, since you left?" Gavlin asked.

chapter 25

"Where will we find yer family?" the father called back to us after a lengthy three hours I had no desire to ever repeat in my life.

Rowan was the first to speak up. "They are staying at the Hilton in the downtown area. I understand if you don't want to maneuver the motor home downtown. We'll be able to walk, and I can call them when we stop."

"We are planning a visit to Phoenix Park in Dublin. We can stop on the north side for ye."

"Sounds great. Thanks for the ride here. Our family will be very appreciative. Would I be able to see your map to have an idea of where they'll drive to pick us up?" Rowan inquired, eyeing the large folding map the mother had spread in front of her as we neared the interior of Dublin. Personally, I was a fan of iPads and electronic maps due to my nature to fail epically at reading anything without a self-locating option and turn-by-turn directions. Rowan seemed to have no issues scanning the crumpled map passed back to him.

263

"Thanks," he said and correctly folded and passed the map back toward the front passenger seat.

The RV took a bit of a wild turn to the right, narrowly managing not to take out the cars in the other lane and sending all of us in the back struggling to keep our seats. These buses are not meant for someone without a good grasp of space perception, and how a thirty-five-foot vehicle is engineered to turn. I was elated we would not have to travel into the center of Dublin any farther. Pedestrian death appeared imminent if such action were pursued. We hit the next left curb, sending a basket of fruit on the counter flying into the aisle and a collective grimace on a couple of faces. We only started picking up a few rouge oranges and mangled bananas from the floor when the bus took another wild right turn, sending Riley, who was bent over on the floor, flying to the ground. Riley eventually picked her self up, rubbing her hip and scrunching her face up from the pain that comes with being sent to the ground. Additionally, I was slammed into the back of the poorly padded couch as the momentum rocked backward.

"Enjoy the wedding. The best to the bride and groom!" the father called from the driver seat, still not concerned that his driving was bound to wreck some vehicle or person in the near future. His wife, on the other hand, was white-knuckled, hanging onto the armrests of her passenger seat lounge chair.

Collecting my backpack and following Riley down the couple of stairs, we all waved good-bye prior to being dumped onto the sidewalk in Dublin. The narrow street was lined with small homes of a beige or brown variety, indicating our presence in a residential area a couple miles from the hub of the city. We watched the door of the motor home slam, the retractable steps creak inward, and heard the whooshing release of the air brakes and an unsettling, grinding sound as the Magic Bus pulled away from the curb. Haley pulled up on the window blinds and waved to us. Enthusiastically waving back at the thin windows, we were all still dumbstruck at how we managed to snag that ride across Ireland. Regardless, I watched as the exhaust poured out the back, and the bus made a lurching turn left only to hit the curb once more. I grimaced thinking about the suspension, which I am sure would be the least of their problems when the engine finally blew up, its warning screams silenced by a missing bulb in the jacket pocket of the person standing to my left. By then, we could only hope they were in the next county and we were in the next country.

"I am not anticipating the walk I am about to endure in the next two minutes," Falon commented. She had since given up on the fact she had not showered in days, but remained concerned with fixing what details she could of her appearance in the reflective surface of a parked car.

"I have no clue what walk we're in for. Ask Rowan. He's the only one who looked at the map," I answered.

"About eight kilometers to the shore."

"A little shy of five miles," I said, doing the quick conversion in my head.

"I'm not even going to ask why you'd know that," Gavlin remarked.

"I like numbers?" I replied, considering that most people would probably have to use some Internet-based research for such information.

"And that will take how long?" Falon questioned.

"If you want to run it, forty at a slow pace. Walking, a little over an hour."

Downtown Dublin was a nice change from some of the larger cities. Nevertheless, we were still playing a guessing game as to where and how we were planning to swim across the Irish Sea to Britain. From the number of tourists to locals, we were clearly not traveling during a high season, which we knew would not work to our advantage. Less people meant less ability to hide. So far, we appeared to be in no real danger. The corporation organizing our manhunt obviously lost us somewhere between the private plane, horses, and motor home ride across Ireland. I feared as we closed in on The Hague, there were only so many paths to place guards and even fewer ways to physically get to the international safety of The Hague.

Inside a small Irish souvenir store, we asked an older gentleman propped on a wooden stool behind the counter if he could point us toward the port where we could catch a boat to the UK. His response was a little muddled and, as interpreted by Gavlin and me, we just needed to head down the road to the left, and we would see some signs. I think he said a couple of ferries could take us to the UK.

Riley spotted the first sign for the Holyhead Ferry as she skipped ahead of us, turning backward occasionally to wait before continuing down Upper Sheriff Street. It was a relief because I feared even Gavlin might have reached the point where he would have beat a certain someone over the head for complaining. We all sympathized that five more miles was too much walking, but unfortunately the cash stash was numbered.

A cruise ship-sized ferry waited ominously, her white sides reflecting the few rays of sun coming through the generally overcast sky in the harbor, and rocking slightly as the waves rolled into the port and climbed up the retaining walls before subsequently descending back into the dark ocean. On the other side of a large building labeled "Stena Line," the ferry company with a monopoly on all trips between the Irish Sea and English Channel, cars waited in lines to be consumed by the open belly of the ferry. Walking into the building, we found ourselves looking at a fairly open commercial space with a stretch of desks. Receptionists catered to the needs of the few individuals waiting between stretches of rope lines. We stopped at the end of a line behind a young couple and their two children. The children were both near the age of four and were more interested in running under the ropes forming the physical barriers of the lines than anything else. I looked up at the times available for our upcoming ferry journey. It was currently 18:47. The next ferry departed at 19:30 for Hardwich, Britain. For the second time toady, we were winning after the epic fail this morning. At this point, it was all about enjoying the little wins. Then, I saw the cost. It would cost a total of around 161 euros, or 210 dollars. Forking over the final bit of cash we had would be suicidal, considering we still needed to make it from Britain to the Netherlands. The losses for the day were definitely out numbering the wins now.

"Where is the last of the cash?" Rowan asked me.

"We'll have just barely enough. Once we use the rest of it, we are out and stuck a couple of hundred miles from The Hague."

Riley had already reached in her lightweight backpack to pull out a couple of the euro bills I told her to keep in case we were separated. Falon chimed in, "I do not believe there is any other option at this point in our travels, Devon."

I hated being pushed into a corner without any sort of semi-logical rebuttal. "I just hope we will have some of our earlier luck leftover," I said, skeptically.

Gavlin inserted himself into our conversation. "Guys, I might have an option." He pulled a credit card out of his pocket.

"Explanation?" I questioned, a bit displeased at how he managed to have a credit card this entire time, without our knowledge.

"I kept it after Zermatt. We could use it."

"And become instant bait?" I realized how much I had raised my voice after the fact.

"Don't blow a gasket on me." He put his hands up in the air, palms flat toward me, as if fending off an attack.

Riley jumped her way into the conversation and stated, "*Use it now. We can use the cash later. There is a better chance to escape in England than near The Hague.*"

"See what I am sayin'?" Gavlin emphasized.

"No. All I see is a solution to my problem that just causes a larger one." I refused to accept the idea that this could end our trip prematurely when the end was only a hop and a skip away.

"The tag is on Gavlin. We can split," Rowan said, accepting the newest idea.

"The tag is on all of us. You forget we come as a nice match set after the last few days. The likelihood it is disabled is high as well," I chimed in.

"They would keep it on to track us. It's now or later, you said," Rowan rebutted, glaring straight at me as I stood with my arms crossed in front of my chest.

Falon bent over to block the space between us. "You two have approximately twelve seconds to decide because we need to make this ferry in less than thirty minutes."

"Twelve centuries might not be enough time. What's one more risk?" Gavlin walked from the circle, with Falon following, and straight to the black desk, where a middle-aged woman waited to assist them. The two of us stood for a couple of seconds longer until I turned to join them at the desk. Eventually, Rowan stepped behind me near the front service desk. If they came after us, he was going under the bus first.

Since we were passengers without a car, tickets were simple to obtain, and Gavlin passed off Riley and me as under sixteen, which worked fine. Taking into account we were using a credit card, price did not appear terribly significant. As she took the card from him and prepared to swipe it through the computer, my senses went on instant high alert. As soon as the card's magnetic strip card hit the card reader, I was ready for red flashing police lights and blaring sirens to come flying down from the ceiling. What was more likely to happen was rejection of the credit card for some type of hold, and a warning on the computer screen in bolded blinking red lettering that would send the unsuspecting women rushing toward the back room with a reason to have the police detain and arrest us. Before my delusions could occur, she smiled and handed the card back to Gavlin, along with five printed boarding passes for the ferry departing to Holyhead. They were currently boarding passengers.

With Riley eyeing the tickets, Gavlin was more than happy to hand them over and allow her to rush ahead of the group in her normal fashion. He fell back in the group with me as we headed out a couple of glass doors to the port.

"You're so tense," Gavlin said, reaching over to me. At the same time, I instinctively ducked down and ran a couple of steps outside of his reach.

"I'm fine."

"You're sure tense. The two of you are great to watch. I hate ending tense situations between you two," he joked to my un-amused facial expression.

"Yeah, funny. We are almost there." I hoped.

chapter 26

Our luxury ferry anchored at the Holyhead port in England, a little over two hours after departing from Ireland. The sun had only set about a half hour before we arrived, casting striking orange and furious red rays across the choppy waves of the Irish channel. For the duration of the trip, we situated ourselves at a nice table alongside the floor-to-ceiling windows just under the top deck, soaking up the passing of another day and the sand in our hourglass running lower. Tomorrow would have to be the last push toward The Hague. By the time the ferry landed on UK soil, we were an anxious mess from the realization that our pursuers would likely be awaiting us on the other side. As soon as the doors opened, there was no telling what or where a trap could be set. This round would be won by who could make the first move. I vowed for it to be us. Still, sitting and waiting for the ferry to be properly anchored to her home-port in Britain, there was absolute silence. Rowan paced, Falon dazed outside, Riley moved the zippers around on my backpack, Gavlin stared outside while tapping his foot, and I resorted to examining my non-existent nails. Ideas about what we planned to do were flowing as fast as a dried up riverbed in the desert. Logically, there were only so many ways on and off the ferry. Unlike the plane, I had yet to find an emergency exit with a bouncy slide. The ferry had a simple layout, though the sheer size of the ship left enormous numbers of smaller hiding places, staircases, and doorways. There were only so many exits: one for larger vehicles, and a handful for guests on foot. I had no plans to stay on this ferry any longer than necessary. Then an idea came to me.

"Follow me," I said, motioning to the group as I took off at a half-jogging pace toward the back staircase. I had not heard mention of any other ideas, and we were too low on time for explanations, not to mention possible unwanted and unneeded rejection of my plan by a certain someone. I knew from the layout of the ferry printed on a poster on the main deck, where we were headed. There was one place they would not be expecting us. Landing off the last flight of stairs at the very bottom of the ship, I threw open a metal door to reveal the hull of the ferry. Stashed carefully in the hull were various cars, buses, and trucks waiting in a giant, floating underground parking garage. Most people were in their cars, while a few were mulling around on the outside and waiting for the ship to open her hull and release her cargo onto solid land. Off to the left side of the cavernous space, I noticed a couple of workers in uniform chatting and waiting for the signal to start directing traffic out. My plan was to just hang around with the passengers below and sneak out between the vehicles when the door opened. The likelihood our "friends" would expect us to depart with all the cars below was lower, but not impossible, considering who we were dealing with. Rowan, on the contrary, had a different idea, always attempting to outdo me. I was unaware of his thoughts before he said something rapidly to Riley and whispered something to Falon, before they both took off at a determined pace toward the ferry workers.

"I hope one of you two can drive a manual," he said to Gavlin and me.

"I can," Gavlin answered.

"My car at home is an old manual," I said.

"Even better. You two are driving." He snuck off toward Falon and Riley.

"We missed the plan," Gavlin said, looking over at me.

"Guess the invitation was lost at sea. I swear he is going to get us all killed if we have no idea what's happening. I suppose we'll stay over here and make it look like we are busy and waiting for someone."

"I think this is where we're splitting."

"I would say that's a fair judgment."

I saw Gavlin light up with a little bit of a grin. He faced the direction the other three had taken off to. "Thank god that Falon is hot, and Riley has innocent down."

"Great...what are they doing now?"

"The usual, using the girls as bait." It was definitely not the first time this act had been used. "Riley and Falon are distracting the two workers. Riley looks to be writing something down, and Falon looks to be flirting with them. The one is young enough to fall for it, and the other is like old and wicked creepy."

"Not sure how I feel about that." I desperately wanted to turn around, although I understood it would only draw unwanted attention in their direction.

"And Rowan found some type of rack behind the counter. Looks like keys?" Gavlin strained to look.

"They probably transport cars for people."

"I give him credit. We have rides. I hope he checked for some nice ones before just grabbing anything. I want a Roadster."

"This is not what I had in mind. For all we know, those cars are going to be jammed against a wall, and instead of actually getting out of here, we are going to be a bunch of carless, dead ducks," I said in time to have Rowan stride up and shove a pair of keys in both of our hands. I was hoping he'd heard.

"These two are parked on the outside," Rowan instructed.

"And exactly what is the plan?" I threw out.

"We drive into the sunset toward the Netherlands," Gavlin joked, obviously thinking this was as far as we needed to think.

"No. We talked about splitting up, and from the map in the ferry there are two routes to the Netherlands by ferry. One from Harwich and the other from the north at…Hull, I believe. There will be no time to stop once we get outside this ferry because I am almost certain they are going to be waiting. If they do not find us here, they will be anticipating us at either place, but more likely Harwich, because it is the most direct route. We need to have a head start on them if we are going to make it ahead of their convoy," I summed up for them.

"We take both routes. The less anticipated and shorter route is to Hull. We send some of us to Hull, to alarm the system without any of the documents. The others to Harwich," Rowan offered.

"So, theoretically, your plan hinges on the fact that the other group makes it on the road. How can you guarantee that? If they don't, the plan is not even going to come close to working," I disputed.

"A risk we have to take," Rowan replied.

"I still think we should leave together."

"Um, won't we need two cars to split?" Gavlin inquired.

"Better to get one later that they do not have the plate and identification for, unlike if we take two here," I argued.

"I'll let you break into the other one then," Rowan said. I never thought of it; still, my plan was as risky as his.

"Who'll be there first to the Netherlands?" Gavlin asked.

"If I've calculated correctly, the group from Hull will have a longer ferry trip in the morning, which gives the other group time to get into the Netherlands before they expect us. Hopefully, both groups will be able to make it out of the chaos," I explained.

"So, the riskier port is what?"

"Harwich," both Rowan and I said, simultaneously.

I continued to say, "The security will more likely be there because it is the most logical choice. The key is that the group at Hull will be at the British port first to give those guys at Harwich time to hopefully board the ferry. Harwich also runs the risk of having all the paperwork, while the others will be caught empty-handed and therefore without any legal reason to detain them."

"Then, my car is headed to Harwich," Gavlin insisted.

I was more than fine with allowing Gavlin to walk the line of fire. I was just more upset than anything that I would not be with him. Prior to any rebuttal, Rowan added a change to the plans. "Gavlin, you are heading to Hull. You have international coverage with your status. If you're caught, it'll be too hard for them to detain you without evidence. They'll let you go, and whoever is with you, to avoid the media."

Gavlin was not pleased, yet he had nothing to counter the valid point Rowan had made. Surprisingly, I could not take his side either. If we were going to guarantee safety for the most people, this had to be the way, despite how much I was not in agreement. "We send Riley and Falon with him, as well. The less people with me the better, because I want more people alive than not if something goes wrong," I said.

"You two are going to kill each other," was all Gavlin could manage to say, swiveling his eyes between the two of us.

"Not if they kill us first," I regretted saying. I was not trying to dwell on the grim future facing us outside the metal walls of the ferry's hull; it is just that it was already knocking.

Gavlin just sighed. "Where are the other two?"

"I told them to look for a 'lost phone' and to stay together. They know the plan. Signal them when the car is ready to move."

"Riley has some cash, but take this," I said, reaching into my bag. I grabbed a handful of bills and handed them to Gavlin. "This should be plenty for you all to get tickets. Get to The Hague. It is sovereign, international territory. Okay?" I gave him the best advice I could in this situation. Seconds later, I heard the creaking of metal from the hull opening her berth, the night sky entering the well-lit interior, and car engines roaring to life.

Gavlin reached over and gave me one of his warm hugs that lasted much longer than a quick goodbye; it was not supposed to be forever. I guess none of us really knew at this point. Pulling away, I took one last look at those yellow eyes, with the exotic combination of olive skin, and tried to remember the details not just of his face, but the goofy smile to match his easygoing personality and the way he thrived on any type of challenge.

"See you at The Hague when we're laughing our asses off at those people who tried to stop five teenagers from destroying a country," he smirked.

"Yep," was all I could manage. We hugged one last time, and both ran off. Gavlin jogged between a row of cars, and I was left to find my copilot for the upcoming five-hour drive to Harwich. And I thought the three hours from Boyle to Dublin was long. This could be a bloodbath.

Cars were slowly making their way down the ramp from the ship. I knew we would be moving soon so I started to scan the crowd more diligently for Rowan. I glanced down at the keys in my hand to see the logo for Ford. When I looked back up, Rowan was standing one row of cars to my right. He quickly explained something to both of the other girls, waited as Falon forcibly gave him a hug, and then grabbed Riley in an embrace. I raced toward them hoping to say good-bye. Falon was already in tears when I arrived. I quickly gave her a hug, which she returned, sniffling and delicately wiping her eyes. Afterward, Riley latched on to me, tears streaming down her face. Eventually, I knew I had to let her go. There was only a miniscule amount of comfort in the fact that I was leaving them with someone I knew would take a bullet for any of us. Riley kept pushing her sleeve up to her face to wipe away her tears and the wisps of hair sticking to her face.

"I love you," I signed with my right hand in a type of universal symbol that she returned. She ran to her brother one last time and, immediately following, we were forced to split. They took off to the right, where I saw Gavlin beckoning them to hurry from the right side of a little, red compact car. The space behind him was open, and he clearly could not afford to wait much longer.

Spinning around to Rowan, I said, "We have a Ford; you know which one?"

"Hit the unlock button."

Doing as he asked, I pressed the button in hopes that maybe a large neon sign would drop from the ceiling and point me in the correct direction.

"That one," he said indicating to something behind me. He raced around me.

It was an American-made car, but the wheel was on the right side. This was going to be a new challenge, and I could only hope that

277

the route southeast would be composed of straight highway roads. Given the opportunity, I would be back on the wrong, right side of the road. Inside the burnt-red, compact Ford Fiesta I inserted the key, started the engine, and adjusted the seat and mirrors quickly. To my relief, the gas tank was around three-quarters full, and with luck the other car would be the same. Looking in my rearview mirrors, I noticed there was enough room behind and in front of me to treat this like a bad case of parallel parking.

I threw the car in reverse, backed within inches of the car behind me, cranked the wheel to the left, and drove forward. It took a few rounds of shifting back and forth until enough space had been made to just turn the wheel to the left and drive straight forward in the gap between a row of parked cars and the wall. I quickly shifted back to reverse. Alternating gazes between three mirrors, I flew backward knowing I could back a car up pretty quickly and efficiently. After passing about half a dozen cars, we came to the end of the row. I whipped the rear of the miniature Fiesta between another car and the wall, aiming finally in a forward direction toward the exit.

Everything was moving smoothly, and my gut told me it would be short-lived. Lo and behold, I eyed two guys showing badges to the ferry attendants on duty, who were directing cars onto the brightly lit port. To the naïve eye, they appeared to be just undercover cops. I knew in an instant, though, that they were not. They were after us, whether it be the English popo or hired guns. Both men began to stop cars as they passed through, having them roll down the windows and open large trunks. My first thought was in regard to the other three. In an ideal world, they had escaped with the earlier cars and were already cruising the open highways northbound. Regardless, there was little we could do for them. The only exit for cars was down a one-and-a-half-car-wide ramp to the port, which passed directly through the two men and others originally hired to direct traffic. I considered the possibility of squeezing next to another departing car, in our clown car, but with the stop-and-go nature of the traffic, we would be stuck at some point. Additionally, the large tour buses and shipping trucks farther up would no doubt stop our progress. The only way to effectively avoid the issue would be to create enough space between the guards and me to guarantee a modified exit. I noticed the way the traffic guard stood fairly far away from the exit ramp, while directing the multiple lanes of traffic into an orderly, single-file line of vehicles.

chapter 27

"I know how to drive a stick; just do not say anything," I made clear to Rowan, as I joined a couple of other cars waiting their turn to become part of the straight exit line.

Since the two men in search of us had arrived, three others had joined them and were helping to search additional cars. The process still remained slow. As the car second in our line, I eyed what the intersection of cars looked to be. There were two lines off to my right side. The traffic director from the ferry stood between all three lines, waving cars as he saw fit to keep the lines equal and prevent too much congestion farther back in the hold. He would wait a couple of minutes until the single line at the checkpoint was three cars long before allowing other cars to add to the line. Soon it was our turn. There were three cars in the exit line, and we would be the second people to add to the line. He waved to the car in our line, and those of us following, to commence our exit. The first car rolled smoothly forward, taking its time to make it toward the front. A green van at security could be seen bounding down the ramp after successful completion of the security examination. Showtime.

Grinding the gears in our car as I falsely pretend to be clueless about the manual transmission, I slowly made a wide and sweeping left-hand turn. When I calculated our position to be far enough forward to block every lane of traffic, I completely stalled the car. It came to a slow, stalled halt, and I put on the most shocked and confused facial expression. I attempted to re-shift back into neutral and act as if I had pretty much no clue in the world as to what I was doing. I stomped on the clutch and the gas, and pulled the shifter back at the precisely wrong time in order to keep us from budging an inch. The attendant was clearly annoyed with my poor driving, which was delaying his process that had once moved smoothly and efficiently. He continued to boldly wave me forward before finally noticing I was struggling to restart my engine. Instead of offering to help, he just stood his ground. I silently thanked him. It was exactly how I wanted him to be: not helpful, which would help my escape plan. I looked past Rowan out the passenger seat to see there were still two cars being searched. Thankfully, the searches had slowed down traffic so that when cars exited onto the port and were forced to drive around a large, red-brick building, there was no congestion.

"Hurry up," I mumbled under my breath, fiddling around, but starting the engine to a quiet hum. "Hold on. If you believe in any type of God, now would be a good time to pray to him," I advised Rowan. One car left.

I shifted the car into first, spinning the wheel to straighten her out with the narrow ramp. The guards had just opened the trunk of the last vehicle in the exit line. Satisfied we were not stowed away in the pint-sized trunk of a sedan, the guard slammed it closed with a forceful push of both hands. The force reverberated throughout the car, and he signaled to his comrade near the driver's window to release the car. And then, I took off. With the newer clutch, the manual shifted much smoother than I was accustomed to with my car at home, which only stayed in the gear I wanted if it was in the mood. Locked in a lower gear, I was ready to see how much our Ford Fiesta could manage. The tires faintly squealed against the concrete as we zipped past the signaling man; the look of his face read nothing short of bewilderment as he jumped back. I would not have hit him anyway. Bearing down with only a couple hundred feet before the guards, I had no plans of slowing down. Foot on the accelerator and hands tightly on the wheel, my vision tunneled to include only what lay directly in front of me. The last car was just bounding down the ramp, where I knew it would turn slightly to the left and around the brick building dead ahead. The guards obviously took notice of the stunt I was pulling and jumped out in front of me as soon as they heard the tires squeal and the whirr of an engine not designed for this type of beating. Desperate times called for a lack of morals. I just kept going, knowing I would have to anticipate the limited space from the car not far in front of us. The car was more a concern, the people not as much; people are logical, and instinct would tell their bodies to back away from a speeding car.

Time slowed as we raced toward them. The only two people dumb enough to stay out in the open were two of the private security men. Then I saw one of them reach for a gun. My foot never came off the pedal as I kept honing in on them. Fortunately for their lives, they jumped to the side. With a light "thump," I tagged one on the left corner with only enough force to maybe leave a broken bone or two and some bruising. Shaking with adrenaline and fear, I heard the crack only a bullet leaving the barrel of a gun could make. As a large, close target, it was no surprise when the ping of at least one bullet made contact with the rear of our car. The tires were still intact, and it sounded like the worst damage was a suspicious hole in the back trunk. The unsettling bump down onto the ramp would have ground out the front of a car with any lower suspension, and I quickly downshifted before sliding slightly as we careened left around the unforgiving brick of the near building. My hands were death-gripped on the lower part of the steering wheel, only leaving momentarily to shift the car. Never in its life did any little Ford Fiesta expect to be pounded to death in this manner. I could see the bright brake lights of the white Volkswagen off to right side of the thin path that exited on to the main road. Without an illuminated blinker nor the option of heading straight, the driver clearly had not a clue where to go. Not waiting, I threw the car as far as I could to the left, narrowly missing our friend by inches, and swung out in front of the Volkswagen to make a right on the main road without taking the time to look for the headlights of oncoming traffic. It was not a central road in the city, and I hoped the speed limits around here would allow an oncoming car to stop before careening into me. Luckily, the man in the nearest car was far enough away to slam on his brakes, as I flew out and gunned it away from the port. My headlights soon became the primary source of light, and I was outdriving them.

"I told you I can drive," I had to remark to Rowan as we sped excessively down the road. Between choosing roads to turn down and looking out for other traffic, I kept compulsively checking my rearview mirrors for signs of flashing police lights in the black night. The first turn I could make to the right, I took. We raced alongside uniform, stucco dark-colored housing complexes with cars parked on the side of road, often occupying space on top of the curb. Speeding along narrow English streets, obeying the whole left-side-of–the-road rule and the fact that the headlights were not illuminating the road as quickly as our shadow could catch it, made this all incredibly challenging. Still seeing no flashing lights after a couple of more right-handed turns and a left, I slowed our pace to what I though would be a bit more normal, and attempted to blend in with the few cars on the road at this hour. During the adrenaline rush, I had been failing quite epically at driving on the correct side of the road. Now, I really needed to blend before some pedestrian decided to report my reckless driving. After the relentless pounding I had done to the car's engine and to my own heart, I took a deep breath, unaware I had been holding it a majority of the time. While I knew there were no lights trailing our path, I continued to compulsively check my side mirrors, ready to take off at the slightest sign of trouble.

"There is A55. Take that," Rowan directed, obviously remembering the route from the maps we had perused during the ferry trip.

Once on the four-lane highway, it was open territory lined by large shrubs on the side of the road. I set the cruise control at one hundred twenty kph. As long as we were not pulled over for speeding, I had a feeling the international powers of the private guns were not capable of having the British police devote itself to a full-scale manhunt for us, without too many questions.

"You should have found me a BMW or something." I attempted to start a conversation, knowing that it would be a long four to five hours, and the chance of finding anything on the radio was slim.

"The way you drive, I thought you would've killed a couple of those people, or us." I realized he had turned to face me when he talked instead of his normal staring straight ahead. Figures, since I needed to watch the road.

"I wasn't even close. At least this one is a newer car, which makes life a little easier to shift and control."

"How many speeding tickets do you have in that red racecar you own?"

"A couple, maybe. And I never told you that it was red."

"Just a guess."

"You guessed correctly. So do we have a map or anything?"

"I have an idea, but we should stop if you see somewhere," he said confidently and unconcerned.

"Glad someone besides me will be reading the maps. I rely strictly on navigation systems and the "Where am I?" button on my iPhone. Best invention ever. Being stranded without it ended badly last time for me."

"They only work well with reception," he added, to play the devil's advocate.

"I am going to guess that the mountains aren't very reception friendly when you are driving your pickup truck around." I took a guess as to his car, knowing he did not drive a manual and he lived in the mountains.

"Yes to both."

"I am awesome," I mocked him.

"Don't get too full of yourself." He reminded me how much we both pushed each other's buttons to prove who was the more knowledgeable one. I glanced over to catch him looking straight at me with those green eyes that had taken on a little bit more life since we'd first left. Beyond the death of his father and our life-threatening journey, the real Rowan was finally showing. It was still the same stubborn, to-the-point Rowan. Maybe in the next four hours, I would be able get something out of him. People always say "stay close to your friends and even closer to your enemies." As

I turned my eyes back to the open road, I considered the fact that maybe enemies, like in those old spy movies, always become something more than just two rivals.

I glanced at the electronic clock near the radio. We had been driving for roughly three hours, including our stop to check a map. It was 1:20 in the morning, and we were still careening along M6 outside of Coventry. At least that was what the last sign, a few minutes ago, stated. Despite my usual ability to stay functional on minimal amounts of sleep, my body was objecting to the fact that I was concentrating on the monotone road ahead of me at this hour, and after a lot of stress and a couple hours of walking. Not even the moon illuminated the road, and we were without the company of any other headlights. The world slept quietly. I bit the inside of my mouth to see if the sharp pain would arouse my body to keep my fluttering eyes from closing.

"Either you need to keep punching me awake, or we need to stop before I kill us." I broke the pleasant silence we had fallen into about thirty minutes prior.

"The first ferry doesn't leave until morning. We should stop," Rowan offered, without staging any opposition.

"I wish these roads had more ways to get off," I yawned.

He looked out the window to concentrate on finding any signs anchored along the high-speed roadway. "A426 is up a few kilometers."

"Hopefully, there'll be nothing more than a small town. We'll pull off, and I'll park." I was glad to have the option of sleep, regardless of how short, in the near future.

A couple of miles later, I was able to exit off toward the left and circle back around to a road on the southern side of the highway.

I noticed a fair amount of lights and what looked to be a town in the distance. On the other hand, my rearview mirrors showed a smaller road without any nearby signs of life behind us. We needed to lay low, so I scanned the road for any oncoming headlights before pulling a bat turn in order to head over a bridge to the much quieter side of the highway. The overgrown trees encroached on the narrow road. A few homes were spread along the road in the first kilometer, their front lights illuminating only a couple of hundred feet. I kept moving until open grassy fields and deciduous green trees surrounded us. I pulled the car off to the left, testing to make sure the ground was not damp from the constant overcast and rainy spring weather of the English countryside. The tires did not sink down. I pulled completely onto the low shoulder and put the car in park. I looked over to Rowan with my raccoon, bloodshot eyes, and he returned my gaze.

"I'll stay awake," he offered. The risk of parking a car in a ditch in the countryside and receiving questions from the locals was legitimate.

"Thanks. Wake me at four o'clock so we can be in Harwich no later than seven o'clock." I was proud of myself for being able to subtract three from seven, in my current state.

Rowan nodded and I looked to the back seat, deciding that if I only had two hours to fall into one cycle of sleep, at least I was going to stretch out on the back seat. Instead of opening the door and walking around, I pulled my feet to my chest and planned to climb over the thin console straight into the back seat. I paused, still propped up on the balls of my feet, with my one hand balanced on the center console.

"Did you really mean what you said on the plane?" I blurted.

"What plane?"

"When you said you didn't want me to get hurt. Do you really think Gavlin would do that, after all of this?"

"No. I don't think he would. I think you'd do it to yourself. You're the person who traps all of their real emotions. This trip will be the breaking point."

"How would you know?"

"Because when you're stuck in the same place, you're the only one who knows what is actually going on. I locked you out because I couldn't let you in. It would destroy the way I handle my life."

"If this is going to be my breaking point, then what about you?"

"I'm not sure. That's why you scare me."

"It's always nice to have a little company. Maybe in a few days we'll both be ready to accept that."

I jumped into the back seat before he had the chance to shut me out. Laying down and looking at the seat with my back to him, I fell asleep without any real time to consider what he said.

chapter 28

Four a.m. came entirely too early when I heard Rowan's voice beckon me to wake up. The sky was not any lighter than when I had drifted off the sleep, making me want to curl back up and bury my head in the dark seat. My neck and left shoulder were not appreciative of my awkward sleeping situation, which included indentations from seat belts digging into my back.

"You might be better off dozing in the passenger seat," I mumbled while attempting to stretch the knots out of my back and shoulders. As I had done last night, I pulled myself over the center console and into the driver's seat. A couple yawns later and with the realization we would be on the road for three more hours, I buckled up and wondered if Starbucks had yet to reach the country roads of rural England.

"Right about now…" Rowan remarked at 6:30, after a long stretch in silence that had defined my morning. He had not slept a wink since we had hit the highway for the final leg.

"Now what?"

"They should be ticketed and boarded on the ferry to Holland."

"I am sure Gavlin can handle the situation. Well, maybe not the immature and misguided youth he is, but at least we sent Beauty and the Brainchild. With the celebrity status added in, that should cover any situation."

And silence. I attempted to revive the conversation. "After we jump onto another form of transportation, make a mad dash to The Hague, take down a national government, and finally sit down for a feast complete with celebratory Portillo's chocolate cake and vanilla ice cream, how do you plan to continue on with life as we now know it to be?"

"I'm surprised you can think past ten seconds into the future."

"Hey, I am just holding onto the thread of sanity that tells me some part of normalcy will return. On the contrary, living this way is going to make everything else appear hopelessly boring."

"You'll be happy for consistency, again," he said before displaying what looked like a different version of the sign for "horse."

"What was that supposed to mean?"

"It's obvious."

"It is not polite to talk with your hands if I can't understand a word you're saying."

"Failing as a student." I saw the first mocking grin since we'd started our banter.

"I've only had like four days. And you have had what, fourteen years, to master sign language?"

"Ten."

"Wait…but that would have made her four," I stated. "If she was four, why did she not talk?"

"Even with a powerful implant she was not going to hear. Instead of wanting to keep "fixing" her like some people wanted, it was a new way of life. She went to a school for the deaf, learned ASL, and became a part of Deaf culture," he plainly stated before adding, "She doesn't speak, unless she has to, but she went to speech therapy and can speak."

"Why not around us?"

"Why should she have to speak our language?" he replied.

"Regardless, to convince a four-year-old girl her life was no longer the same had to have been no easy endeavor."

"The seven-year-old was more of the problem at the time," he plainly remarked, and it took me a couple of seconds to realize that he was referring to himself.

Resisting the urge to just prod and antagonize, like I know he would have done to me, I said, "Well, it doesn't look like she's holding any grudges with you. If siblings do anything for you, they teach you how to deal with that kind of love. And it makes life a whole lot easier when you leave home and live with other people."

"Only children just don't function with people besides themselves," he said, receiving a slap from me on the side of his arm. "Point taken."

"I ought to run this little clown car off the road and into that metal road sign on your half of the car, wait! We are getting off in Harwich?"

"Yes."

"Thank you very little, my handy copilot," I remarked while veering the car toward the exit.

"Right, left, and around in a circle we goooo," I was half-singing to myself as we followed the circling road around some straggly bushes on Parkseton Roundabout. Having driven via A120 and winding our way through a couple of small neighborhoods in Harwich, we were now alongside some creek and hopefully heading toward the ocean and the Stena Ferry Line. "Oh look, another roundabout, but this time we just get to look at brown, dead shrubs."

"Left here," Rowan said from the passenger seat.

"Last time you said that, it was a left here, which turned into a right, and then a 'just kidding' turn left," I joked, wishing we could have pirated a car with a GPS system.

"Drive."

"At least there is hope now. I see an increasing amount of concrete, parking lights, semis with cargo, and loading areas. I would not want to live in any of these houses," I commented about the homes alongside the narrow road leading into the port and between rundown patches of tangled shrubs. "I see blue and what looks to be a large cruise ship with something that says '…ine'."

"Stena Line. Park to the left, and follow it around."

"Planes, trains, automobiles, ferries, horses, and skis. Have I forgotten anything?" I added.

"Walking."

"Running. Falon would not have let me forget that."

Once parked among the tens of other small European favored cars in front of the Stena building, I glanced at the digital clock on the dashboard: 7:35 a.m., which left us with about three-quarters of an hour before boarding. We were hoping that somehow people would not have the desire to wake up for the early ferry, and tickets would be available when we went inside. We were armed with nothing more than minimal cash and a couple of falsified passports that had hopefully not been tagged as false.

I slammed the door shut on our crispy red-orange Fiesta and swung my backpack over my shoulder. "As much as I loved you, little car, in our time of need, I have to admit I will not miss the way you drove."

I received only a judging glance from Rowan as I tapped the car on the roof. Then we headed to the low industrial building of Stena Ferry.

I was pleased to find the lines considerably short as some families mulled around and attempted to corral small children who should not have been this peppy at this hour of the morning. I was surprised to see multiple dogs straining at their leashes, in excitement for the upcoming trip. A young Labrador mix received a giggle from me when I watched him wrap a leash around the bags and legs of an unsuspecting mother, while she fixed the blonde hair of a four-year-old girl. It was only when the puppy yanked the leash to sniff some other smell, dragging a suitcase into the pair, that the mother came to a realization of her new predicament.

"We have ninety-five pounds," I reminded Rowan as we stepped up to the counter.

"Good morning. Two adults," Rowan announced to the older gentleman behind the desk.

"Are you bringing any vehicles, pets, or bicycles with you today? Would you be interested in any onboard lunch packages or seating in the Stena Plus Lounge?"

"We're on foot. How much are your rooms?"

Looking down at his computer and typing in a couple of simple commands, the man replied, "We could provide you with the simplest two-person room, without a window, for seventeen-point-ninety-five pounds. May I suggest upgrading to a Comfort or Captain room, with a window and additional space?"

"The room for seventeen-point-ninety-five pounds and the two tickets will do," Rowan politely replied without asking me how necessary I felt a room would be for our quick day trip. At this point, a nice lounge chair would suffice.

"It will be ninety-three-point-forty-six pounds."

"Cutting it close," I remarked as I handed over the cash and passports while propping my body against the counter.

"Please show your passports at the gate when you board," the man said, handing the documents back to Rowan.

Rowan thanked the man and turned to me as we walked toward the lines to pass through security before boarding the Britannica to Holland. "And close only counts in horseshoes and hand grenades."

When a person says the word "ferry," I associate the word with a small ship with simple seating and economical usage of space in order to efficiently travel from destination A to destination B. Our previous ferry ride, aside from the room below for cars, was equivalent to what I had pictured. Standing on the port now, I realized there was a reason why the Stena Line fleet had evolved into the largest thriving ferry company in the area. The Britannica was not simply a ship. Under the "Stena Line" logo painted in blue down her white exterior, she was a massive cruise vessel designed for short-distance trips between the island known as the United Kingdom and the rest of Europe.

Walking up the shaky stainless-steel scaffolding-like ramps to the ship, we were greeted by an enthusiastic staff guiding passengers in various directions, with oversized smiles and crispy uniforms. The décor was clearly done with effectiveness and cheerful colors. In the ten seconds I was aboard, it became too overwhelming. If I would have seen another bright blue or red, I might have lost it. The sleep deprivation from driving was catching up to me, and I was now, though I would never give him the satisfaction of knowing, thrilled for a room with any form of a bed. I followed Rowan as he weaved through a group of tourists numbering about twenty and toward a set of elevators. He briefly looked at the number printed on the cardholder for the room in his hand and pressed the elevator button down. Once crammed inside the claustrophobic box with a generous crowd of people, it was only three floors downward. About one-quarter of the way down the hall on the left, among a sea of bright and dizzily printed carpeting, a narrow wooden door matched our key. Once the door was open, I saw that the room was no wider than a king-sized bed and only about as long as one and a half of them. The tiny bathroom door on the right side opened into anyone who might have been standing in the narrow hall boxed in by the main door and closet. On the left was a cherry-red, poorly stuffed, narrow couch placed below a large flat-screen television. The right side of the room consisted of a narrow bed and an additional one folded up on the wall in bunk bed style.

Rowan ducked into the bathroom as I wedged myself between the door and the wall before collapsing on the bed. Backpack still on my back, I could not find the energy to move from my sprawled position, with my face jammed into the tightly pulled, scratchy sheets. The dull sound of the shower running floated through my ears and enticed my exhausted brain with the option of a hot shower. At home I would have filled up the claw tub in the master bathroom, locked the door, and waited while the steam swirled around, filling my sinuses as I sunk below the toasty water. A shower would have to do. A much needed shower. It had been a few days.

In my minimally conscious mindset, I let the scalding water run over me for some period of time, losing track of time and place.

Stepping out of the shower, I reached into my backpack, which had been tossed haphazardly between the toilet and the wall. The only remaining survivors of our rogue adventure were a hoodie and my fleece jacket. Not in the mood to be concerned with who actually had ownership, I slipped the hoodie on and wrapped my dripping hair into the standard issue white towel found neatly hanging on the wall. Then I slipped my jeans back on. What I would have given for one of my oversized T-shirts and a pair of my baggy, college-branded sweatpants.

Opening the door to the bathroom, I saw Rowan propped up against the wall while sitting on the bed and surfing through the channels on the television. "I just drove here. I am not sleeping on the couch. Move it."

He pretended to be infatuated with the blabbering idiot box on the wall and flipped through a couple more channels. Instead of just grabbing a blanket and choosing the easier option, I took three steps over to the bed. "Put the top one down," I told him, pointing above his head.

"You can."

"Ugh," I mumbled and crawled onto the bed. My attempt to yank the covers up so I could crawl underneath was a failed venture, with his body mass holding them hostage. All I wanted to do was sleep—end of story.

"Nice sweatshirt," he mocked, watching me struggle.

I looked down to see it was the Colorado Springs one he was wearing at the airport on the first day I met him. "I clearly do not care."

He finally picked up his feet, releasing the weight on the sheets. I yanked them up with a wimpy amount of strength and wrapped them into a proper cocoon around myself. At this point, I had no energy to verbally embark on a losing battle to make him move off the bed. Instead, the last thing I remembered was drifting off into never-never land and being oddly pleased that someone was there with me.

The digital clock on the television read 16:23. I had been asleep for about six hours, which felt wonderful. If we were not supposed to be off the gentle rocking ship in the next half hour, I would have turned back over and fallen into another coma.

Lying next to me with his back to mine, I called to Rowan. "Get up. Thirty minutes to showtime."

About twenty seconds later, he sat up, rubbed the sleep off his face, and sent a hand through his misguided head of hair. I followed suit by sitting up, which landed my face, and a tangled knot of fluffy hair, next to his. Before I realized what was going on, he had leaned in. And then I did. I was still wrapped up in the sheets when his embrace pulled me close, and my head came to rest on his chest. I could feel his slow breaths moving his chest up and down and his arms wrapped around me. Sitting there at my worst, with minimal sleep, dirty clothes, and unparalleled stress, I felt like everything was not crashing down and suffocating me in a pile of rubble. There was still the pile of rubble; I had just found a way to breathe. There was no fighting time as the moments passed. The little voice of logic yelled in my head that I should not be sitting here relying on someone else to protect me. Yet, a new voice was telling me that when your life might only last a matter of a few more minutes, there is nothing like knowing there is someone else. To take it all on by myself was not possible.

chapter 29

"I would like to say that while Converse shoes are wonderfully comfortable to walk in, after two and a half hours, they are way past their roaming abilities. Probably any type of shoe would have been past the point of comfort. After all of this, I plan on never exercising again, or walking, unless it is to the refrigerator to get a bowl of vanilla ice cream, or to my car to drive somewhere to buy myself more ice cream. Honestly, I am starving. I think the last time we ate was probably what, more than a full day ago? It is already sometime near six o'clock at night, and we still have another hour until we reach The Hague. Personally, I think it is going to be a wonderful rendezvous when we are dodging the secret service or CIA or whoever they are in those black uniforms. Likely, they are more than willing to hold a gun to our heads if we do not cooperate. Did I tell you how much I am enjoying my life right now?" I managed to rattle off at mach speed while Rowan and I were walking along the North Sea Cycle Route after leaving the port in Hoek van Holland.

Once landing on solid ground in Holland without any of our "friends" present to snatch us up and throw us in the back of an unmarked van, we followed a large crowd of people and a couple of signs, which were in English, to the train station conveniently located near the port. Unfortunately for us, we could not produce near enough money for the hour-long train ticket to The Hague, so we scrounged up the couple of remaining bills and bought a map. A wonderful gentleman pointed out on the map where we needed to be and wished us the best, remarking that bicycle was the way to travel in this country. If only we had been lucky enough to not be lying when we said we had a couple to use for the day. Regardless, we left the low, chocolate-brown brick building and headed north to the Peace Palace.

The walk through the small port town of Hoek van Holland was simple, with large amounts of greenery, cookie cutter brick homes attached in townhome style, and plenty of sidewalks. Eventually, the town gave way to more open space, and we took a path slightly to the west before encountering what our map called "Noordlandsepad/ Route 1" or, in English, the famous North Sea Cycle Route. Along the way, we could feel the damp, cool breeze coming from our unin-terrupted view of the shoreline. The roar of the waves slowly col-lapsing with a crash on the fairly desolate beach added to the peace-ful trip uninterrupted by the roar of car engines. The only form of human contact we encountered consisted of a few bikers and others choosing to explore the path by horse or foot. Rowan was still not much for talking, so I blabbered to myself at high speed about noth-ing in particular. The silence bothered me. It was nice for us to be tolerating each other. There was no other way to describe the newest development in our relationship. In order to make it to The Hague before sunset, we needed to walk briskly. Near the third hour, we were no longer on the path near the seaside and were forced to follow the rumble of cars on S100.

The sun began to descend from the sky, and the air was cooling off quickly. Our simple sweaters would not have sufficed if we had not been walking quickly and producing our own body heat.

"We should only be one kilometer away," Rowan commented when we paused along a street corner to take in our bearings.

"Which would be about point sixty-two miles," I added, with my Americanized orientation. "Think we might run into the others?"

"Depends on where they came in. If they walked, like us, then they should be an hour or two behind," he said, handing the map back to me to shove into my backpack.

"I hope they make it before sundown." I watched the brightening orange rays of sunshine coming through the narrow gaps of the buildings and blinding me from the west side of the street. I found the street we were walking along in the city of Den Haag absolutely charming. Instead of the plain, dark brick of all the other homes, these were a washed-out red brick with large windows facing the street, outlined in sharp white trim. They lined the entire street in one long, connected complex going up three of four stories into the sky. A narrow street wove through the center, accommodating only small vehicles. The antique-style lampposts along the sidewalk added character and made me want to dance around as I starred in my own black-and-white film.

For another quarter of a mile, I admired more buildings of similar design, except those with the occasional glass shop window across the first story. Few people came and went between the shops and homes on this weekday night—business as usual in Den Haag, Netherlands. We acquired a fair amount of stares and puzzled looks from the locals as we casually made our way down the street. If we had been anything aside from a couple of American touristy-looking kids, it might just have been a hair easier to blend in.

Unexpectedly, I felt Rowan tense up slightly as he stood a couple of inches taller and strained to see what occupied the space a couple of streets ahead of ours.

"Who do you see?" I asked, my nerves shooting adrenaline through my system to prepare for a fight-or-flight reaction. I started to scan every inch of the street for any peculiar movements, or cars suspiciously slowing down.

"We should've given them less money," Rowan said, relaxing a little as we continued to walk faster down the sidewalks while dodging the few people and a multitude of lampposts.

"Where are they?" I demanded to know. It was a bit unreal that despite many hours, different forms of transportation, and splitting up almost a day ago, we would be seeing each other not tied up with duct tape on our mouths in an abandoned warehouse.

"Corner on the left," Rowan responded.

After walking a few more blocks, I noticed they were still standing on the corner debating which way they needed to turn in order to achieve the correct destination. Falon was insistently pointing left, Riley was shaking her head and politely trying to correct Falon, and Gavlin stood by waiting for a decision to be reached, bouncing on the balls of his feet.

"Hey, I thought we got rid of you three!" I half-shouted across the street to catch their attention.

Gavlin looked up first, followed by the other two, who followed his gaze straight at Rowan and me. I could see a huge grin on all of their faces, which no doubt mirrored ours. We waited for a blue Smart car to zip by before Rowan and I crossed over the side street to meet them. I broke into a jog as soon as my feet hit the paved street, jumping up onto the curb ahead of Rowan.

"And we thought you two were on a plane to the Cayman Islands by now, with daiquiris and sunshine," Gavlin mocked, grabbing me in a hug.

"Although really, how'd you make it here before we did?" I asked.

"The train station at the port had two connecting trains, which placed us a few blocks away. Now we appear to be a tad lost while trying to make it the last few blocks to The Hague. I would also like to mention we decided to travel the back route instead of directly, in case they were potentially waiting," Falon added.

"Should have traveled with you all. We were a bit strapped for cash, and food was not even on the list," I said.

Riley looked a little puzzled and asked, "*Walk?*" while pointing at her brother and me.

I sarcastically said, "*Yeah, walked.*"

"That had to have been a hell of a walk," Gavlin said.

"Three and a half hours," Rowan said.

"I would like to *die* now," I moaned.

"Do either of you know how much farther, and in which direction, we need to travel?" Falon brought the conversation back on point.

"Half a mile in that direction," I guessed, and pointed in the opposite direction from which Rowan and I had just come.

"This road will take us straight there," Rowan said.

"*They will be waiting,*" Riley signed, helpfully reminding us how far we still had to go, despite the minuscule physical distance.

"Yeah," Gavlin agreed.

I voiced the obvious question. "Are we going to break up or stay together?"

"Split," Gavlin responded, instantly.

Riley waved her hand to catch our attention. "*No.*"

"*Why?*" Rowan said.

"*Together we can focus their attention. We bait them over to one place, then split quickly at the end.*"

"Would that not run the risk of everyone being surrounded instead of giving some people a better chance?" Falon questioned.

"They have enough resources to surround all sides. There'll be people everywhere, even if we divide. This could be our only option. I'm more concerned with who takes the information. We're not going to split it," Rowan stated.

"Why would we risk it all on one person?" I asked, strongly opposed.

"If we know who has it, then we get that one person in. If anyone else is caught, there is nothing to hold them for."

"And if that one person is caught, everything we've risked in the past week will not have been worth it," I rebutted. "We are already shy one set of documents. We split the three and hope at least one person makes it in. There would be proof to our claims about producing more similar documents, and help from officials. Otherwise, it's the word of a teenager against high-ranking officials with a preconceived agenda."

"No. Minimize the risk to everyone else. Someone needs to bite the bullet to keep everyone else here alive," Rowan strongly stated, standing like a stone in front of me.

No one else dared interrupt our heated argument, even if it was deciding everyone's fate. "Fine. Who is it going to be?" I dared him.

"You."

My head was spinning. Ten minutes ago, I was under the impression Rowan would be the one taking the bullet while the rest of us did not look back. Now I was standing on a street with the sun setting, deliberating how the rest of our possibly short lives could end.

I wondered how I could have ever trusted this kid. Last time I trust anyone, I decided. My breath was caught in my throat, and my legs felt like concrete pillars. The four other faces surrounding me were blurred. It was just me, in a time warp, battling my stupid emotions and waiting for the logical part of my brain to kick in and do its job.

"Devon. Devon!" Gavlin's voice reached my subconscious.

I looked at his concerned face, his golden eyes. I thought about how he had kept the other two alive and how he was always my comedic reprieve in this ride. I saw a striking Falon with hair hanging down from a messy bun and not a trace of makeup on her face. She had lost her posh image, but underneath it all was a mentally exhausted teenager breaking apart, pieces falling like teardrops more frequently. On my right was the youngest, who we all had grown to love as our own. A little bit of inspiration and a whole lot of brains in a bubbly, energized fourteen years. It was simple. I had been forced into it, but I would be doing it for the right reasons.

"Fine," I said.

"Devon, I can do it. I should do it," Gavlin offered without hesitation.

"Really, you could take this wonderful burden off my hands, except you worked all too well with Falon and Riley, and we need you three to make it through. The one who offered me up for this sacrificial lamb position," I said, glancing sideways at Rowan, "will be the distraction for me."

For a moment, no one uttered a word. Gavlin could not rebut. He knew from our previous agreements that he would not win. Rowan was content to have his way and had no intention of modifying the situation, despite the twist I threw into his plan.

"*OK,*" Riley said, recognizing that the decision had been finalized and that this was how it was going to be. "*Better get going. The sun is setting fast.*"

"*Agreed,*" I responded.

"How far will we be together?" Falon asked while we started to walk up the block.

"I'd say until we spot trouble. We need to make sure they radio for everyone to come to this side before we split. After that, further splitting is going to be 'play it by ear' and discretionary," I replied.

"*What?*" Riley asked me for clarification.

I attempted to fill her in, and she replied, "*Play by ear? We are amazing at that!*" I could only hope our good luck and luckier timing from earlier would prevail. Thirty seconds later, that dream was crushed when Rowan grabbed Riley and Falon and forcibly swept the rest of us onto the nearest available side street. Our guests had arrived.

chapter 30

"How many and where, exactly?" I demanded in a whisper.

"Block ahead, standing on the corner. He was looking at a black car across the street," Rowan replied, ducked over as we all huddled together.

"Could be a normal car," Falon said.

Rowan looked slightly frustrated that we would not just take his word. "It's not the typical hybrid car found around here," he said.

"Did they see us?" I wanted to know. It had been a fairly quick exit off the street, and the plan was riding on diverting all of their attention to our location.

"Not well enough." Rowan read my mind.

"Is it time for a random song and choreographed dance in the streets? Do you have the *music, Riley?*" Gavlin attempted to lighten the mood.

"Music? I lost my iPod back in São Paulo."

"We need to move. Song and dance during the end credits, my friends." I rallied the group in an audible whisper. "We are going to calmly walk back to the street. When they see us, we keep going. Anyone can call the split when they start to crowd us. In that case, Riley, Falon, and Gavlin head off to the left and keep going north around the backside of The Hague. Take any entrance in. Rowan and I will keep heading directly there. The men should take off toward the three of you, but you will be ahead, and Rowan and I will have less distance to cover."

"Yep," Gavlin replied for the group.

We remained silent as we reluctantly walked back onto the street. There was no small talk, which might have helped to ease the image of our tense shoulders and darting eyes for any signs of suspicious movement. Though my head kept scanning the streets for other cars or killers, it kept jumping back to the single man on the corner nearest a large black sedan. The man was sporting a black suit pant with a medium-weight outer coat that looked too awkwardly bulky to only be covering up extra poundage around his hips and lower gut. A crew cut, brown hair, and heavy eyebrows above trained falcon eyes, accented his hard jaw line. The thought of his muscular five-ten frame sprinting down the narrow streets of Holland, after us, was not on my agenda and, given our history, I thought he might just resort to firearms. We had outrun, outsmarted, and out-lucked these guys when it came to our evasive techniques. Mentally, I am sure every one of them was not willing to return to his master with his tails between his legs and ego bruised, to say a handful of untrained teenagers were still on the loose.

My main motive for continuing to look in his direction was to determine if he was going to call over anyone else because, as soon as that happened, we would have a matter of seconds to scatter like cockroaches. This plan was going to be the thinnest line we had balanced on our whole trip, aside for almost being grabbed at the ski mountain and the airport, and the other half a dozen locations. This trip was like walking a tightrope between two skyscrapers on a windy day. Closing the distance of the few blocks between us, I saw the man reach into his pocket and pull out an iPhone. He proceeded to speed dial someone and make a very brief statement. The entire time he attempted to not make eye contact with us. Yet, I could see his beady eyes glaring us down and waiting for the moment to strike. He was not going to let us get away this time. He paced a couple of steps back and forth on the corner after hanging up and shoving his phone back into his left jacket pocket. We followed the sidewalk up the street to a point almost a block away from where he and the car remained.

"Now?" Falon said, as I opened my mouth.

"You read my mind. Now or never," I replied softly.

"See you in another life, brother." Gavlin quoted what I recognized to be Desmond from the television show *LOST*.

"Until then," I responded. The next side street branched off to both the left and right. Gavlin, Riley, and Falon quietly slipped around the corner to our left and headed down a slim street. I caught them beginning to sprint out of my peripheral vision. It took me a second to realize that the blue signs with a red "x" indicated that the street was a one-way. At least we knew the car was not going to have an easy time following them in the near future. One for us, and none for the bad guys.

The guard on the corner must have realized, after a couple of seconds, we were now short more than half of our group. I suddenly registered a change in his movement as he took off at a full sprint toward us. With so few obstacles, it was going to take him no time at all to reach us. The squealing of tires also gave away their next move.

JACQUELINE BOYLE

I turned around to assure my brain that my ears were not deceiving me. Indeed, the black sedan was racing down the street in our direction. The roads were definitely going to come to our assistance because in order to be on the opposite side of the street, where we were, the driver would have to weave in between the lampposts down the divided road on a small median. At that point, he would then be dodging oncoming traffic. He would also need to drive through the cars parallel parked along the street and the line of trees placed only a few feet from each other that formed a blockade between the road and the pedestrians on the sidewalk. I reminded myself to thank the Dutch street planners if we made it through this excursion.

After realizing they were quickly gaining on our brisk walking pace, I whipped my head forward and sprinted off. I had seen the map earlier, and it lingered as a fuzzy image in my mind. I knew the only way would be to keep going straight until we hit the back corner of the presumably fenced Hague Academy of International Law. Rowan was right next to me, adding to the footsteps pounding down the sidewalk. Hoping for a side street, we were out of luck. The solid brick buildings with sharp white trim continued on as we ran. I checked behind us after a minute to see our friend closing the distance. I prayed our young, nimble bodies would be able to take in more oxygen and run longer. He was obviously in running shape and doing well. The car I had been concerned about was not in sight, but that did not mean it was out of mind. I could only hear the huffing of my breath as I considered how my numb feet were mercilessly hammering into the concrete sidewalk. My whole body stopped feeling anything, and I felt like I could run forever. My light backpack bounced against the lower part of my back, and I was glad I shortened the straps earlier for easier running. If we stopped, there would be no way to get me going again. I looked back. We were alone.

"Where…did…he go?" I gasped.

Rowan slammed to a halt. While my physical body foll my mental state told me not to. "I have no clue," Rowan said, his eyes darting around.

I noticed that the buildings around us had changed to an older style with more character; we were in the historical district of Den Haag. There were slight breaks between buildings that allowed for more greenery in the form of matured trees. The road no longer had the central median and bent off to the left slightly. I could see a wrought iron fence clearly extending around the corner. All of the trees within the fence stood erect in a perfectly manicured fashion. We had made it. We were standing on the edge of The Hague. We could see it, but we could not touch it.

"Damn it," Rowan mumbled.

I looked ahead to where his shocked look was focused on two cars racing around the corner at an ungodly speed. Before I had ten seconds to respond, he grabbed my shoulders and spun me to the left.

"The entrance should be that way." He pointed ahead. "Run!"

I wanted to have the last word because I always have the last word, but nothing would come out. I was a deer in headlights with my heart pounding through my chest. I looked at him standing there. His chest was taking in air quickly, and his face reflected a manically determined look. His green eyes were set intently on the two cars beating down on us and scanning for escape routes. It would only be for a few minutes.

I was thanking the street gods for the millionth time today when a one-way street appeared ahead. I raced up the wide sidewalks under the cover of tall, mature trees casting splotchy shadows on anything beneath them. Once one of the cars saw what I had done, it slammed to a halt, and two men immediately jumped out. It had taken them a few hundred feet to decelerate enough for a safe exit, and I was already running fast, pounding the pavement hard, with every other part of my body obediently cooperating. The two men who jumped out were holding guns at the ready. The few people meandering along the streets shouted in some other language, and a middle-aged couple in my path jumped out of the way and pointed behind me. I considered zigging and zagging, but the corner was only a couple of hundred feet. If I could only get around to the front... The front was sure to have some security guard who, hopefully, was competent enough and had a gun. With enough witnesses, releasing a bullet in my direction would cause some serious international legal issues.

I glanced backward while keeping up my pace. The two cars were both stopped. For a brief second, I could have sworn I saw Rowan running to one of the car doors. Running blind was not an option, so I looked straight ahead once more. I bore down quickly on the corner and, as I turned, I got one more look at the situation unfolding behind me. The men were still pursuing me, though I could tell something was bothering them. How had Rowan managed to get so close to the cars? I could never have guessed, but Rowan was there and holding something in the air as bait. It was not the documents. Still, it sure looked close enough to a flash drive from my distance.

I had to tell myself that it was almost over. I was almost there. It was pertinent to keep running.

Soon, a large intersection materialized ahead. It had to be the entrance, because if not, I was surely dead, and Rowan was a lost cause. The Hague appeared before my eyes behind a large wrought iron gate that served as the security stop for incoming people and cars. The bottom stone archways of the building built up into light red-brick and stone-edged windows along the front. On the left, a tower rose high above the three-story, shingled black roof. The roof itself was nothing plain; spires extended into the sky, and a shorter, but equally detailed and beautiful tower on the right adorned the castle structure. The ground lights poured fluorescent illumination onto the face of the building and into the blacking, cloudless sky. The world's international court demanded respect.

I dodged around a few cars, sprinting toward the gate. The security guard looked completely taken aback by my sudden appearance. As I was about to cross over onto the grounds of The Hague, I heard gunshots from where I had just run. It took all I had not to turn back around and sprint toward them, but my backpack weighed me down for what this trip meant, for what the last decades meant, for what my mom, Rowan and Riley's dad, and Gavlin's parents meant.

"English? Call the police!" I demanded to the guard in gasping breaths when he emerged shocked and dazed from his post. He immediately returned back to his small stand and dialed someone without even asking. This could have been a teenage trick, though my current physical and mental state must have sent off its own warning system. The gunshots might have sold it.

I collapsed onto the ground right there on the sidewalk, taking in air and scanning the entrance for a sign of anyone else. I needed to go back out there, but I knew I was hopeless against guns. The security guard slipped back to my side and bent down to make sure I was still alive.

"Police. You call? They have guns," I said again.

"Yes. Who is it? Are there more people?" he questioned in heavily accented English.

"They are dangerous and armed, and hired by a private company. Four more." I had finally caught my breath and was standing back up. "How long?"

"Not long," he responded, while looking at my ragged appearance. He paced back into the security booth as I saw a security car from within the gates race to the front. I needed the real police. I was barley wrestling my mind into logical submission. I was helpless to aid the four people who had saved my life and were probably the only thing I would have left at the end of this. I needed to go back out. I needed the documents to be safe.

A graying man, older and in good shape, opened the door to the security car and jogged over to where I was now nervously pacing back and forth, with my eyes on the road and my arms crossed defensibly across my chest.

"Are you fine?" he looked me in the eyes, which caused me to briefly stop.

"There are men with guns out there after four people. I need you to get the police out here or anyone with the power to stop them! This is life or death!" I did not mean to yell at the man who was hopefully going to be helping me. My mind was not thinking so politely at this point. He gave me a look like I was some crazed kid who was high on drugs.

Thankfully, the other security guard came running over and started rattling off information in Dutch. With every word, I saw the older man's jaw tense and eyes widen, and subconsciously he reach down for the gun on his hip. Off in the distance, I heard sirens. I was hoping they were heading this way. It was our only salvation. Timing was essential. The police needed to be out there before our pursuers fled, possibly with any of the other four captive.

"Can we go out there?" I cut into their conversation.

"The police are coming. How many are there?" the older, police-trained security officer asked.

"They had two cars and at least four people. I took off, but my friend is over there."

"You need to stay. I will return," he offered before saying a couple more words in Dutch, jumping in his car and peeling off. I watched helplessly as he turned the corner, with the tires squealing against the pavement.

My patience was nothing. I paced back and forth, fighting the instinct to say the hell with it, leave, and go find everyone else. Sitting idle and waiting while the rest sacrificed their lives left me with a gut-dropping feeling. I doubled over, wanting to hurl. The world was too vivid from the emotions, the pressure, the adrenaline, and the gun shot sounds reverberating through my mind.

Moments later, three bodies appeared from the opposite direction, running at a decent jog toward us. Impossible to see that far, I still would have bet my life on whom it was. Within seconds, I could detect Riley in the lead, with Falon and Gavlin working hard to keep up. They did not wait for any of the lights to change before dodging traffic and making their way onto sovereign territory. I ran out to meet them in the middle of the paved entrance, nearly careening into Riley when I grabbed her in a hug and would not let go. Her light-brown hair was tangled around her face, and she pulled away to take a deep breath. Falon was bent halfway over, dying to find air. Now *I* needed to go find our missing link. I was holding on to the hope that in the next ten seconds he would come sprinting out of the trees across the way and join the rest of us. If not, I was going after him.

"Falon and Riley, hold on to these." I ripped the backpack off my back and halfway threw it to Riley. "Stay here," I demanded.

"I'm coming," Gavlin demanded.

"Fine."

Riley was clearly not pleased we were going after her brother without her, indicated by the most angered look I had ever seen her give.

Her glare threatened to light me aflame. Falon was out of the loop and paid no attention to anything aside from her own breathing.

"If anything happens, those," I said, pointing to the contents of the backpack, "tell our story. We will be back," I promised to her as I took off, hoping I would be able to keep that promise.

chapter 31

Gavlin took the hint quickly and sprinted off after me. Just as we were turning the corner, I caught sight of the police lights whirling around. The blaring of the sirens warned oncoming foot and car traffic to be prepared for a detour of the area—the area where I left Rowan to fend off too many people. My conscience was telling me I was selfish person for thinking that I could just leave him there and save my own hide. He had told me to, and at least now the documents were safe. His mission was accomplished. It still did not ease my guilt. Six squad cars and two ambulances were parked around the corner when we came racing over. The area was a general collection of white cars with blue and red stripes, and police officers fanned out. Some officers guided passing foot traffic to continue walking while another two helped with the recent traffic predicament. Between all the hypnotic, unsynchronized lights and the blocked street, it was impossible to tell if any of the hired guns chasing us were still present. The blue lights reflected off the streetlamps and bathed the area in color. The alarms became silent in my mind, and only the quick chatter of responding voices floated by me, increasing in volume as we neared.

I could not see the security officer I had talked to back at the entrance. He knew me, and I needed to know what was going on. A young officer in the standard white shirt, and black tie and pants greeted us in Dutch. It was clear that he thought we were a bunch of rowdy kids trying to snoop around. When I noticed that he was not letting us advance any farther, I was not going to stand for it. I ran around him before he could do anything, and squeezed my way to the center of the action where they had pulled the ambulances and surrounded them with police cars. There were shouts behind me, yet they were muffled. I shimmied sideways between two squad cars and bullied my way past a stationary officer with his back to me. The shouting I ignored had caused a ruckus, and so had my definitive actions. Instead of being free on the other side of the police car blockade, someone snatched my right arm, leaving a burn I would not notice until much later. He turned me around to face the exterior of their circle, hiding whatever was going on, and restrained me long enough for Gavlin and the man I ran past to appear. I knew fighting would do no good as I rapidly scanned the crowd for a familiar face in uniform. I saw him only ten seconds before he took notice of the scene surrounding me. He took up a light jog toward us. The older gentleman must have explained the situation in Dutch because I was free ten seconds later. I whipped around and emerged into the world they were attempting to protect from the real world outside.

A handful of paramedics and multiple police officers surrounding them were the center of attention. I took in the scene, and my first instinct was not what I wanted it to be, though somehow I knew it was right. There was something wrong. Instead of the panic to rush whoever was on the ground to the hospital, they were moving as though already defeated. Between the feet of the officers, I could see blood across the cold concrete.

And then I crumbled to the ground while the world swept me away into an ocean of black tears.

chapter 32

At some point, I found out that the torment of the sky's thunderous state does ground you.

When we arrived, there were five place settings at the table. One just sat at the head of the table. No one touched it for a few days. A place setting waiting for a fifth person to walk through the door from venturing around the wooded area that surrounded our safe home tucked away in the European countryside. Finally, at 3:00 in the morning, I put it away.

We all waited for someone when we first arrived. Eight footsteps echoing silently off the wooden walls.

Gavlin received a phone call from his older sister about their parents. The funeral was completely arranged, and because of our precarious situation for the next couple months, it would be held without his presence. I overheard a few mumbling words before he disappeared into his bedroom. Despite the warnings by those overseeing our protection, he left through the window and disappeared into the woods. Our personal security guards and supervisors said nothing when he slipped through the back door at 2:00 in morning. He was not much for talking when I tiptoed down to his room and sat for a few hours in silence. The next day, he was looking onward. Two less sets of feet roamed our halls. He was our usual comedic reprieve and our reminder of adolescence. Though sometimes, we knew the laughter was his way of trying to move on or sometimes cover it up. Gavlin would return to his professional career and live in his California home when we returned to the real world. He was the youngest in the family, leaving him alone in a house of old memories. It was hard for him to be on the ground around here. It was as if when he finally came down, life dealt him the hardest hand it could find.

It would only be a few more months in this safe house in Europe, with the location unknown to even us. There was only a secure Internet connection for mail messages and a direct phone line to those working to keep us alive. Within this group, my father and Falon's were serving as the leaders, living at headquarters and working through the documents, the litigation, and tracking down a collection of people with connections to everything that started decades ago. Unknown to us at the time, my father had managed to redeem an old favor from a friend who had escorted him into the Netherlands. He was only blocks away when we arrived that night at The Hague. I only vaguely remembered him from that night.

Despite proving ourselves capable to fend for ourselves against the world, it was nice to be in the company of Falon's mamá y papá a week into our "prison" stay. I think it was a godsend for Falon. Still, Falon's mental and emotion state was on thin ice. There came a time when getting her to make it through a conversation without tears was an achievement. It was not just what had happened at The Hague. She was well on her way down that spiral before all this. Her emotions were open for the world. It was a blessing as much as a curse. I wish I could find it in me to express that kind of openness. Eventually, I found her in the bathroom with her designer clothes and makeup. It was a relief. It was her way of dealing with the world. Her aunt and uncle did their best to create a normal family dynamic, but we were much more accustomed to our parentless version. Regardless, no one objected to being liberated from adult responsibility.

As far as Falon's real father, she met him once, before they dropped us off in the woods. It all happened without her permission, and there may have been half a dozen words before she turned her heels, stepped into the black Suburban and slammed the door. She never mentions him, and in conference calls their interactions never extend beyond cordialness. In those two sets of identical eyes, I see one with a glimmer of longing dampened by years of thunderstorms and the other with the fury of lightning and thunderous booms. How strong is the blood coursing through a person's veins when compared to all the blood from skinned knees healed by kisses and cartoon Band-Aids?

Custody has been an issue with Riley. Taking her away from Colorado would cut the last string holding her to her previous life, but so far there has been no progress. Her immediate family has children and is only willing to take her if she would move. Every part of me just wants to protect her, but I still am trying to figure that out.

While it is an impossible thought at the moment, in a few months I will be packing my bags for college at Washington University in St. Louis, three hundred miles away from home and away from everything I once knew, until it was shattered only a short time ago. Maybe it is actually coming just at the right time.

Now, I am sitting outside on our porch swing and waiting for the sound of the back door and someone to come back into my once lonely world.

When the back door swings open and a hand gently guides it back to its resting place, I know it is still not who I am waiting for. The figure with black tightly-fitting jeans sits down quietly on the other side of the swing, causing just a slight rocking motion. I continue to stare out into the woods. He reaches over and takes me in an embrace. Not previously accepting of even a simple hug, I just allow someone else to be my protection from the world I seem to have lost back on a street in Den Haag. Curled in his arms with my head on his chest, I know someone is keeping the world at bay. While I could sit in his protection, I know I am still the one who has to fight the world. I never lost that part of me; it was just misguided for a little while. It called to say it was five minutes away. The pitter of the rain begins to fall upon the deck, the overhang of the roof keeping the inner part of the deck dry.

"I love you. And so does everyone else. It just takes time," he whispers and squeezes me before getting up and heading back inside.

I have a tendency to lose track of time recently. It is the kind of lost time you never really lose; you just spend it in your head. Returning to my view of the grassy opening and the woods off our backyard, a small figure in a black raincoat with no hood, and dirty blond hair, wavy from being soaked, jumps into my vision. Red rain boots sloshing in the large puddles from the sky's tears, arms spread out wide, face catching droplets, she twirls like a ballerina wearing a carefree expression. Riley. If I could bottle up an ounce of her strength and acceptance, world peace would be within reach. Tears came too easily for three days when she had the time to think about it. We took turns keeping her busy—a hard task when Gavlin and I were the only marginally mentally stable ones. Most teenagers would have kept hidden under the comfort of the blankets in a warm bed, but she made it up every morning with a genuine smile and held it for as long as she could. She lost everything, and yet, here she was.

Under the wet hair and the rain dripping off her delicate features, she catches my eye. For a second, I can see Rowan in her, and everything floods back as a tsunami. Then it all screeches to a halt. I see her. I see the rain. I slowly unfold from the swing and walk across the deck, feeling the wet ground freeze my bare feet for only a moment as the icy rain hits my face.

Made in the USA
Lexington, KY
02 April 2013